The Long Walk Back

A Novel based on the life of a Maritime Woman

by

Elizabeth Savoie

© Copyright 2004 Elizabeth Savoie. All rights reserved.

No part of this publication may be reproduced, stored in a retrieval system, or transmitted, in any form or by any means, electronic, mechanical, photocopying, recording, or otherwise, without the written prior permission of the author.

Printed in Victoria, Canada

National Library of Canada Cataloguing in Publication Data

A cataloguing record for this book that includes the U.S. Library of Congress Classification number, the Library of Congress Call number and the Dewey Decimal cataloguing code is available from the National Library of Canada. The complete cataloguing record can be obtained from the National Library's online database at: www.nlc-bnc.ca/amicus/index-e.html

ISBN 1-4120-1648-7

TRAFFORD

This book was published *on-demand* in cooperation with Trafford Publishing.
On-demand publishing is a unique process and service of making a book available for retail sale to the public taking advantage of on-demand manufacturing and Internet marketing.
On-demand publishing includes promotions, retail sales, manufacturing, order fulfilment, accounting and collecting royalties on behalf of the author.

Suite 6E, 2333 Government St., Victoria, B.C. V8T 4P4, CANADA
Phone   250-383-6864   Toll-free   1-888-232-4444 (Canada & US)
Fax   250-383-6804   E-mail   sales@trafford.com
Web site www.trafford.com   TRAFFORD PUBLISHING IS A DIVISION OF TRAFFORD
                             HOLDINGS LTD.
Trafford Catalogue #03-2025 www.trafford.com/robots/03-2025.html

10   9   8   7   6   5   4   3   2

Acknowledgments

I would like to thank all those who helped and encouraged me in writing this novel. They are too numerous for me to mention them all by name, but first I would like to thank my friend, Brenda, who over the years told me bits and pieces about her life and gave permission for me to use them in a story. Also I remember the people who read and critiqued my original draft and told me that I had a story to tell. Then there were those who worked with me at the Writers' Workshops at the University of New Brunswick, helping me to hone my craft. I would also like to thank my proof readers who red-marked my manuscript for typos and grammatical errors, and those who assisted me with the technical problems with the computer. And all those who simply inquired, "How is your novel going?"

Thanks!

*This novel is dedicated to
my children
Mark Savoie
and
Joy Savoie McQuade
who never got tired of hearing me talk about my novel
and always encouraged me.*

Preface

Miriam felt the solid surface beneath her shift suddenly and give way. She flung her arms out, struggling for balance, but there wasn't any solid ground under her. There was only ice, and the ice only appeared to be solid. It was shifting, moving, breaking, tilting. Then there was water rushing around her, closing over her, and she went down, down, into the cold and dark. She struggled against that cold and dark, the water all around her.

There was light somewhere. She reached upwards toward the light, threshing, fighting towards the light. She had to reach that light. It was life. And around her the darkness and the cold were death.

She almost made it! She gasped for air. There were others around her, their hands reaching out to her, grasping, grabbing, begging, desperate for help; help from her. And there was no one to help her.

There was a child with her in the water, its hands reaching out to her. She had to save the child. She renewed her struggle.

Then she was cold, colder than she had ever been before in her life. Cold to her very innermost parts, to her very being. Cold had replaced the water. It was the enemy. Cold swirled around her; cold and darkness were sinking into the depth of her life force. And again, people were there with her in the cold and the dark. People sobbing quietly, people crying out, people shouting at her; asking, demanding something of her. What did they expect? She was cold, so cold, and so exhausted. Why didn't they leave her alone so that she could submit to the cold.

She saw Bruce! Bruce was surrounded by warmth and light. He was coming for her, reaching out to her. Bruce had come to help her. And in the light she saw someone with him: a child like no other, a child with curly black hair and shining eyes: a child that glowed with warmth and light. She knew this child, even though the last time she had seen it, it had been a baby, and now it was a child of uncertain age. She recognized her child even before Bruce spoke.

"Look, Miriam. I found Elizabeth. She was waiting for us. She came for me. Come with us now, Miriam. Come. We love you. We want you."

The child was reaching out to her. "Mummy, mummy, come with us."

Miriam was cold, oh so cold. They offered warmth and light. They wanted her. They could pull her from the cold and the darkness and save her. But what about the child whimpering in her arms?

"Bring him, Mummy. Bring my little brother."

Somewhere another child was crying, screaming, pulling her into the darkness, away from these creatures of warmth and light. Somewhere in the swirling cold other hands were reaching out to her. Other voices were shouting at her. She was torn. There was love and warmth and comfort on one side; and so many demands on the other; a never ending struggle but in it she would find her strength and the place where she belonged. And the child would be with her.

The Long Walk Back

Miriam Taylor was excited. Today, she was beginning a new adventure. Today she was starting school.

She pushed her unruly brown hair back from her face as she hurried after Hannah, her mother. Her short, chubby legs tried, unsuccessfully, to match her mother's long strides. Ahead her two older brothers, Jack and Bill, ran along the lane tripping and pushing at each other while her sister Annie tried her best to look dignified as she walked along, actually matching strides with her mother's.

They reached the end of their lane and passed their grandparents' small cottage, where Miriam waved to her grandfather who was splitting wood in the door yard. She smiled as she skipped past the two mailboxes that marked the beginning of the gravel road which led down towards the forks, and beyond to the village, where several other roads joined, forming the main road which meandered to Saint John, over thirty miles in the distance. Except on very rare occasions the mailboxes were the furthest she had previously been permitted to venture. She had been waiting all summer for this day.

Soon, in that fall of 1949, Miriam would be six years old; old enough to venture beyond her lane and begin the long walk down the road to the school; old enough to long for the adventure, freedom and knowledge that she imagined school would bring to her, as she had practiced her letters and numbers at the kitchen table throughout the summer and made her plans. Too young to notice her mother's deep concern, to be aware that formal schooling might be just a dream, to reason out the facts. After all, the school had been closed for most of the previous year, after the young and inexperienced teacher had thrown up her hands in despair in the middle of one particularly difficult day and rushed from the class-room crying. Two days later word had come from her home in the city that she wouldn't be returning. The school board had tried their best to replace her, but the term had slipped by into summer, and even by late August they hadn't found anyone willing to come to this isolated backwater of the school to deal with these unruly and unappreciative children.

But school was opening on time. Just last week two men from the school board had come down the lane to the Taylor place. They sat out on the veranda and talked a while with Miriam's father, Johnny, before calling Hannah to join them. The very next day, after Gran had paid her usual call, Hannah announced at the dinner table that the school would be opening on time, and she would be the teacher. Miriam was delighted with the news, her six-year-old mind never questioning why a busy farm woman with seven children, including an infant, would agree to teach school.

Gran had arrived earlier than usual that first day to look after Paul, Davy, and baby Gracie, while Miriam joined her mother and older siblings for the long walk to the school house.

Now they were passing the LeBlanc place. Miriam looked curiously up the lane to the house. She certainly had never been permitted to go there. Once in a while Maurice LeBlanc, with Louie in trailing along, would come over to hang around with Jack and Bill, and once this past summer Claudette and Suzanne had come over and played on the swing with Annie. Miriam had hung around until Annie chased her away, threatening to 'Tell Mum'. Later Miriam had listened to Annie whining for permission to return the visit.

"Please, Mum. It's not far. You can see their house from here."

"No, Annie. You know that's out of the question. You can play with them if they come here, you can even meet them at the line-fence, but I don't want you going to their place."

"But why not?"

"Annie, I said, 'No'."

Miriam was working up her courage to join in. "If Annie goes, can I go too." but before the words were out of her mouth Gram spoke up:

"That's no place for a decent girl to be hanging around. The mother doesn't even speak English."

Miriam didn't understand. "Doesn't speak English?" Then how would she talk? But then she remembered. Some people spoke French. Maurice had taught Jack and Bill to swear in French. But that was just a few words. Could people actually talk to each other in French? Could they actually say things like: "Pass the potatoes." "Time to get the milking done." "Get ready for bed." using strange words that didn't make sense? She wished even more that she could go into that neighbouring house and listen to the people talking their strange language, but there was no sense arguing.

Gram's word would be final. Annie wouldn't be permitted to go to the LeBlanc's, and if she couldn't, then

Miriam couldn't either. Annie was three years older and was permitted to do lots of things Miriam couldn't.

"Maybe," Miriam hoped, "now that I'm going to school, I'll meet some friends of my own."

She suddenly became aware that Jack and Bill had stepped off the road down the slight embankment. Pushing aside the bushes, they were looking at something in the long grasses that grew along the almost dry brook. Hannah walked on by, but both girls stopped to look too.
"Look here. A dead rabbit. I bet a hawk got him, and recently too," Jack exclaimed.

"No. It was more likely a fox. We must have scared him away just as we came up. We would have seen it if a hawk had taken off."

"Maybe it was the LeBlanc's cat," Miriam butted in, anxious always to be included.

"Don't be so stupid. A cat couldn't kill a rabbit this big. No, it had to be a fox."

"I still say it was a hawk, or else there would be tracks here in the mud."

Annie shuddered, "Poor little rabbit," but then lost interest in the mangled remains and turned to hurry after her mother. Miriam reluctantly followed her, leaving the boys to look for feathers or tracks to support their arguments.

"Annie, tell me more about school. Who will be there?"

"Well, my friend Jane. She's in my grade. And Suzanne and probably Claudette, though she told me that she thinks that twelve is too old for school."

"What about Grade One? Who else will be in my grade?"

"Well, probably Little Robbie Marshall. He's older than you. He started last year but Mom says that because nobody finished they will all have to go back to their old grades. I think that's mean. Jane and Suzanne and me will still be in Grade Two. It's not fair."

"But who else? Will anybody else be in my grade?"

"How should I know, Miriam? Maybe Suzanne's little brother. Yea, Louie LeBlanc. He'll be in your class."

"No girls?"

"Like I said. I don't know."

"What will it be like at school?"

"I've already told you a million times. You and Robbie and Louie will have to sit in the little desks up at the front. Grade ones always sit there. Then us Grade twos just behind, and the bigger kids behind us. You have to sit still and pay attention to the teacher. You can't talk at all until recess, and you can't get out of your seat."

"And you learn to read, and do arithmetic, and write, and do all sorts of stuff."

"Yeah, if you're smart and you pay attention."

"I'll pay attention. I want to learn. I can hardly wait to get there."

"It's not going be as much fun as you think." Jack had caught up with them. "All this yakking about school and you don't know what you're talking about. There's nothing fun about school. It's just sitting still all day and looking at the blackboard and getting yelled at for every little thing."

"Yea," Bill added. "If you make a mistake, you get yelled at. And sometimes you get the strap."

"Yea. Sometimes you get the strap for no reason at all."

"Mum wouldn't do that." Miriam cried in alarm.

Bill went on, "She won't be 'Mum' when we're at school. She'll be a teacher and all teachers are mean."

"I wish she would stay at home like other women. Whoever heard of a guy's mother teaching school?" Jack grumbled almost to himself.

"If she wasn't teaching the school would be closed again, and maybe we could cut some wood and earn some money, or maybe Dad could get us jobs at the mill."

"But I want to go to school," Miriam protested. "I want to learn to read."

"Yea," Miriam was surprised when Annie agreed with her. "We have to have a school. Everybody has to learn."

"Look who's talking," Bill laughed. "You can't even read yourself."

"Can, too."

"You call that reading. 'See Dick and Jane. See the Baby.' Wait until you get into the hard books in grade four and five. Then see if you can read."

"Besides," Jack joined in. "I already know how to read and write and figure. Look at Dad. He told me himself he only went to grade four, and anything he learned after that he learned in the army. Remember he drove a supply truck -- and after that he trained new soldiers -- and I bet I can read as good as him."

Miriam ignored her brothers and hurried again to keep up with Annie who had adopted an air of aloofness when they began their teasing. She felt a surge of excitement as they rounded a turn in the road and approached the forks. In the distance was the high-pitched whine of the sawmill where their father had been working since seven that morning, and directly ahead was the small one-roomed school house. Hannah was already crossing the yard toward the door, key in hand. A neat little white house stood directly across from the school, and a small boy that Miriam guessed must be Little Robbie Marshall was hurrying out the door with a new white softball in his hand. Miriam was too shy to wave to him.

A tall, handsome teenager was approaching up the main road. Jack and Bill were waving to him.

"There comes Charlie Smart. He must have decided to come back again. Boy, am I glad." Jack sighed. "I was afraid Maurice and me might be the oldest boys in the school. Hey, Charlie! Over here."

Annie turned her attention to a small group of children approaching from the left fork.

"There's my friend Jane, and Eva, and the rest." She paused to wait for them, but when Miriam stopped too, Annie practically shoved her on ahead.

"You can't be hanging around me and my friends all the time. Go over into the school yard and wait until Mum — wait until Teacher rings the bell. Then go in and sit where I told you. And don't embarrass me." Annie ran to meet her friends, while Miriam stumbled across the school yard. She didn't feel dejected for long however. A whole new world was opening up to her. She was going to school. She was going to make friends, and she was going to learn to read.

Chapter Two

At first school was everything Miriam had hoped for, and she loved it. All summer she had been asking questions and she knew immediately what was expected of her. She marched into the classroom and took possession of one of the small desks at the front of the room, folded her hands neatly before her and awaited instructions. Robbie, almost two years older and having already attended one term the previous year, slid into the desk beside her, and they both turned their heads to watch Louie silently struggling to escape as his sister dragged him into the classroom and shoved him into the third small seat. Miriam and Robbie looked at him in bewilderment, wondering what he was sniffling about, then both turned their attention to the teacher, listened attentively and then eagerly snatched the sheet of simple number facts that Teacher handed to each of them. Quickly Miriam began coloring: one kitten, two shoes, three apples, four rabbits, already realizing that she was in a race with Robbie.. Within a few minutes Miriam called out: "Mum, I'm done."

"Miriam! If you want to speak out you have to put your hand up and wait until I notice you. Remember that from now on. And in class you must call me 'Teacher' like the others do. If you are finished, you may turn your page over and practice making your numbers on the back. I am working with the older grades now."

Miriam bit her tongue between her teeth and pushed the pencil with her stubby fingers, forming her numbers as best she could. Before long she was bored with the work and began to look around the room. This was more interesting. She listened intently as Teacher reviewed work with the older grades, trying to find the levels at which they would be starting in each subject. Miriam waited expectantly for someone to raise their hand, as she knew they should, and give an answer. Young as she was Miriam could sense Teacher's frustration, and she longed for a question to which she might hazard a guess.

Everyone was relieved when 10:30 came. Teacher tapped the bell on her desk, dismissing them for recess and they raced outdoors, gathering in small groups. Miriam hung around the edges catching bits of conversation.

"What does she expect from us? We never took that long division last year."

"Yeah, no wonder we got them wrong. We don't know how to work with them big numbers."

"What kind of a teacher is she anyway? I'll bet she's going to be strict. Jack, how come your mother wants to be a teacher, anyway?"

Miriam waited for Jack to defend their mother but he just shrugged and muttered: "Don't ask me. I just wish that she'd stay home like every else's mum."

Miriam was about to protest. Jack should stick up for their mother, but she caught Bill's scowl and knew that this wasn't the time to butt in.

"Come on, guys," Jack lifted his voice. "Let's not waste time. How about getting a ball game started." He grabbed a bat and the boys followed him over to the rusty backstop where they quickly began choosing sides. Miriam started to follow them but then noticed that the girls turned in the other direction and began lining up for skipping. Miriam hurried in behind Annie, but Annie turned and hissed at her: "Don't always be hanging around me, I told you. This is for big kids. Go find someone you own age."

Robbie had already joined the older boys in the ball game; accepted despite his small size because it was his ball. Louie was sitting forlornly on the steps. She went over and sat down beside him. He inched away. She inched closer. He moved again and again she, catching on to the game, crowded closer. He moved to the very end of the step. She inched over aware that if he moved again he would fall off the side. Suddenly he turned and shoved her, hard. She scrambled to keep her balance, looking around to see if anyone had noticed, while he jumped up and ran around the side of the building where he slouched in the gloom under a cedar tree until the bell rang calling them back inside, and once more his sister had to drag him in. Miriam reflected that recess hadn't been any fun at all.

Then while she and Robbie copied their letters on another work-sheet and Louie sat with his head buried in his arms, Teacher began calling the older classes up to the front to read. This should be interesting. Miriam ignored her own work to listen to the stories from their books, but they stumbled so badly over the words that it was difficult to make sense of anything they read. Finally even Teacher seemed to be bored and she suggested that beginning tomorrow each class would review the previous year's reader.

Within a week Teacher had the entire student body reviewing their phonics during the first few minutes after opening exercises each day. Miriam was delighted. Grade ones were starting phonics. She would get a chance to work with the big kids. She sat on the edge of her seat, her hand itching to be raised. Sometimes she got it up before

Robbie or even the grade two or three kids knew the answer. Louie never participated, and the older boys and girls slouched in their seats and feigned boredom, but before long everybody seemed to be reading more smoothly. Now Miriam found herself rushing through her assigned work each day, so that she would watch and listen while Teacher called each class up in turn to read aloud. Now that they were reading at a level at which they had some competence some of the stories became interesting, and Miriam couldn't understand their complaining about having to read "Baby" books.

It was the same in arithmetic. Teacher soon had the entire student body reviewing the simplest number facts and, as Miriam caught on, she delighted in getting her hand up – before Robbie, sometimes even before Annie and the other kids in second grade.

At recess Miriam divided her time between pestering Louis, who continued to wander around on his own, and watching the older children at their games hoping to be permitted to join in. Most of the time Annie had simply ignored her, after explaining that skipping, hopscotch, even hide-and-seek were too difficult for a six-year old. The other girls followed Annie's lead. Eventually Miriam might have been included, but before long they were resenting her 'showing off'.

Teacher was doing a quick drill: addition, subtraction, multiplying. Hands were shooting up around the room. Four plus seven. Most of the hands in grades one and two were up, the older kids slouching in their seats not willing to answer the easy questions. Teacher called on Suzanne. "Ten," Suzanne mumbled. Miriam waved her hand wildly. Robbie and Annie both had their hands up.

"Eleven, teacher. Four plus seven equals eleven." Miriam shouted out without waiting for Teacher's attention. The bell rang and the children charged for the door. Suddenly Miriam felt her feet tripped out from under her. She fell hard against the door frame, grabbing for balance, and looked up at Suzanne's sneer: "How do you like that, Miss Know-it-all?" Miriam swung her fist at Suzanne's face but Annie grabbed her. "No fighting. You know you're not supposed to fight."

"But . . . But . . ." Miriam was sputtering mad.

Annie pushed her backward and she almost fell down the steps. Several children laughed. Betrayed and embarrassed, she fled to the other side of the school where the boys were gathering for their ball game.

"Look who's here. The little Miss-Show-Off." Charlie taunted. "You might know who'd be the Teacher's pet." When Jack and Bill didn't show any response, he turned to them.

"What's the matter? Can't you teach your sister any manners?"

If she expected them to stick up for her she was disappointed. Jack simply turned away, while Bill hissed at her; "Go away." Then he picked up the bat and, ignoring her, hurried after Jack.

Miriam ran to the back of the school, hoping to hide among the cedars, and there was Louie pushing a stick around, making marks in the dirt. He was someone her own size, or just a little bigger, and he was Suzanne's brother. Miriam attack, fists flying. Over and over they rolled in the dirt, punching, poking, kicking, and calling names. When they pulled apart both seemed about ready to cry. Miriam turned back towards the school. There was Annie waiting for her.

"Don't you dare tell Teacher. There's nothing worse than a tattletale."

Miriam sat on the step by herself until the bell rang.

Fortunately the afternoon lessons were even more interesting than the morning ones. Teacher read books about Social Studies -- she pointed to maps and talked about brave explorers and people who lived in far away lands. Then the big kids had to copy notes from the board so that they would be ready to answer questions the next day, but Robbie, Miriam and Louie were just expected to colour a picture. Miriam tried to make sense of the words on the blackboard. She noticed Robbie staring at them too. Someday soon they would be able to answer the questions just as well as the big kids. And get picked on in the school yard, Miriam realized. But it didn't make sense. Nobody seemed to pick on Robbie and he was just a smart as she was. She looked over at Louie. No need to worry about him. He was just making marks on his paper with his crayons, not even colouring very well. She purposely bumped his elbow. He kicked her under the desk. It hurt. She looked up to see if Teacher had noticed but she was busy on the other side of the room. She decided to ignore Louie until she got a chance to get him good. Anyway Teacher was going up to the big desk at the front of the room and choosing a book. This was Miriam's favourite part of the day. As teacher read aloud, Miriam found herself transported from the classroom to a raft floating down the Mississippi River with two boys named Tom and Huck. Another time she would be running down the red roads of Prince Edward Island with a little redheaded orphan, or struggling through the snows of the frozen north where a dog named Buck was pulling his master from the clutches of the half-frozen Yukon river. Only half understanding the stories, Miriam would allow her imagination to drift until she was startled back to reality by the ringing of the three-thirty bell.

Despite the bullying that continued off and on during recesses and lunch hours that fall, Miriam thrived in the one room school, knowing instinctively that Robbie was her biggest rival. Everything was a race to see if she could catch on and complete her work as fast as Robbie did, and he was just enough older and further advanced that it was a continuous challenge. Louis didn't matter at all. He just sat all day sniffling and even after Teacher took time to give him individual instruction he just pushed his pencil aimlessly around his paper, never seeming to know what to do or how to do it. It was almost as though he didn't know what they were talking about, and couldn't understand what he should do, like some little kid, even though he was bigger than Miriam herself. Miriam didn't realize how close to the truth she was. Louie understood very little English. She soon learned to ignore him, except when he leaned over trying to see what she was doing, and then she would crouch over her paper covering it up so that he couldn't copy her work. And whenever either of them got the chance they would exchange sneaky punches that hurt, but not nearly as much as those of the older kids on the playground.

The challenge was always to try to keep track of everything going on in the classroom, to rush through her own simple assignments, or simply put them off, and watch and listen and try to comprehend, and occasionally to throw her hand in the air, panting under her breath, waiting for Teacher to acknowledge her so that she could hazard an answer. "Quit showing off," Annie would mutter as she jabbed her in the back with a pencil and Miriam would fight the urge to turn around and punch her. Worse than Annie's jabs was the fact that sometimes, instead of acting pleased, Teacher would scold, "Miriam, have you finished your own work yet?"

It was hard to concentrate on finishing her own work, especially after Teacher stopped preparing individual work sheets for Grade one and expected them to laboriously copy their work from the blackboard like everyone else. Then at the end of the day, after listening with rapt attention to the story she would realize that she hadn't completed her assignments and she would have to 'stay-in'.

Other kids hated to 'stay-in', but Miriam knew that she should too, but actually she didn't mind so very much. Hannah encouraged all four of her children to stay after school and walk home with her. She always had to stay behind at the end of the day, giving children extra help, marking assignments, preparing next day's lessons. Usually it was well after four o'clock before she was ready to lock up. "Look on it as an opportunity." Miriam heard her explain. "You can finish up your work and do your homework for tomorrow. Or you can read books or work on special projects."

Reluctantly they all hung around. Then Bill objected, "I can't stay late tonight. Dad wants me to go down to the far pasture for that dry cow. I don't know why. He just said that he needed her home early tonight. So I can't wait for you'se guys."

"That's right. I remember now he mentioned it this morning. All right, Bill. For today. And Jack, you'd better go with him. He may need help if she's in the swamp."

A few days later Miriam heard Jack telling their mother, "I promised Gran that I'd come home directly. She wants me to dig some potatoes for her."

"Yea," Bill added. "And I said that I'd pick her some apples. She told me that she's been wanting to make some pies, but it's almost supper time when we get home, and after supper it's too dark."

There was no arguing with that logic. All farm children had chores and were expected home to do them. The next week the boys begged off again.

"Dad told us to get that dry wood into the shed before the next rain. We better get to it right away. We don't know when its going to rain."

"What about your homework?"

"Maybe we'll get here early tomorrow and hurry through it before class."

Before long, the pattern was set. After school while Hannah finished her teacher duties, Miriam studied eagerly, Annie reluctantly, and the boys hardly at all.

It was seldom that anyone in Miriam's family took work home. Miriam couldn't understand. Teacher insisted that the other children take homework with them, standing by the door as they left to remind them if they forgot, but she didn't insist that her own children do so. However after a few times that either Miriam or Annie took a book or project home with them, Miriam caught on. No sooner would she sit down and start to concentrate than Gran would find her a chore to do. And after Gran had gone home and supper had been eaten and the dishes washed and put away, if she got it out again her father would mutter, "If there is one thing I can't stand is for everyone to be sitting around with their nose in a book. Anyway, you'll ruin your eyes reading by that lamplight." Hannah was probably one of the few teachers who didn't take her work home with her. Except for the occasional Saturday newspaper brought home from a trip to town the Taylor household was not a reading household.

Soon, too, Annie was copying the boys.

"I can't stay today. I promised Gran I'd be home early to help with supper. You know how mad Dad was when it was late last night."

Hannah sighed. "Okay, Annie. Just this once."

"I'll stay, Teacher," piped up Miriam. "Can I help you with anything?"

Hannah sighed. She didn't seem as pleased as Miriam had expected her to be. "Yes, Miriam. If you've finished your work you can go and clean the blackboard erasers. Then you may choose a book to read."

As the autumn wore on, Teacher sometimes would glance at Miriam's waving hand and give the slightest of head shakes, and if Miriam continued Teacher would pointedly ignore her or speak sharply, "Miriam, have you finished your arithmetic?"

"Almost, Ma'am."

"Then finish it. Then you may get a workbook from the back shelf and do a page of extra questions."

It hurt that Teacher didn't appreciate her contribution but insisted that she continue to copy that boring work from the blackboard. The workbooks were interesting at first, but by late November Miriam started skipping pages of easy questions and trying the harder ones at the back. Sometimes then they didn't seem to make sense. How could you subtract 19 from 24? Nine was bigger than four. Everybody knew that the biggest number had to be on the top. Maybe there was a trick. Maybe the biggest number wasn't always on the top. Maybe you subtracted four from nine: then one from two. No, it didn't make sense, but Miriam struggled and completed the page as best she could and finally satisfied she put it in the pile of work to be marked.

That afternoon when the older children were busy copying a story about Eskimos from the blackboard and the little ones were supposed to be drawing a picture of Eskimo life as they understood it from the book Teacher had read, Miriam heard her name called.

"Miriam, come up to my desk, please."

"Yes, Teacher."

"Miriam, you've done this page completely wrong."

"Sorry, Teacher." She hung her head, her cheeks burning. This was embarrassing. The LeBlanc kids, Eva, sometimes even Jack or Annie sometimes got called up for teacher to point out their mistakes and make them do a page over, but never Miriam. She hoped that no one was noticing.

"Miriam, we haven't covered this work yet this term. Look at all these skipped pages. These are the ones you need to be doing for practice. Work from the front of the book."

"But other kids skip pages."

"Only if they have already covered the work. Don't argue with me. And don't jump ahead unless you are sure you can do it. As I said, this page is all wrong."

Miriam slunk back to her seat. Humiliation! She had made mistakes! She had been singled out and scolded! Surely the kids would tease her now. She had a hard time holding back her tears, but that would only make matters worse. Only babies cried. And sure enough, after school she had to listen to Annie brag. She had a gold star on her arithmetic and Teacher had praised her for working diligently.

The next day after opening exercises, Teacher again went through her quick drill of number facts then directed the Grade Ones to their questions, near the bottom of the board. Miriam resolutely picked up her pencil and copied down the first question and automatically filled in the answer. This was easy, and boring. The only hard part of this work was copying the question, trying to keep within the lines on her scribbler and being reasonably neat.

Miriam looked up. Teacher had finished her review, assigned work for the older classes and was giving her attention exclusively to the second grade.

"Pay close attention now. Today we are going to work on a new concept in subtraction. It's called borrowing and we use it when working with big numbers."

Miriam glanced back at Annie. Annie's knuckles were white where she had her hands clasped in front of her and she was frowning as she tried to give all her attention to the teacher. 'Annie was probably hoping that today's work would be the same as yesterdays and she could get another gold star. Now she's scared that she won't catch on.' Miriam thought as she turned her attention back to the board where Teacher was demonstrating the lesson. When she glanced again at her sister she could see that while Annie was still staring straight ahead her eyes had a glazed, vacant look. 'She's probably thinking about recess,' Miriam concluded. 'She needn't bother. If she doesn't pay attention, she won't get it right. Then she'll have to stay-in.' Miriam turned her full attention back to Teacher who was starting to ask questions.

"Now we've gone over it a couple of times. Who would like to try this one? 24 - 6?"

Slowly Jane raised her hand. You could tell by the quiver in her voice that she was guessing. Then Teacher went over it again. And again. Jane and one of the boys were getting a few questions right now. Then Robbie raised his hand for a question. Teacher acknowledged him and he proudly gave the correct answer. The next question. Teacher was looking directly at Annie. "Why don't you try this one?"

Annie had broken out in a sweat. She tried frantically to count on her fingers, out of sight under the desk, then she made a wild stab at the answer.

"No, Annie. Weren't you listening? Does anyone else know?"

Suddenly Miriam realized how it worked. Of course. You borrowed from the next number over. Her hand shot up, waving frantically. Teacher had acknowledged Robbie; surely she would call on Miriam as well. But Teacher pointedly ignored her eager gestures and announced that they would go over it one more time. Annie and Suzanne should pay special attention.

Miriam bent over her simple assignment, hurrying through it so that she could get a workbook from the shelf. Now she could do the hard questions at the back of the book. Regardless of her frowns and head shakes, Teacher must be proud of her. And she could do better than Annie.

As they hurried out of the classroom for recess, Annie tripped her roughly and as she fell face first in the dirt she heard Annie muttering, 'You think you're so smart. Always showing off.' Miriam looked up to see Jack and Bill and their friend Charlie laughing, but this time they were laughing at Annie.

"Ho, ho. Even your little sister is smarter than you." Charlie hooted. Annie rushed away to hide among her friends, and the boys turned to their own interests, leaving Miriam to brush the pebbles off her hands and nurse her skinned knees by herself.

That afternoon, despite Hannah's suggestion that Annie stay late and practice her subtraction, Annie insisted that she had to leave with the boys after rushing through her homework.

"I told Gran that I would help her make a cake for supper."

******

Annie and the boys escaped immediately after school with the usual excuses. Jack and Bill had barn work to do. Gran needed Annie's help. Only Miriam waited, occupying herself around the classroom, while Teacher prepared the next days work. Then she skipped happily beside her mother during the long walk home. She had shown everybody! She was just as smart as they were! She'd show them at home too!

But at home life was different. At home Annie seemed capable of doing almost everything, helping in the kitchen and around the house and taking care of the baby, while Miriam was assigned the simplest and most boring chores, gathering the eggs, drying the dishes, carrying kindling in from the shed, fetching and carrying for the older ones.

Now maybe things would change. She was smart. Surely she could help.

They reached the house. Gran was already watching for them, her jacket on her arm, anxious to get home to Gramps. Mum hurried to the kitchen to help Annie finish preparing dinner. Miriam wandered into the front room.

The baby was fussing in her basket.

There was always a baby in the house. Miriam didn't even remember when Paul was born. Then there was Davy; now Gracie. Annie was so protective of Gracie. Miriam could remember her bossing, "No. You can't carry the baby. You're too little. You're not supporting her head properly. And you've got to be careful of the soft spot."

Mum was better. Sometimes if Miriam begged, Mum would tell her to sit down and then she would place Gracie in her arms. Miriam would rock back and forth feeling proud and grown-up. Gracie was so little and cute. But before long Miriam's arms would start to get tired and she would try to shift the baby to a more comfortable position. Then Annie would shriek at her.

"You're not doing it right. You're letting her head flop all over the place. Give her to me."

But not today. Mum and Annie were busy in the kitchen. Gracie was fussing. And Miriam was so much bigger and smarter than she had been. She would help. She would settle the baby.

At first she just reached into the basket, patting Gracie. Gracie still fussed. Making faces didn't help.

Neither did singing a lullaby. Obviously she needed to be picked up. Gingerly Miriam wrapped her arms around her and carefully carried her over to the chesterfield. There, she was quiet again--for about two minutes. Before long Gracie's fussing turned to howls. Miriam was struggling to lift her up to her shoulder to pat her back as she had seen her mother do, when Annie burst in from the kitchen.

"Mum, Miriam's got the baby out of the basket."

"She was crying."

"No she was just fussing a little before she settled down for a sleep. I already gave her a bottle for Gram. Don't you know anything? Now you've got her all worked up and she'll never settle. Give her to me."

Mum was right there too, siding with Annie. "Miriam, you know you're too little to pick up the baby. You're lucky you didn't drop her."

"Mum, look. She's not even supporting the head right."

"Sorry, Mum. I was just trying to help."

"You can help by going out and checking on Paul and Davy."

Miriam wandered out into the yard and watched the little boys who seemed to be completely absorbed in making marks in the dirt with a pointed stick. It didn't hold her interest for long and she hurried back into the kitchen letting the door slam behind her. Again Annie yelled at her.

"Don't slam that door. Me and Gran put a cake in the oven before she left. Now we'll be lucky if it doesn't fall."

Miriam shrugged her shoulders as if to say, "How should I know?" and looked around for something to do.

The little boys' shouts indicated that Johnny was getting home from the mill and Mum hurried out to greet him. Miriam noticed that her mother had just taken a roast of pork from the oven. She would get a knife and cut it up. Mum would be pleased.

But Annie was shrieking again.

"Mum, Miriam's trying to cut up the meat with the paring knife. Give that to me before you cut yourself."

Miriam couldn't take it any longer.

"You shut up and leave me alone. I am going to help."

"You help? You're too stupid to help. You're just in the way. And making more work for Mum and me. Put that knife down."

"No. And you can't make me."

Gracie, who had finally fallen asleep, woke suddenly and began crying loudly. Mum hurried back to the kitchen, just as Johnny roared from his rocking chair.

"Settle down in there. If there's anything I can't stand it's a bunch of females squabbling. Can't a man enjoy a smoke in peace?"

Mum took in the scene at a glance.

"Miriam, put that knife down, right now. Annie, hurry and get the potatoes mashed. I'll finish the meat and make the gravy."

"But I want to help."

"You've already upset your father. Now you can help by setting the table."

Miriam couldn't understand it. Annie had been shouting more than she was but Annie didn't get blamed. Besides, even with their arguing they weren't making half as much noise as Jack and Bill who had just stopped hammering on a tree house they were building to have a knock down, tumble over, kicking, punching fist fight, and Paul and Davy were chasing each other around the door yard yelling war whoops. Why should Mum let Annie boss her around all the time just to keep the peace, and why was everyone expected to keep out of Dad's way and not upset him?

After supper Miriam dried the dishes that Annie washed, in an uneasy truce. Each knew how it would be--Miriam might excel at school but Annie would rule the roost at home.

Chapter Three

Paul took time to shout, "Mum! Mum! Come quick! Come and see!"

Then he and Davy leaped from the veranda and raced down the lane.

Hannah scooped up Gracie and followed Annie and Miriam as they hurried outside. Dad had taken the older boys with him for a walk to the village that morning. He was back, driving past the gate in a car! They watched in amazement as he pulled up to the veranda steps in a swirl of dust. Everybody was talking at once.

"Is it really ours?"

"Where did you get it?"

"Can I go for a drive?"

"Me too! Me too!" Even Gracie was caught up in the excitement.

Jack and Bill strutted around, showing off.

"It's a Chev."

"Only three years old – hardly broken in."

"Look at it bounce." Bill threw his weight down on one fender and the car swayed several times. Jack kicked the tires.

"I put my foot down. Told him I'd give him six hundred cash and not a penny more," Johnny explained to Hannah. "I guess he could see who he was dealing with. Want to go for a spin?"

They all piled in. Dad, Mum, Davy and Gracie in the front. Jack, Bill, Annie, Miriam, and Paul in the back, pushing for position until Dad shouted, "This car isn't going anywhere until you settle down." But you could tell that he was in a good mood.

Finally they settled. Annie and Miriam at the windows – Jack and Bill had had a turn on the way home -- Paul standing between his big brothers' knees, leaning over the back of the front seat.

"Wow!" They couldn't believe it. They had a car.

Miriam thought of the changes that had taken place in the last few years. Brightly colored curtains had appeared in the windows, paint and wallpaper, linoleum on the kitchen floor. Then last year – electricity! Electric lights in every room and one in the door yard; a refrigerator. They must be rich! And now a car!

They were no longer isolated at the end of the dirt road. They could pile in the car and go anywhere they wanted– visiting the neighbours, in to the village, even all the way to Saint John a couple of times in the year.

The visits were the best. Miriam loved it when after lunch on a boring Sunday, Johnny would announce: "I think we should take a run over to Ernie's place on the ridge." Or Mum would murmur: "I'd really like to see Bessie's new baby."

That was a signal. Quickly they would finish up the dishes and be ready for a drive. Miriam loved visiting. Regardless of where they went there was always a hearty greeting:

"So glad you dropped by."
"How have you been?"
"Haven't seen you in a dog's age."
"Come in, come in."
"You're looking good."

Maybe there would be a word or two to the children, "My, you've grown."

Before long all but the babies would be shooed away.

"Run along and play now."

"Show your cousins the new pigs."

"Go try out that swing Ernie just put up."

Off they'd go to admire a new farm animal or see the new tree house or swing. Soon they would be racing through the fields, chasing each other in wild games of hide-and-seek, kick-the-can, or cowboys and Indians; climbing trees after the early apples or just to see how high they could reach; racing down to the brook to catch frogs or skip rocks or hop from rock to log to rock trying to get across and back without falling in. These were all things that they could do alone or with their siblings but so much more fun with company.

After a while their games would pale for Miriam. The old teasing from school would start up again, or she would simply find herself left out. The kids all seemed to be several years older than her, and try as she might she could not keep up with their games or their jokes. If she wandered back to the dooryard and tried to play with her little brothers and the other little kids, their activities soon bored her.

If she wandered into to the house Miriam would inevitably find that the adults had divided themselves into two distinct groups: the women in the "front room" and the men out on the veranda, or in the shed, or even the barn. Only later, when one of the visitors stretched and remarked about the time and that they must be getting home, and the hostess would say, "'So soon, where does the time fly. I was about to make a cup of tea", would they get together for a cup of tea and homemade bread and preserves, or cake or cookies.

Miriam soon found that a child, if she was quiet and didn't butt into the conversation, and spoke only when spoken to, could sometimes join the fringes of either group. They would ignore her and sometimes even forget that she was there as she listened in on the conversations.

Annie and the older girls sometimes joined the women, and might be permitted to help with the quilting, or work on a needle work project, or to sit and knit with occasional praise from an adult. When the lunch was served they would be allowed to pass the cookies or sweetbreads. Perhaps because she felt so awkward at them and had been criticized so often by Annie, these activities didn't interest Miriam.

She would creep out to where the men were gathered and listen to their discussion about crops and hunting and work at the mill, or discourses on the government, taxes, poor roads, few services. More often than not the men would begin swapping stories about the war. It was supposed to be common knowledge that returned soldiers didn't like to talk about the war, but Miriam didn't find it that way. Her father and the men she knew talked and talked - not about hunger or wounds or death of friends and companions, but just about everything else.

Miriam treasured one evening when she sat curled up in her father's arms.

"I signed up right at the beginning," Johnny was saying. "I was one of the first from this area. As soon as I heard they were taking recruits in Saint John, I hitched right in. I didn't have to go. No, siree. I had the place here. I was married. Goodness, I had Jack and Bill, and the wife was expecting any time. Annie was born before we shipped out of Saint John. So I didn't have to sign up. In fact I could have got a deferment. But no, I told them. 'My daddy fought in the last war, and I'm in this one.' Next thing you know I'm in the army, over at Camp Aldershot near Kentville, and my folks are helping the wife and kids with the place here."

"Then you must have been with one of the first regiments to go overseas."

"No. That's the hell of it. I should have been. They got us outfitted, and had us training. God, that training. Get in shape.

Break in your new boots. Learn to take orders. Jump here, run there. Always on the double. We had this old sergeant from the first war. Always on our backs. But that's another story. Anyway, there we were. Ready to ship out. We're actually in Halifax ready to board ship. For the last two or three days I'd been having this awful pain in my gut. I tried not to mention it. I didn't want anyone thinking I was a coward, trying to find an excuse not to go. So, I'm really suffering. A few of the guys find out and they're covering for me. But finally, Perly Smyth -- remember him, from up the ridge, he didn't come back. Finally he just says to me, 'Ya gotta report to sick bay. You can't get on that boat like this. You'll die before you're out of sight of land.' So I let him talk me into it. Anyway to make a long story short, while my regiment are on the seas headed for England, I'm lying on the operating table having my appendix out. And sure enough, the doctor says that I would have been dead within 24 hours if they hadn't caught it."

"So, you went with the next batch?"

"No. They don't do things like that in the army. Anyway, it seems I'd put off the operation too long as it was. Full of infection, I was. Took me a damn long time to get out of the hospital. It was touch and go for awhile, I can tell you. Sick? Man, I never want to go through something like that again. Now-a-days with penicillin and all them wonder drugs, appendicitis isn't so bad. But back then, once it burst, a lot of people died. Even after I got up and around, I was weak as a kitten. So they sent me back home and I got to spend some more time with the wife and kids. I tried to teach Jack how to help out some around the place. He was pretty little but growing all the time. He and Bill were following me all over. And Annie was sitting up and babbling and grabbing food off the table before the army remembered me and I got my orders to report to Petawawa."

"That's that big camp in Ontario. Why did they send you up there?"

"Who knows why the army does things? I didn't ask questions. There I am back in boot-camp, but now instead of taking orders, I'm giving them. Yes, made me a sergeant and I've got me training raw recruits. Some of those city boys, from Toronto and that, they are so smart and cocksure, and they don't know one end of a gun from the other."

"So, you stayed stateside. You never did get overseas?"

"I'm coming to that. It sure looked like I'd missed my chance. But then, a good two years after I signed up, orders came through. The whole kit and caboodle of us were to take a train for Halifax. Us Maritimers were given a week's leave. So I got off the train in Saint John and hitched a ride home. A few days later we sailed from Halifax. I was in England when I learned this one was on the way. She was past two when I first laid eyes on her."

"Boy, you're some fast worker. Only home for a few days you say."

"I'll bet you were relieved she looks like you."

Miriam, half dozing, and not half understanding the conversation, suddenly realized that she was the center of attention.

"'Yeh, Johnny, there's no mistaken that one. She's yours."

The men guffawed and slapped their thighs, and Miriam squirmed from her father's arms. Embarrassed and sure that somehow she had done something wrong she hurried in to hang around her mother's chair.

Chapter Four

Jack tramped around the kitchen in pride, sharing the story again. He and Bill had spotted the deer down in the lower pasture browsing on the alders near the brook. They had crept closer, using the old log fence for cover until he could get a clear shot. Then, just as he had raised his gun, the deer lifted its head in alarm. It was starting to leap in the air as he pulled the trigger. Then it fell.

Bill took over then. "I raced down with my knife. It was still kicking, so I had to be careful. But as soon as it stopped, I reached down, grabbed an antler and slit it's throat."

Miriam saw Mum shutter, but then she praised the boys, pointing out how much the meat would be needed that winter.

"And now that you've got a deer and the hunting season is almost over, I hope that you'll be just as eager to apply yourselves to your studies."

The mood changed suddenly as everybody looked at Mum. Finally Jack spoke.

"I've been meaning to tell you, Mum. I'm not going back to school."

"What do you mean? Not going back?"

"It's like this. I've missed a lot of time this fall – what with the potato picking and farm work, and then the hunting. And I've been talking to the old man over at the mill. I think he'll take me on in the woods this winter."

"But Jack. You're in grade eight now. Just this winter and you'll be finished."

"No I won't. Not with the time I missed. I'll be away behind. And you'll fail me. You know you will."

"It's not for me to say. The Department of Education sets the standards. But if you apply yourself. If you really work at it and let me give you extra help, I know you could do it."

"It's not that big a deal. Anyway, I'll have a job. I'll be earning money to help the family."

From the corner by the wood box Bill spoke up. "If Jack's not going back to school, I ain't either."

"Oh, Bill, no. Of course you'll go back."

"And be the only one sitting among those little kids in the school. Charlie's been working with the mechanic since the summer, and I'm damn sure Maurice ain't going back."

"Charlie finished grade eight in June. Bill, you're working at grade level now. And you're smart. You'll need an education."

"Not if I can get a job. If the old man takes Jack on, he'll take me too. I'm as strong as Jack."

"But Jack, Bill! It might not seem to be a big step now, but education is important. Don't you want to say that you went as far as you could in school."

"Dad didn't. And he's done alright."

Miriam watched as Hannah looked at Johnny. Perhaps he would say something to stop the boys from arguing with Mum. Miriam could tell that it upset her, and Miriam didn't like anyone to upset Mum. Maybe Dad could tell them that he wished that he could have gone further. Though teenagers now, the boys would still respect their father's opinion. Instead he took their side:

"Leave them alone. Let them make up their own minds. If they can get work, let them. They're strong enough to do a man's job. If they don't, then they can go back to school.

"But it will be too late then." for a moment Miriam, listening from the sidelines, actually thought that Mum in her 'Teacher' role would argue further. She almost hoped that she would, but was afraid at the same time. Nobody argued long with her father. Then Hannah's shoulders dropped and she was just 'Mum' again, murmuring something about, "If you think it's right." before she hurried into the front room to check on the younger ones. Miriam couldn't remember ever hearing her parents argue for more than a word or two yet she was always afraid that it might happen.

It was different at school now. The room was full of little kids. Paul and Davy were both attending, and there seemed to be a lot of children their age, born in the years after the war when the men came back from overseas. But the older boys were missed. Sitting at the back with their feigned indifference and their muttered comments, they had set the tone for the school. Now Annie and her friends were the oldest, with Miriam, Robbie and Louie trying to keep up and fit in.

Miriam found it easier now. Without the older boys tacit approval, she wasn't teased and picked on when she knew the answers, and she was learning as well not to show off. She let others have a turn with their hands up. She was contented to know herself that she was doing good work and she took pride in completing her assignments and then volunteering to be teacher's helper, a privilege given to the older ones who completed their work.

With so many little ones, Teacher appreciated any help she could get. Miriam often found herself sitting with the Grade 1s or 2s, hearing their ABCs or their counting, or checking their work pages. Louie LeBlanc had repeated his first difficult year while struggling with his shyness and the challenge of studying in a language he barely understood.

Now he occasionally accepted Miriam's help with his grammar. But Miriam sensed his resentment and remembered with shame how she had covered up her work so that he couldn't copy it when he really needed to.

She got along better with Annie now too. Occasionally the older grades were assigned projects where they worked together and Miriam learned to appreciate Annie's meticulous attention to detail and fine penmanship, while Annie was willing to let Miriam research the subject and sketch out the first draft.

Then one Sunday when several families converged at one house for an impromptu visit to a shut-in, Miriam came in from running around playing kick-the-can to get a drink of water in the kitchen. For a change she remembered not to let the door slam, and as she stood quietly she overheard her name mentioned in the next room where the women had gathered.

"Hannah, my Rob says that Miriam is one of the smartest children in the school." Mrs. Marshall was saying. "I wonder why you're holding her back. Why don't you move her up a grade?"

"Oh, I couldn't do that. The most up-to-date teaching pamphlets really don't recommend it. They think it's best to keep children with their age-mates so they develop properly socially, and let them do outside reading or projects. It's called enrichment, rather then advancement."

"But you advanced my Rob after that first year, and your own Bill a while back I remember."

"That was different. If a child is behind his age level because of sickness, or because the school was closed for a time, then its all right to move them up, if they are interested and can handle the acceleration."

Another voice, "Goodness, with some of the teachers we had for a while before you started teaching, there must be a lot of kids behind for their ages. Why don't you advance them?"

"Yes. Your Annie was one of those who missed out. But you've never moved her up."

The 'Teacher's' voice again, but somewhat hesitantly, as though she was not sure how much further to carry this discussion, "Some children are better off if you don't push them too hard. Sometimes they are contented to do well at the level they are presently working even though it might be behind the expected 'standard' for that age. They'd rather do well in the grade they are in now than struggle and risk failure if they try to catch up, especially if they lack confidence. Believe me, I've given serious thought to Annie, and to each of the other children. At first Annie was frustrated at being behind where she thought she should be, but now she has settled in nicely and is happy. Perhaps as she gets older, I'll see what can be done so that she can finish by the time she's sixteen, but not right now. All children have abilities and talents, but not all are academically inclined or interested. Annie's main interests seem to lie elsewhere, which is true of many of the children."

Just then several other children burst through the kitchen door and raced for the water pump, and Miriam pretended to be busy tying a shoe, while she overheard a few words of Teacher slipping back into the role of mother/housewife. "Sadie, that was excellent crab-apple jelly your daughter brought me last week. Could I have the recipe?"

****

Now that they didn't seem to be competing as much at school, but actually working together occasionally, Annie and Miriam were getting along better at home too. Under Gram's tutelage Annie seemed to have mastered all the intricacies of cooking and homemaking, and now Gran left for home, where Gramps was feeling his age, as soon as they were home from school. Together with Mum when she had time, Annie passed on what she had learned, showing Miriam how to make sauces for vegetables, gravies, spices for meats - how to have a light hand with pie crust, and how to kneed bread until it was elastic to the touch. When Miriam had dough sticking between her fingers, and half way up to her elbows, and pasted to the table cloth and the rolling pin, Annie no longer called her stupid and pushed her away, but they had a good laugh together before Annie, patiently if a bit haughtily explained, "Let me show you again. Just a little sprinkling of flour, and a light touch of the rolling pin. Like this. Now you try again."

It was the same with knitting and embroidery. When Miriam dropped a stitch, or got her threads tangled, Annie would patiently pick back to the mistake and help Miriam get started again. Finally Miriam knit herself a sweater and proudly showed it off to her father pleased that Annie didn't try to take most of the credit.

There was one area, however, where Annie jealously guarded her domain. She was the one who helped Mum take care of Gracie. By now they had both realized that a baby's head would not fall off if it wasn't properly supported, and Gracie had grown from a helpless infant to a little girl. Miriam might occasionally play silly clapping games with her, or teach her nursery rhymes, but it was to Annie that she ran when she was unhappy, or tired, or wanted some babying. Annie petted her and rocked her, fixed her snacks of bread and jam, and slept with her at night. If occasionally Annie entered a room and found Gracie curled up beside Miriam while Miriam read to her or told her a fairy story, Annie would call Gracie away with a tempting treat, or a declaration that it was time to get washed up for bed. Then she would glare at Miriam as if she had done something wrong. Gracie always obeyed Annie and willingly followed her around, treating her with the same deference and respect that was due her mother and Gram.

It was with her younger brothers that Miriam found pals. At school they looked up to her as a sort of teacher's helper. At home they were glad to share their adventures with her. Miriam would look back on this as the happiest time in her childhood.

Jack and Bill had tentatively entered the world of men, and they could look tolerantly and affectionately on young girls and little children. Through the winter they took it upon themselves to show Paul and Davy how to set rabbit snares. Miriam, who remembered being laughed at and humiliated when she tried to keep up with Jack and Bill and set snares with their discarded bits of wire and never catch anything, now watched while they showed Paul how to measure out a length of wire, twist it around on itself so that it would pull tight around the hapless animal's neck, and anchor it to a springy sapling. That was it. She needed the proper materials to work with. When they shared a generous length of wire with her and she set her own snares and enjoyed her successes and the occasional rabbit stew added variety to their winter diet.

In the spring she followed along when they showed their little brothers where the best fishing holes were and learned to cut a sapling for a rod and attach a length of fishing line. She developed a light hand with a fishing rod, sensing when the time was right and setting the hook with a quick jerk and then pulling the trout out of the water with hardly a splash.

She watched Paul in his eagerness jerking the line whenever he felt a nibble. Often he would pull the hook right out of the fish's mouth. Other times he would yank the rod up and the fish would go sailing over their heads and the line would become hopelessly entangled in the alder bushes growing by the stream. Then Miriam would help him to sort out the mess and begin fishing again. Like Miriam, Davy developed a lighter touch.

Chapter Five

Jack and Bill had their own car now: a beaten-up, second-hand rattle-trap, but it got them around. Miriam hung on the fringes listening as they bragged about cruising around the neighbourhood with Charlie and Maurice, and driving in to town on Saturday nights to meet other young people, hanging around the hotdog stand. Occasionally they would mention venturing further, perhaps to a drive-in movie or a dance and she wished that they would take her along.

That summer the boys sat out on the veranda with their father and talked man-talk of farming and woods word and politics. Occasionally other young people would drop around and after a while Johnny would come back into the house, and as Hannah put on the kettle for a cup of tea, Annie would jump up from her handwork and hurry out to the kitchen to fix a snack for the boys.

Miriam couldn't understand.

"For heaven's sake, Annie. Why are you waiting on Jack and Bill? Let them do it themselves."

"Because we've got company. It's important to make them welcome."

"Company? It's only Charlie and Maurice."

"Yes. And you stay out of the way now. They don't want to be bothered with little kids."

Then, when she took out the tray, instead of coming back in like Mum would have done, Annie stayed out on the veranda, laughing and joking along with the boys. Usually then Mum and Dad sat in the kitchen, drinking their tea. Knowing that she was unwanted on the veranda, Miriam would join them, listening for odd snatches of conversation and Annie's high pitched laughter, not realizing that her parents were half listening too, until the evening Johnny slammed his cup down on the sideboard. "Just listen to her out there with that foolishness. And with that no good LeBlanc boy at that. Catholic, too. Doesn't she have any sense?" He glared at Hannah: "If you don't call her in, I will."

"Annie. It's time to come in now. There's a chill in the air this evening."

Miriam smiled in satisfaction. It served Annie right for all the airs she put on about being grown-up when she was just causing friction between her parents.

Then a few weeks later Annie came in, "Mum, we're going to take a drive in to town to see what's going on. Is that o'kay?"

"Ask you father."

Miriam expected him to object, to point out that no girl should be running the roads at all hours of the night, but instead he agreed, "With Charlie and the boys? Okay. But be back by 10:00 or I'll come looking for you."

The screen door slammed behind Annie, and Miriam heard her giggling. Miriam watched from the window and noticed that instead of going with her brothers, Annie was climbing into Charlie's car. She felt a tinge of envy, wishing that she was old enough to join them. It might be fun to ride around town on a Friday evening.

Miriam was in bed when Annie got home, just under her curfew, smiling and humming. Obviously she had had a good time.

When school opened in the fall, Annie made it clear that she no longer had time for Miriam or any little kids. She was in her final year and instead of joining in the schoolyard games she linked arms with Jane and Suzanne and walked around the grounds, heads bent together whispering. At home she spent her free time experimenting with hair styles and trying on lipstick, and Friday and Saturday nights she was permitted to go out with her brothers and their friends. If Miriam asked where they went or what they did, Annie would shrug her shoulders or toss her head, "Oh, we just drove around." If pushed for more details she would snap "None of your business." Miriam began to feel left out but she wasn't much interested. She wasn't much attracted by the boys who chummed with Jack and Bill and teased Annie. Even Charlie Smart, who always seemed to be coming around, and whose tall, broad-shouldered, blond good-looks always sent Annie into a flutter, but who ignored Miriam as though she wasn't there, didn't interest her much.

The only boy she really talked to was Rob Marshall at school. He was the only other person she knew who really seemed to enjoy studying. Like her, he eagerly read all the books on the back shelf - not just the ones assigned for a book report or an essay. He was a year ahead of her now, in his final year in the little one-room school, but often the older grades shared assignments and usually he and Miriam chose each other as partners on a project while Annie worked with her friends.

It just seemed natural that they would start eating their lunches together; and sometimes when they were talking about something interesting after school he would walk to the end of the road with her, and they would continue their conversation leaning against the mailboxes, sometimes until Hannah came hurrying along with Gracie after having finished up at the school. Miriam never thought of these walks together as dates. She just enjoyed his company.

Miriam didn't like to think of what might happen when Rob finished school in the spring. She realized that he wouldn't want to start work in the woods or at the mill like Jack and Bill, Charlie and Maurice, but what else would he do? Then, early in June he told her; his family had decided to move to Saint John.

"I think that they're probably moving so I'll be able to go to highschool. There're so few opportunities around here. Sure, sometime in the future they'll probably build a bigger school in town and there'll be school busses, but that won't happen in time for me. Once you're out of school, it's darned hard to go back. I've already had to catch up once."

"I'd forgotten about that," Miriam muttered, too shocked to say anything more, but he didn't notice as he went on, "Just think, Miriam! Highschool! There will be a whole library of books. And a chemistry lab where I'll be able to do experiments. And all sorts of new experiences. And different teachers who are experts in their fields. Goodness, maybe I'll even be able to go on to university. There's no limit to what a fellow can do if he gets an education."

Rob seemed so excited that Miriam didn't mention how devastated she felt. He never once mentioned that he would miss her, but she already knew how lost and lonely she would be without him.

****

The boys were gone. The first to leave was Charlie, in the early spring. Miriam heard Annie lament: "I'll hardly see him anymore."

But it seemed every weekend he was back, hardly taking time to stop at his place before heading for the Taylor's where he would sit with Johnny and the boys and brag, "I got my chance. The Old Man heard they were looking for mechanics down on the docks. Hell, I've been working at that all year. So I just went down and put in my name and now I'm a junior mechanic, working for my papers. And earning good money at the same time. There ain't nothing here to hold me. This place is a dead end."

A few weeks later as the mill began it's seasonal layoffs, he was urging the boys: "They're hiring down there all the time. Come down. I'll put in a good word for you."

Still they were home every weekend, and it seemed to Miriam that was all Annie waited for, welcoming her brothers and asking about Charlie. Then after supper they would hear his car in the driveway and Annie would rush out onto the veranda, anticipating his call, "Come on Annie. Let's go for a drive."

Then as the summer dragged on, more and more often Miriam heard Annie talking about the opportunities for work in Saint John. At night in their bedroom Annie whispered to Miriam in an unexpected confidence: "Charlie wants me to come to Saint John." Miriam didn't know what to think. What would life be like on the farm without Annie bossing her, but also occasionally confiding in her?

"You couldn't do that."

"Why not?" Annie was suddenly impatient. "I'm not a child like you. I'll get a job and a room somewhere."

"What could you do?" Miriam sneered.

"I could wait on tables, or work at Zellers or Woolworths. There's lots of work in Saint John."

"Dad would never let you go!"

Miriam felt Annie harden and they both knew that would be the problem but unlike Miriam who never wanted to cause a family quarrel, Annie was willing to plea, "Please, Mum. Talk to Dad. I could get a job. I know I could."

It was no surprise that her parents agreed that she was too young to go to the city by herself. Besides she was needed at home. Gramps had suffered a stroke and Gram needed to stay at home to care for him. Begrudgingly, after school started Annie took over the household chores, cheering up only when she heard that the boys were coming home for the weekend.

Everyone was excited on Friday nights when Jack and Bill arrived home with treats for the little ones and sometimes a gift for Hannah or the girls. Miriam noticed that they were treated as company. Supper was reheated and dished out to them while Johnny questioned them about the happenings in Saint John and brought them up to date on the farm and the neighbours. Mum asked about their room. Was it comfortable? Were they getting enough to eat? Only Annie held back waiting until she heard Charlie's car in the driveway.

****

Miriam's final year at school had started with no other students in either grade seven or eight. As she had expected, it was lonely but she adjusted to it. Often her mother outlined a course of study for her and she worked away at it on her own, taking breaks every now and then to help out with the younger classes.

Thirteen years old and in her final year in the little one room school, Miriam looked around the classroom and wondered how long it had been getting shabbier. A few years before when Paul and Davy and then Gracie had started school, the room had been full. Instead of two or three children in each grade, there had been five or six. New desks and chairs had been purchased, and crowded into the room. There was some talk about expansion, adding another room and hiring another teacher, when enrolment more than doubled and there were over thirty-five children in the school. No wonder Hannah had permitted, even encouraged, the older children to help the younger ones. But now there were empty desks piled up in the cloakroom, and enrolment was dropping again. People were abandoning their houses and homesteads and moving into town, or more often than not into Saint John. Sometimes two or three families left in a year, pulling three or four children out of the school at a time.

Miriam began to wonder what would happen to her at the end of the term when she would be finished school. Would she end up helping Annie keep house, or more likely take over the housework, for Annie was again talking about moving to Saint John.

"Everybody my age wants a life of their own. Ada's married and living in town. Jane's in Saint John."

"That's a little different. Her whole family moved. She'd look cute staying in that big house all by herself now wouldn't she."

"Claudette and Susanne are working in Moncton."

"No doubt they've got family there. Lots of French people live in Moncton. But until you're eighteen you will live with us."

"Maybe Charlie and me will get married. Then nobody will stop us from moving to town."

"Not until you're eighteen," Johnny slammed his foot down. Miriam shuttered. She admired Annie's courage in continuing to argue, but was afraid also. She didn't like confrontation.

"And why not? Goodness Ada's not much older than me and she's been married almost a year, and she has a baby."

"You notice Ada's not my daughter, either. Enough of this foolishness."

Miriam thought the issue was closed, but then she overheard bits of whispered conferences between Annie and her mother, and then between Hannah and Johnny; and during the Christmas break there was a quiet little wedding at the house, and Annie had her way. After New Year's she moved to Saint John as Mrs. Charlie Smart.

For the rest of the winter, Hannah and Miriam hurried home after school to get supper on the table for Johnny and the kids, and laundry and cleaning were done on the weekends.

Chapter Six

Miriam was sitting at the kitchen table enjoying the late afternoon sun as she stemmed strawberries while her mother peeled potatoes at the sink, when her mother told her that the family would be moving to Saint John as soon as the school year was over.

Miriam leaped up in surprise almost knocking the berries over. A million thoughts raced through her mind at once. Saint John! Annie and the boys! Shopping! Movies! Then the sobering thought of leaving home and the only life she had known.

"But what about your job, Mum. How will you be able to teach if we live so far away?" As soon as she asked, Miriam knew that it was a stupid question.

"The school is being closed."

"Why?"

"The Moore's are moving. They told me a while ago. That leaves only two families besides us."

"How will their kids get to school?"

"I'm not sure. I imagine the Smith's will get their girls to school in town. They live closer. And I think likely the LeBlanc kids will drop out, I couldn't get the older ones to stay once they reached their teens. But you'll like living in the city, Miriam. I don't know how Paul and Davy will like it. They'll miss their pets, and the open fields and the woods. But you and Gracie will like it. Especially you. Maybe you'll be able to go to high school. Anyway, it's just about settled. Charlie and Annie found us an apartment down by the waterfront, not far from where Dad will be working. Jack and Bill have a room nearby, and Charlie and Annie are just a few blocks away."

But from the words 'high school' Miriam hadn't been listening. High school! What would it be like? Ever since Rob had talked so excitedly about it she had wondered about high school. Would Rob be in the same school? Would he help her find her way around? Show her where things were? Introduce her to his friends? He was older and in a different grade. Did young people from different grades chum around? Would they have any classes together? There would be separate classrooms for different classes, and different teachers would teach different subjects. Goodness, she had never had a teacher other than her mother. What would it be like? Would she fit in? She had never taken subjects like music, art, French, or phys-ed. Would the other kids laugh at her? Would she be able to find her way around the big building? How would she find the bathroom? What about her clothes? How did the high school girls dress? Did they wear make-up to school? Would she even know how to talk to city girls? Maybe they would think she was an ignorant country hick.

One thing she never questioned was her ability to do the regular work. She knew that her reading and math skills were up to par. 'Teacher' never permitted anyone to complete the eighth grade without being able to pass standardized tests. With her extra reading, she felt confident in her knowledge of social studies (called history and geography in high school) and nature studies. And the school would have a library. That had been one of the things Rob had been excited about. Not just a few books on the shelves at the back of the classroom, but a whole room devoted to books. Yes, she could go to high school.

Eventually she would become a teacher. Yes, a teacher. She loved teaching, and she had had so much practice when helping the little ones.

    Miriam decided that it was worth leaving the only home she had ever known, if she could continue in school. She would have opportunities. She would have a future. With this in mind she cheerfully helped her mother pack up whatever household goods and furniture they would be taking with them.

******

    Although they never discussed it with her, and she didn't expect them to, Miriam knew that her parents must have had a difficult time making the decision; and even with hindsight it was difficult to know if they had made the right one. When she considered it the move seemed inevitable. Rural populations were moving to the cities. That's where work, and social life, and opportunities were--not isolated at the end of some gravel road. Hannah had been right: the school did not reopen in the fall. During the summer the Smiths put their small house on skids and moved it to the edge of town, and with the Taylors gone there were no small children beyond the forks. Within a few years the whole hamlet would be grown up in brush and weeds: the school deserted with the wind blowing through the broken windows. The mill would be closed and the machinery removed. The empty houses would stand forlornly, sagging on their rotting sills. Only the LeBlanc place would remain occupied and even it would look overgrown and neglected. It was several years before the regional school opened in town and then the bus would only run out as far as the forks. Perhaps they had moved at the right time.

In their small apartment with thin partitions there were few secrets. As Miriam lay awake at night, keeping still so that she wouldn't disturb Gracie sleeping beside her, she would hear her parents talking in the next room. Often the discussion turned to money. First there was the rent. Miriam couldn't believe it as she heard Johnny raise his voice and swear about how much they had to pay for their four rooms. Never before had the Taylors paid for accommodation. Their land had been in the family for generations. They had added buildings as needed -- additions to the house, barns, sheds with their own labour. And there were the additional expenses for water and sewerage–water with added chlorine so their tea tasted off, and the children complained unless they could make Koolaid that had previous been a treat.

The city offered conveniences. It seemed heavenly to have a bathroom – a tub to soak in and a flush toilet. No more outhouse with its smell and its flies – even worse in winter with the snow and cold. And they were freed from the drudgery of cutting, splitting, piling, carrying kindling and wood, for now they cooked on an electric stove.

However, Miriam realized that she and Hannah still spent a lot of time in the kitchen preparing meals, while the Paul and Davy hung around bored.

"We hate this place. Why can't we go back home?"

"There's nothing to do."

"You could go down to the store and pick up a few groceries. I've been making a list." Hannah suggested and the boys who had taken it for granted that they should slop the pigs, and gather eggs, and work in the garden if they hoped for fresh vegetables for supper considered a short walk to the corner store an imposition that deserved a reward:

"Then can we each get a popsicle."

Miriam heard her mother sigh and watched her reach for the old sugar bowl where she kept her spare change. They could run a tab at the local store for groceries, with Johnny going in on payday to settle up, but Hannah had a rule that treats had to be paid for at the time. "Here you are. There's enough for one popsicle. You'll have to share."

Yet Miriam wished that she could ask for a popsicle too. It was so hot in the apartment. Then as she heard Hannah call after the boys to bring home a can of Kam for supper, she found herself thinking of walking down across the pasture to the stream, feeling the coolness she cast her line into the water and waited for the thrill of that first nibble. Then when she had her stringer full, she would pick wild berries on the way home and Hannah could make a pie. Her mouth watered for fresh brook trout and blueberry pie rather than Kam.

But there was school to think about. That made it all worthwhile. In the fall they would start school. The boys and Gracie would make friends and not be so whiny. And she would go to highschool. She thought of Rob. She had hoped to run into him in the city but she had no idea where he lived and would have been too shy to go to his house anyway, but even in that big school, surely she would see him. Through the summer she waited.

It was almost like that year when she was little, waiting to start school, chatting excitedly about her anticipated adventures, and not noticing the worried look on her mother's face. Then one day in August when the boys were throwing a ball around listlessly under the clotheslines in the back yard, and Gracie was over at Annie's place, 'helping' with the baby, Miriam looked through the Eaton catalogue trying to figure out what city girls might be wearing to school:

"Mum, do you think that I could have a new blouse for the first day of school. I think it might be important to make a good first impression. I don't want to look like a hick."

"Miriam, Dad and I have been talking. I know you're heart is set on going to school, but this is a bad time. We can barely afford to outfit the boys and Gracie."

"Then maybe I could make some new clothes. Surely we could afford some yard goods, and I could make some for Gracie too."

"No, Miriam. That's not what I mean. It's more than clothes. You'd need shoes, but we'd manage them somehow. But then there's books as well. And you are looking at four years of high school. That's a lot of time."

"I know, Mum. And then there's another year at Teachers' College in Fredericton before I could get my licence."

"That's the point, Miriam. We just can't afford it. Not as things are now. Not with three younger ones just to get through elementary school." Hannah glanced at Miriam but then looked back down to the sweater she was knitting for Gracie.

Suddenly Miriam realized what Mum was saying. But it couldn't be true. It couldn't!

"Surely you don't mean that I can't go to school."

"I'm sorry, Miriam. That's the way it is. We've talked and your father has made up his mind."

So that was it. Miriam didn't know what to say. She had never learned to argue with her parents like Annie used to. Miriam always worried about hurting or disappointing her mother, and to protect her mother from any unpleasantness as well as herself she always tried to keep peace with her father. But this was important, even if she had to plea. Surely Mum could intervene on her behalf.

"Why, Mum? Why? Dad's working steady at the docks now. I heard him say that he's earning more than he ever did at the mill."

"Expenses are up Miriam. We never dreamed how much it would cost to live in the city. We don't have the farm to fall back on any more. And I'm not working." Suddenly Miriam realized why her mother wasn't looking at her. Hannah was trying to hide her own discouragement. She didn't want Miriam to read it in her eyes. Miriam turned away too, looking down at her hands. It was almost too awful to bear her mother's pain along with her own. Yet she couldn't leave it alone.

"I suppose you'll want me to get a job, though I don't know what I'll do. You always said that a person had to have an education in today's world." Miriam felt almost as though she had struck her mother physically but she continued, "Maybe I could wash dishes somewhere and earn my keep." She dashed out of the house, brushing past her brothers in the back yard and walked for hours, not coming home until long after supper, when she ignored the plate that Hannah had kept warm for her and fled to her bedroom, crawling into bed and under the blankets next to Gracie before her brothers came in to climb into their bunks.

She lie there staring at the ceiling. She heard Hannah and Johnny talking in the kitchen but it was too far away for her to make out what they were saying. Once Johnny raised his voice, but her mother 'shss'd him'.

All Miriam could think about was that she had to quit school. All her hopes, all her dreams - gone. 'We've decided that it would just take to long.' Who decided? Who made the decisions? Where? When? How had they even discussed it without her knowing? Without consulting her? Wasn't this her future they were talking about? Didn't she matter?

Jack and Bill were out on their own though they hung around the apartment enough you might think that they still lived there. They had their freedom, they were doing what they wanted. 'Teacher' had urged them to stay in school as long as they could and they had refused. Annie was married, with her own place, and everybody making a fuss over the new baby. Mum had helped her, kept her in school until she was sixteen, even though she was so far behind. Miriam was only fourteen. Surely she was entitled to two more years, just to be fair.

She timidly broached the subject at breakfast but her father turned on her.

"Didn't your mother tell you last night. It's been decided. I'm not made of money. I bust my ass every day just to put food on the table. I can't be throwing money away. And what good is another two years of schooling going to do you. How much does a girl need to know to peel potatoes and change diapers?"

So that was it. It came back to Annie. Annie, married and with a baby. Annie putting on airs, and not yet eighteen.

"But I'm not like Annie."

Suddenly Miriam caught her mother's eye and couldn't go on. She choked down the last of her porridge and sneaked out onto the fire escape where she sat with her head in her hands until she knew the kitchen was empty. Dad was off to work. Mum had Gracie in the bedroom with her as she made the beds and picked up the laundry. The boys burst out the back door and past her on the landing without so much as a glance. She went in to do the dishes. Despite the fact that her world had crumbled around her, there were still the chores to be done, the routines to be followed.

It was a few days later that Hannah invited her to sit down together after lunch.

"Miriam, I've made some inquiries. There's a business college in town. They'll be starting a new term soon. Would you like to think about it?"

Miriam didn't know what to think. Was this perhaps something she could look forward to? "Maybe."

But there were obstacles. Didn't Mum know? "But Business College costs money Mum. It's not like school. You have to pay tuition. I don't have any money and Dad's not going to give me any."

"I have a little put away. Each year while I was teaching I saved some in case it was needed. There's just enough for the short course – eight months, and you would have a certificate and be able to get a job as a clerk-typist or receptionist.

"Would I qualify though? Don't you have to have high school?"

"Only for the advanced course. Otherwise they take girls with grade eight. There's just one problem thought. You're supposed to be sixteen to enter."

"But Mum. That doesn't make sense. If I'm smart enough, if I've got my grade eight, I should be allowed to go. I'll just pretend to be sixteen."

'Could she pull it off?' Miriam wondered. Annie might have. Like her mother Annie was tall and slim. But Miriam took after her father who was short and solid. As a child she had been chunky and now she only came to her mother's shoulder, but with puberty she had developed some shape. She looked down at her chest. She had developed early. Her breasts were bigger than Annie's. Annie sometimes made snide remarks about them. Her brothers and Charlie teased her and she sometimes felt embarrassed by uninvited stares on the street and even though the movie stars and entertainers seemed proud of their big breasts she was ambivalent, sometimes pleased with her development but other times wishing that they were a little less conspicuous. But now it they helped her to look older they would be an asset.

"I'll wear high heels and put my hair up. That will make me look taller."

"It might work. You're right. It doesn't seem fair to make you wait two years when you already qualify. I know that you could do the work."

Miriam thought about it. She'd rather be a teacher than a secretary, but that was impossible. Dad had put his foot down. Now Mum was suggesting a possibility. It would be better than working in a restaurant. But there were still so many obstacles. Only a few days before Mum had been explaining how little money they had and how many expenses. Now she was proposing something that surely would be expensive. Didn't she know? Was she somehow getting Miriam's hopes up, only to have them crash again.

"Mum. There will still be books and clothes and things. And I won't be earning anything for the house while I'm studying. Dad will be expecting me to pay my way. He did with the boys, remember. As soon as they quit school Dad insisted that they contribute to the household. I don't see how we can even think about it."

"I've considered that. It was different with the boys. They made their own choice. I've looked around and I'm taking a job at the lunch counter at Woolworths as soon as school starts. It will be part time, but Gracie can go over to Annie's after school and the Paul and Davy can manage on their own for a few hours until somebody gets home."

Miriam felt her face burn with shame as she realized the sacrifice that her mother was making. Hannah, who had been a teacher, with a degree of independence, and the status that went with being a professional, was willing to work at a lunch counter so that Miriam wouldn't have to. Hannah was making it possible for her to make something of herself after all. She would have to live up to Hannah's expectations.

"You won't be sorry, Mum."

During the next week Miriam wavered between hope and despair. Deep down in her heart she knew that she would rather be a teacher, but as she walked over to the business district at noon hour and watched the secretaries, receptionists, and stenos leaving their buildings and walking briskly and importantly over to Zellers or Woolworth's, buying their lunches and sitting in the booths chatting and laughing together she realized that there might be advantages to office work. Hannah had always brought a lunch from home and ate with the children before hurrying to get the afternoon work on the blackboard.

Maybe it would be nice to work in an office. Miriam tried hard to develop a positive attitude. But she wasn't sure. She wasn't ready for that life. She still thought of herself as a schoolgirl dreaming of highschool and the future. Wasn't that the whole purpose of moving to the city -- to give the children an opportunity? Apparently not. The boys and Annie had lived at home until they were seventeen. True, the boys had contributed financially from the time they started working, but Annie hadn't. Yet Dad had objected when Annie wanted to leave home. It didn't seem fair. Then she remembered the sacrifice Hannah was making, and she felt her obligation to accept it cheerfully.

Chapter Seven

After an initial adjustment to the Business College - finding her way around in the large brick building, and getting used to having thirty or forty other girls in the class - Miriam realized that most of the class work to be less intellectually challenging than some of the more difficult books she had worked her way through in the old one-room school . She was surprised when some of the other girls struggled to grasp a concept, or shrugged their shoulders in defeat almost from the beginning, and she had a little more sympathy as she thought to Annie. If these sophisticated city girls broke out into a cold sweat at the idea of explaining a bookkeeping entry, it was easier to understand that Annie in a backwood country school might have had the same problems in math years ago.

She knew better now than to volunteer answers. She didn't want to get off on the wrong foot with her classmates and she didn't want to draw attention to herself. She was several years younger than most of the class, more than a year younger than she claimed on her application form.

She need not have worried because no one paid any attention to her after the initial glance around the room on the first day. She realized that she would never fit in with this sophisticated crowd. Her hair was wrong. She set it in rollers each evening, suffering through the night with hard brushes pressing against her head, and brushed it and pinned it up on top of her head, but it wasn't like the others. The homemade skirt and new polyester blouse that had looked just right in the front room of the apartment, looked dowdy in the classroom, while the neat navy jumper and white blouse that she had thought was businesslike, looked more like a school uniform. Obviously she was a country bumpkin come to town.

To Miriam everything was all new and different. Never before had she touched a typewriter. It seemed almost magic to tap a few keys and have words form on paper. It was so much faster and neater than handwriting, and the results appeared so much more professional. But when she looked around to smile in her joy of discovery, the others seemed bored or indifferent, so she went back to studying the keys. It was puzzling why they were not in alphabetical order. Surely that would have made it much easier to find them. When she ask about it the other girls laughed and the instructor shook her head, "I don't know. I never thought about it. But there must be a reason. Just do your exercise and don't question it. If you're having trouble just try not to look at the keyboard. Before long you'll be able to find all the letters."

Miriam felt embarrassed and misunderstood. She was not having any more trouble finding the keys than most of the other girls. She was just curious, puzzled--wanting to understand and make sense out of this new experience.

"Yes, Ma'am."

The other girls giggled, and Miriam was more humiliated, and only after several weeks did she notice that no one else addressed the instructor as 'Ma'am'.

Miriam found lots of time to practice her typing. The room, separate from the regular classroom, was open during breaks and lunch hour for anyone who wished to go in to finish an assignment, type a letter, or just practice. It was a great place for Miriam to hide; for after the first few days when she had shyly approached groups of girls in the cafeteria she realized that she didn't fit in. Many of them already seemed to know each other - from the same neighborhoods or the same school. Even those who came from Sussex, or other surrounding villages, seemed to come in twos or threes, and seemed more confident and worldly than Miriam felt. She didn't know how to socialize in large groups or with strangers. She was too shy to break into conversations. She didn't know what to talk about. These girls didn't seem interested in books. In fact they seemed to spend their spare time talking about boy friends, clothes, make-up, weekend parties, shopping, restaurants. Miriam had no experience in these things to draw upon.

So she practiced diligently - *ju ju ju ju fr fr fr de de de.* Mind numbing repetition, but her short stubby fingers grew nimble, and soon she could find letters with her fingers without even thinking about them. *fr fr fr free free ju ju ju jump.* She was typing words, and then sentences. *The quick, brown fox jumped over the lazy dog.* That sentence contained all the letters of the alphabet. The instructor, who had almost ignored her until the mid-fall tests, began to praise her for her speed and accuracy not only in typing but also in business English and bookkeeping.

The drilling she had received in the 3Rs made the writing of business letters and reports easy and gave her a solid background for bookkeeping which soon became her favorite subject. It was really neat to keep a set of books for an imaginary company and make entries of purchases and sales, to transfer figures from one column to another and finally add them up and have them balance out. Even if they didn't balance the first time, it was rather intriguing to go over each column and find the mistake and work it through. But when she mentioned this to a couple of the girls during a break they looked at her as though she needed her head examined. "Exciting? Yuk. I hate bookkeeping." Later, though, they started coming to her for help - checking to see how she had made a particularly challenging entry. They didn't become her friends; they never invited her to join them for lunch or a stroll during noon-hour unless there was a test coming up or a difficult assignment. She sensed the difference and wondered if she would ever have a friend – someone that she could really talk to and share ideas with.

It was a cool crisp afternoon when she ran into Rob Marshall on the street.

"Rob!"

"Miriam? Miriam Taylor, is that you? What are you doing in town?"

"Oh, didn't you know? I live here. The family moved here last summer."

"Oh. But I've never seen you around school. Where do you keep yourself?"

The next thing she knew they were having a soda together at Woolworth's, and then walking back to her apartment in the late fall shadows. There was so much to talk about. She told him all the news from back home, and what her brothers and sisters were doing. He talked about school. He really was enthusiastic about all the different teachers and the interesting subjects. As he had predicted, he was definitely planning to go to college. She told him a little about the Business College, and her plans to work in an office.

It was so nice to have someone to talk to; she realized how very lonely she was. Seeing Rob brought so much joy. She was absolutely delighted. If he hadn't mentioned getting together again, she was sure she would have, even though her mother and Annie wouldn't approve of her being so forward. But she didn't have to. Before they reached her building, he asked if she was doing anything Saturday night, and suggested a movie.

A Movie! A Date! Her first real date. A boy friend. No. Just Rob. Her old friend Rob. But she was thrilled and excited. Life was wonderful again.

The movie was a comedy starring Rock Hudson and Doris Day. They sat together eating popcorn and laughing. Miriam was no judge of movies, she had seen only a half dozen in her lifetime. Just the excitement of being in the theater, sitting in the dark with Rob, watching the magic on the screen was enough.

During the walk home they had the movie to discuss. They laughed again as they recalled the scenes, and as they reached her building Rob invited her to the up-coming school dance.

Maybe they should have left things as they were - friends, running into each other on the street, sharing a coke and casual conversation, occasionally attending a movie together - because almost from the time Rob called for her the following Saturday things started to feel awkward. Although she had taken extra care in fixing her hair and choosing her clothes, she knew the moment they entered the gym that it was all wrong. She was overdressed, the other girls all were far more casual than she was. The music was loud, making conversation impossible. While she had no trouble following Rob as they danced a waltz and then a foxtrot, she couldn't keep up with the faster tunes. Nobody she knew danced like that. Or did they? Annie and Charlie and the boys went to dances. Maybe they were up on all the recent music, but they hadn't shown her. So Rob sat with her on the sidelines and watched. It wasn't until the intermission that he introduced her to some of his friends, and they sat together drinking cokes.

She had to admit they were polite at first. They asked her where she lived and what school she attended and were surprised when she mentioned the Business College, but Rob seemed impatient. He had heard it all before, and they really weren't interested.

Rob was more enthusiastic when she asked what they were doing. He talked for some time about a project he was working on for an upcoming science fair. He and his partner were working together in the lab, doing experiments, checking reference books. They laughed together about how something had gone wrong and how they had managed permission to skip French class while they corrected the problem and were able to finish on time.. After all, science was more important than French. They were both planning to take engineering at university. Miriam was surprised, not because Rob had plans but because she had never pictured him as an engineer.

"Yes, I guess it would be exciting to work on the railroad. Think of all the places you'll go and things you'll see. And those big engines!"

"What? What do you mean?"

"Well, you said that you wanted to be an engineer. Wouldn't you be driving a train?"

The others laughed and Rob turned to her: "Not that kind of an engineer," he hissed. "For heavens sake! I'll be a Construction Engineer who builds roads, and bridges, and big dams for electrical power."

She nodded, embarrassed and somehow disappointed. "Rob, I never pictured you involved in construction. I didn't know that you had to go to college to build roads. Goodness, remember when they graveled the road out home. Dad drove a dump truck that summer, and the boys both had jobs."

Rob rolled his eyes at the others and shook his head in disbelief. "I'll be designing projects, not digging ditches. God, Miriam, who do you think draws up the plans for all these projects? Look at the Trans Canada Highway — all the work, and planning, and design that went into that. Imagine, a highway stretching all across Canada. Think how efficient it will be. Why, I'll bet it will eventually put trains right out of business." He was getting excited again just talking about it.

Miriam was too humiliated to respond to his enthusiasm. How could she have made such a fool of herself? Of course, that was what Rob would be doing. Sitting at a desk, drawing designs for roads, bridges, dams, buildings. But wasn't that what an architect would do? She wouldn't make a fool of herself by asking. Anyway, Rob wouldn't be driving a front-end loader, or a grader like her brothers would have been proud to do. Rob would make something more of himself. She withdrew into herself, unable to risk further conversation that would portray her ignorance in front of the others, while it seemed that Rob was trying to be extra witty to make up for his sad excuse for a date.

They left early and during the long walk home they found conversation difficult. They had no common ground. They lived in two different worlds. He found hers boring and she could no longer relate to his. All the good will and shared past experiences couldn't keep them together. They didn't arrange to meet the following week.

"I am awful glad that I ran into you again, Miriam." He sounded like he meant it but then he continued. "I've got a lot of studying for exams next month. I'll call you sometime. Is your old man in the book?"

"We don't have a phone."

"Oh! Oh, well. I guess I'll see you around. I'll drop by sometime, maybe during the Christmas break."

But she knew he wouldn't. She was sad as she went into the house and directly to her room without speaking to anyone. Sad, but not heartbroken. She knew that she didn't love Rob. But perhaps she could have, if circumstances had been different. If they had shared a few classes together, been lab partners, met for lunch in the cafeteria and laughed about mutual friends and experiences, groused about the same teachers, and went to school dances and sports events together they might have developed a relationship. But that was not to be.

****

Miriam had been so tied up in her own problems that she barely realized that Paul and Davy were having a hard time adjusting to city life and were unhappy at school. They never discussed it with Miriam but in the evenings when she lay on her bed trying to read her text on office practices she would overhear them from their side of the room. She knew how cruel school yard teasing could be and she would have liked to sympathize with her brothers when she heard them complaining about how the other kids laughed at them and picked on them, but they were angry and resentful when she tried to comfort them.

"Go away and leave us alone. You don't know what it's like."

When Johnny learned that his sons were coming home sniffling after school he was furious, not at the teachers or the other children, but at his own sons. "For God's sake don't come home crying like babies. Fight back. Don't be sissies. After all there's two of you."

So Paul and Davy hung together not expecting sympathy or help from anyone, embarrassed somehow that people knew how miserable they were. Miriam got the impression that somehow they blamed their mother for their problems. It was her fault. She was the one who had kept them in that little one-room school in the country so that they were ignorant when they moved to the city.

By Christmas though Jack and Bill had caught on to the problem. Boxing gloves appeared under the tree and while Miriam helped her mother in the kitchen preparing the traditional turkey dinner, Johnny watched with amusement as his older sons taught the younger ones how to stand back to back and defend themselves with a few boxing moves and some street fighting smarts thrown in. With new found confidence they returned to school in the new year and were able to stand up for themselves. Again as she overheard there conversations, Miriam realized that they were being accepted as part of the gang. But they had learned to keep their feelings to themselves.

As for Gracie, she was quiet and shy at school, and she spent all her spare time at Annie's helping with her little niece, Olive, while Hannah juggled housework with her job at Zellers.

Evenings before bed Hannah became 'Teacher' for a short while as she supervised the younger kids with their homework and Miriam, watching them, longed for the old days back home when she and her Mum / Teacher had held long discussions about literature, history or geography as they worked together in the kitchen during that final winter after Annie left home. She wondered if Mum missed those times. Mum knew even less than Miriam about office procedure. They didn't have anything in common any more.

Chapter Eight

After not hearing from Rob over the Christmas season, Miriam turned her attention back to her studies. Boring though they were, she made up her mind that she would do well. In a few months she was sent out to *Lythcoe and Howard, Lawyers and Solicitors*, for on-the-job experience. Observing the other girls, she had learned something about style, and now that Hannah was earning a bit she'd been able to buy a few new outfits. Nervously she dressed in her new dark plaid jumper, with a crisp white blouse, white gloves and high heels - proper attire she had been taught for a business girl - and reported for work. For two weeks she did some filing, answered the telephone, typed reports and took a few letters from the junior lawyer covering up her shaky shorthand by writing fast and developing her own symbols to supplement those she had learned in class. The school she had attended had a good reputation and had trained her well: smile pleasantly, be quick and accurate with your work, be prompt, be well groomed, be polite, use good grammar, be friendly but not personal. She might have added, 'Keep your opinions to yourself.' The lawyers were patient with her few mistakes and the 'girls' seemed kind, if a bit standoffish.

When it was time to go back to school for her final semester, Mr. Howard asked if she could work a few hours each week for a small wage, and when she finished school in April he offered her a full-time job. At fifteen and a half, Miriam had graduated from Business College and was working in a modern office building with three lawyers and two other secretaries. Surely that was something to be proud of; that and the pay cheque that enabled her to help out her mother at home, and have enough left over to buy a few more clothes for the office and to eat out on paydays. Of course everybody she worked with thought that she was seventeen.

Sometimes when she met girls her own age on the street, dressed in bobby socks and poodle skirts, their hair pulled back in pony tails, carrying school books and giggling together she wished that she were one of them. Once, when she passed the high school while hurrying to the post office to send a registered letter, she saw Rob with a group of friends. He was talking animatedly and didn't seem to notice her so she didn't stop. That part of her life was behind her. Despite her age, she was no longer a teenager.

She didn't have much social life. The other two 'girls' in the office had been there a long time and were twice her age--Sandra was a war widow who lived at home with her mother and her teen-aged son. Agnes had never married; her boy friend had been killed overseas. Sometimes it seemed that they thought they were doing Miriam a favor to have her join them in the tiny staff room where they ate their lunches, or to go out window shopping in the nice spring weather. The lawyers were all older, married men. They were nice enough but they didn't socialize with the 'girls'.

******

The Taylor household had always welcomed guests to drop in at any time. Johnny's army buddies would come around and Miriam would sit quietly in a corner, a book or magazine in her hands, listening to them talk. Or she would join her mother in the kitchen fixing snacks for the men.

Sometimes after they left to walk down to the Legion for a beer and a game of darts, Miriam would sit with her mother in the kitchen and if the little ones were quiet and the chores were done, they would set up the Scrabble board at the table. Miriam treasured these moments when she had her mother all to herself.

Jack and Bill were frequently at the apartment. They would drop over on their day off and take their mother grocery shopping and then come for supper and stay most of the evening. Charlie and Annie often came over too, passing baby Olive over to Gracie almost as soon as they came through the door, and the little girl seemed delighted to take care of her niece, showing off how skilled and responsible she could be in front of the little boys who pretended no interest in the baby.

Miriam found herself resenting their intrusion into her private time she had shared with her mother. She wasn't sure where she fit in at home. At work she was accepted as an adult, but at home her older siblings still treated her like a child. However, she no longer had anything in common with Paul and Davy. They resented her attempts to join into conversations about their school life, and she found their games boring or silly, especially when they spent most of their time arguing over procedures and refused her offers to read the rules and explain them. She gave up with them. Just as Annie had years ago, Gracie resented any attempt that she might make to play with the baby. That was her territory.

So Miriam spent most of her time on the sidelines, or helping her mother. However, more and more often Hannah was joining Johnny for the walk down to the Legion where she had joined the dart team.

Miriam would hang around the front room where the older ones sat up the card table for a game, and she watch eagerly, wishing that they would invite her to join in. When Bill brought his girlfriend over to meet the family, Frances turned to her:

"Bill tells me that you work down town."

She blushed and murmured something about the law office and expected Frances to turn back to the others but instead she continued the conversation.

"I work for the telephone company. That's just a block or two away. Maybe we could meet for lunch sometime." They had something in common, something to talk about. They were both working girls. Then Bill called,

"Come on Frances. Let's play cards – we'll play five handed."

"But what about Miriam. Don't you like to play?"

So they pulled another chair up to the table and Miriam was joining the others in their game.

The boys always brought treats on Friday evenings – chips and pop for the young ones, chips and beer for themselves. At first Miriam helped herself to the pop, but then one evening Charlie handed her a beer. It tasted awful. She would actually have preferred a Coke, but that would have seemed babyish. Frances and now Charlie accepted her as one of the group. She wasn't going to refuse.

There was talk and laughter and fun. Sometimes Johnny and Hannah joined them in the livingroom and they set up two tables. More often it was only the young people playing, while their parents went out. Miriam enjoyed these evenings. Friday evenings she would watch to see if Jack came home with his father; and then as they sat around after supper, the men smoking and talking about work, she would wait and see if Bill and Frances, or Annie and Charlie would show up. She liked Frances, far more than she did Annie, who still had a way of leaving her out of conversations and who ordered her around. "Miriam, put Olive's bottle on to warm so Gracie can give her a feeding." Or "Miriam, aren't you going to put the kettle on. I'd like a cup of tea."

Despite Annie's attitude, Miriam liked to see them come because of Charlie. She enjoyed his jokes and his company. While her quick mind had soon caught on the strategies of the games, she sometimes had trouble shuffling the cards with her stubby fingers.

"For heaven's sake, Miriam," Annie said condescendingly, "That's the third time you've dropped a card. Do you want me to shuffle for you?"

Charlie spoke up for her. "Leave her alone. At least she can play. You don't see her covering her partner's Ace like you did in the last hand."

"Anybody can make a mistake." Annie shot back.

"But not quite as many as you can."

"It's just a game."

"Oh, forget it." He winked at Miriam. She dealt the cards around and then trumped his best play. They laughed together. She wondered how Annie rated somebody as nice and as handsome as Charlie. And she didn't quite understand when Annie followed her out to the kitchen and hissed: "Stop your flirting with Charlie. He's my husband, you know."

Chapter Nine

Annie claimed to be feeling miserable most of the time until her second girl, Amy, was born early in July just a year after her sister, Olive. For the next few weeks Charlie and Annie missed the weekend get-togethers at the Taylor place. Then Charlie came alone, but after he sat around for a hour or so Hannah asked him pointedly if Annie was alone with the babies. The following weekend, they both came, bringing along their children.

It didn't work out though. Olive, who had been a contented baby, was suddenly jealous when Gracie showed more interest in the baby than in her. She let people know that she felt left-out, turning from Gracie to her mother and demanding attention. Amy was fussy and colicky, crying most of the evening. Gracie didn't know what to do, and often Annie couldn't settle her. Even when Hannah walked her, she cried and struggled, only momentarily settled by each change in position. Charlie and Annie left early.

The gathering on Labour-day weekend ended the same with Olive whiney, Amy crying, and no one able to relax. Finally Charlie lost his patience.

"Annie, can't you settle that one down?" But a few minutes after she left the room to try to rock Amy to sleep, he was calling, "Annie, do you want us to deal you in this time. Everybody's waiting."

They went home in a huff, barely speaking to one another. Johnny glared after them, his evening ruined.

Miriam couldn't remember whose suggestion it was that she occasionally give her sister an evening out. Probably her mother's. But from then on it was almost taken for granted that instead of Annie bringing the babies home, Miriam would go over to their place. She didn't mind if they were just going to a movie, but the evenings they were joining the crowd at the folks' place, Miriam felt that she was being taken advantage of. She was being left out of the camaraderie that she had begun to enjoy at those spontaneous gatherings. When she complained however Hannah explained that she was the selfish one. Families helped each other out. Annie often watched Gracie without complaint and without pay. Big sisters helped with little sisters. Younger sisters should watch nieces. After all, once the babies were settled, Miriam could watch TV. The novelty of TV made it worthwhile. Charlie and Annie were the only people Miriam knew who had a TV. What did it matter that it was small, black and white, and there was only one station that broadcast from 6:00 to midnight each evening?

Miriam accepted her position as babysitter, and Annie took her for granted. Usually she found her own way home. It was only a few blocks, and Miriam had never minded being out after dark. Then one night when Charlie and Annie were arguing as they came through the door and Miriam grabbed her sweater to be on her way, Charlie insisted that he walk her home.

"No. Really. You don't have to. I can go by myself." Goodness, she had walked it a hundred times in the past year. As much as she usually enjoyed his company, it did seem to Miriam that Charlie should be home with Annie rather than walking with her.

However Annie was back to treating her like a kid. "Don't be silly, Miriam. Its after midnight and it's not safe for a young girl to be out alone. Besides the night air might help him to sober up a bit."

Somehow Miriam felt that she would be safer alone than with a half-drunk brother-in-law who insisted that he should put his arm around her as soon as they reached the street corner. Was it to keep her warm, as he said, or to steady himself crossing the street? And she didn't know how to react to his mumbled conversation.

"You're going to make some man happy some day."

"Come on, Charlie, let's hurry. It's getting cold out."

"Then let me put my coat around you, and you snuggle in close to me."

"No. Let's just walk faster. We're almost there."

Miriam didn't know how she was supposed to feel. This wasn't much different from her own brother's teasing, and this was her sister's husband - one of the family. But it seemed wrong now when they were alone.

As they neared her building, he pulled her close for a goodnight kiss. She tried to push away without being rude but he held her tight and bent her head back. This wasn't like her brothers' kisses - a rough, dry peck on the cheek accompanied by a squeeze and then a little push away. This was a real, wet kiss on the lips and he was trying to push his tongue in her mouth. She finally got her hands up against his chest and pushed with all her strength. He staggered backwards, almost falling. She ran toward the house as he called after her:

"What, you haven't got a kiss for your own brother-in-law after he was nice enough to see you safely home. You're just like your sister. Mean. Cold. Not very friendly, are you?"

Miriam hurried into the house and into the room she shared with Gracie. Frightened. Confused. What did it all mean? Who could she talk to about it? Maybe if the occasion came up, she could ask Hannah. No. Somehow she knew that Hannah would rather not hear. Annie? Definitely not. One of her brothers? No, they were Charlie's friends. Better just keep it to herself. She was probably reading too much into it. Charlie had had too much to drink, and she was reacting like a scared kid.

Miriam pushed the incident to the back of her mind. The next weekend she went with her parents over to Annie's to watch wrestling on TV, and two weeks later Annie asked her to come over and babysit again.

"I've just got to get out of the house, Miriam. You don't know what it's like being home in this small apartment with two babies. No one to talk to. When Charlie gets home in the evening, all he wants to do is watch TV and then go to bed. By the weekend, we're both just crazy to get out and see someone."

Why not? Miriam had the feeling that her folks were expecting people to 'drop in'. She half wanted to stay and join the fun. But Annie had asked her to help out. How could she refuse? Besides, she was somehow sure that Hannah thought that babysitting was more appropriate for someone Miriam's age.

She told Olive a made-up story half-remembered from a school book she had read a million years ago, and settled her in bed. Then Amy had a bottle. She had to be walked quite a bit after that but finally she settled down. How come Annie would trust her with the babies, anyway? How long ago was it that Annie was complaining that she didn't know how to hold a baby - that she would touch the soft spot on the head or fail to support its neck properly. Somehow they both knew now that a baby's head wouldn't fall off. Yes, she could look after a baby. She had Amy settled down now and in her basket. She'd get a coke and watch TV. Wrestling was always on TV on Saturday night. She would watch some wrestling. Some people were starting to claim that it was fake but Miriam wasn't sure.

Miriam was startled to hear someone at the door. She got up to check when she realized that whoever it was had a key and was letting themselves in.

"Charlie! I didn't expect you back so soon. Where's Annie?"

"She's over at your folks. I told her I had to go out for cigarettes and that I might check back to see how you were doing."

"Fine. They're both asleep."

"Good. Let's hope they stay that way. How about you? You lonesome here by yourself?"

"No. I'm okay. I'm just watching wrestling."

"Oh, I guess you like to see those guys in their skimpy trunks. Show a lot of skin don't they. Who's on tonight? Whipper Billy Watson and Hard-boiled Haggarty for the main event. Good. I'd like to see Haggarty whip the ass off that fancy-pants. I bet you would too, eh? I'll just stay and watch awhile with you. You don't mind, eh?"

Mind? How could she? This was his place.

"Maybe I'd better go home then. I mean, if you're here with the kids. You don't need me."

"Just a minute. I'm only staying awhile. Old Annie will raise hell if I don't get back soon. I can't just leave her there. Anyway, I want to watch it with you. You're real good company and a heck more fun than Annie's been lately."

Miriam couldn't help but feel flattered. She and Annie had always been rivals. Annie always ahead of her in everything except school. Always knowing everything. Always belittling her, putting her down. Even now when Miriam was working an adult job and trying to fit into an adult world, Annie still talked to her like she was a little kid. And now, Annie's husband was telling Miriam that she was better company than Annie.

"Okay. Can I get you something to eat?"

"Just get me a beer from the fridge. Get one for yourself too. Don't bother with a glass. Hell, I always drink from the bottle. Hey, look at that! Haggarty's thrown him out of the ring. I knew it! Fancy-pants can't stand up to him! What are you doing sitting away over there? You can't see from there. Come and sit on the couch with me."

"I'm okay here."

"No, you'll get a stiff neck, looking sideways like that. Hey, maybe that's the problem. Maybe you already got a stiff neck. Maybe you're too good for your brother-in-law."

"No, it's not that."

'Then, come over here. Look. Your hero is winning now. Look at that half-Nelson! Haggardy will slip out of that. That's why he shaved his head. No, Watson has him down for the count. Hey, hey!'

Miriam couldn't resist moving over for the better look. "Yeah, hold him, Whipper! Hold him! Oh, no."

After all, many a time she had sat on that very couch next to Charlie, sometimes with his arm around her shoulders with her sister and parents or brothers present and nobody, not even her sister had said anything.

But then, Charlie was having another drink. He was leaning closer, pulling her up against him. Still watching TV as the fight went on and on. Shouldn't he be leaving to go back to Annie soon? Miriam was no longer enjoying the game. Things didn't feel right. Charlie's hand slid down from her shoulder and squeezed her breast. She jerked upright, trying to push away from him but he roughly pulled her back down. She struggled. There was no pretense any more. He was all over her, his tongue probing her mouth like no kiss she had ever experienced before. His hands were under her clothes. Then holding her down with his weight on her and one arm across her chest, he was fumbling with his zipper.

'Help!'. But it was only a thought. She couldn't shout. She'd wake the children, disturb the neighbors, embarrass everyone. She tried to get her knee up between his legs, like she'd been told too, but he was too quick for her. He pushed her down roughly. "Now you're going to get what you've been asking for, you god-damned tease."

"No, don't! Please, don't! Please, please. Don't!"

She felt his naked flesh, hot and damp against her private parts. She twisted and squirmed in fear and then in pain; then it was over. When he finally let her go, she ran to the bathroom, splashing water on her face, crying uncontrollably, not knowing what to do. She cleaned herself, surprised and frightened by the blood.

When she came out, Charlie was gone. She checked the babies. Thank heavens they had slept through everything. Not knowing what else to do, not able to leave the babies alone, she sat down on the chesterfield held her head between her hands and stared numbly at the television set, not even noticing when the station signed off and the test pattern appeared.

*****

She could tell Charlie and Annie were fighting as soon as they arrived home although Annie tried to hide it. And Annie again insisted that Charlie walk Miriam home.

"No, Annie. I can walk by myself."

"Yeh, she'll be all right. I'm Jes'ly tired."

"Don't be silly Miriam. Go on, Charlie. You need the fresh-air. Besides what do you want? My sister raped on the streets? It's our responsibility."

"Okay, Okay. I'm going. Come on, Miriam. Let's get going."

They walked without speaking or touching, Miriam a few steps ahead almost running, until they were almost to the flat.

"Look Miriam. I'm sorry if I hurt you. I guess you just led me on. I couldn't resist. I'm quite a man eh. And you so pretty and excited and all."

"Just leave me alone."

"Okay. We'll leave it at that. I'm sorry. It won't happen again. But just don't say anything, eh. It would just make matters worse. All in the family, eh."

What to do? Who to tell? Annie? Certainly not. Annie would have a fit, and certainly blame her. Hannah? Miriam tried to imagine telling Hannah. Her mother would be unhappy, upset, and what could her mother do except maybe talk to Annie or to her father? No, Miriam couldn't put her mother in that position. And as for her, herself, telling her father or brothers - never!

They would be angry. They would shout; maybe they would beat Charlie up. But mainly, Miriam knew, their anger would be toward her. No, there was no one to tell. It would be best just to put it behind her, and to avoid being alone with Charlie ever again.

But that was not easy. Annie took it for granted that she would be available for babysitting, and when she made excuses Annie complained to their mother, "I'm going crazy in that place. I've got to get out."

"Then why don't you and Charlie come over for an evening."

"I can't. You know how the baby cried last time we were here for dinner. And evening is her fussy time. Charlie won't take her out. And Miriam won't help me out any more."

"Miriam, is that true?"

"I've been busy when you ask me."

"Miriam, families help families. Your sister says she needs a break. Is there something wrong?"

Miriam looked from her mother to Annie and back again. Was this her chance to explain? Maybe if they had been alone, but not with Annie there.

"No. Like I said. I've been busy. I work all day you know. And I've got things to do at night."

"Like what?" challenged Annie, aware of how little social life Miriam had.

"Like washing my hair, and ironing my clothes, getting things ready for work."

"And you couldn't wash your hair at my place?"

"Miriam," Hannah interjected, "Those are pretty flimsy excuses. Remember everything Annie's done for you."

Funny, Miriam couldn't remember much, but she had never argued with her mother. "All right, I'll go over Saturday night if you want to go out. I didn't say I wouldn't. Just I've been busy."

The first few times she was there, Charlie didn't come back to the house, but just when she was beginning to feel secure she heard his key in the lock.

"I told Annie that I forgot my guitar." He explained, but he was in no rush to leave again.

"Come on, Miriam. I didn't really hurt you that last time. You really liked it, didn't you?"

"No."

"You say 'no', but I can tell you mean 'yes'. Women never say what they mean."

"Charlie, it was wrong."

"What do you mean? It's nature. Come on Miriam. Grow up. You know you were asking for it. If it weren't for me, you'd be looking for someone else. And I think that you like your old brother-in-law."

Somehow Miriam realized Charlie himself didn't think that he was doing anything wrong. Somehow, this was expected of adults, one of the many things that was not talked about but that was accepted. Something like drinking and driving, or buying beer from the bootlegger in the country, or jacking deer. Suddenly Miriam remembered the last fall that they had lived on the farm. She'd gone to bed but before she fell asleep she'd heard a commotion out in the barnyard -- men, her father and brothers, hurrying around with flashlights and lanterns, harnessing the horse, but talking quietly. She'd stumbled out to the kitchen where her mother was nervously poking at the stove, keeping the fire going and the kettle warm. "Mum, what's going on?"

"Hush, dear. There's nothing to be alarmed about."

"But what are Dad and the boys doing at this time of night?"

"I guess you're old enough to know. Jack shot a moose down in the swamp this afternoon. Now that it's dark, they are going down to get it and hide it in the barn."

"Mum! Jack could go to jail!"

"That's why we have to be quiet about things like this."

"But it's against the law."

"It's meat, Miriam. You know that they didn't get a deer all fall, and things have really been slack at the mill. This moose will keep us going until Christmas or after. Let's just hope that nobody heard the shot and comes snooping around. And don't tell the little ones. They just might let it slip to the wrong people at school."

So there were things that everybody knew were wrong yet adults seemed to accept. Families had secrets. There was a boy back at the old school who didn't know that his sister was his mother. All the older kids knew, but nobody told him. His family had been one of the first to move away. Miriam still didn't know if he had ever found out. And the LeBlanc place -- why was it that no decent girl could go near? The old man drank and the mother didn't speak English. Was there anything else, a secret that Miriam didn't know.

Adults jacked deer out of season, they shot moose that were supposed to be protected. They lied. Suddenly Miriam remembered lying her age to get into Business College. Only little kids who couldn't be trusted to keep a secret were kept in the dark.

So this was to be another secret. But somehow Miriam knew that this was different and that it was terribly wrong. She dreaded every time she heard Charlie's key turn in the lock and realized that Annie wasn't with him. Miriam would argue and try unsuccessfully to push him away. If this was what being an adult was, Miriam wished that she had never grown up.

PART TWO

Chapter One

Another morning had been spent in the bathroom fighting nausea before leaving for work. Miriam realized with a sinking stomach that her suspicions were true, that sooner or later she would have to face the fact that her period was almost two months late, and there were other things going on in her body that she could no longer ignore. But how could she admit it? How could she tell her parents? How could she go on day after day knowing that she was pregnant and that the child she was carrying was the product, not of love, but of sin? Somehow, without really knowing how, she had gotten herself into this impossible situation, and there was no predicting how it would affect her family.

She could hear her parents' voices outside the bathroom door, her father's raised in anger, her mother's trying to maintain a calm. She hesitated a few minutes more and when she came out her father was gone.

"Miriam," Her mother was turned away looking into the sink full of dishes instead of at her. "Do you have something to tell me?"

Miriam didn't know how she could talk to her mother about something so difficult. Almost with relief she glanced at her watch and realized that she was already running late. She couldn't take time for a long discussion. Instead she just hung her head and nodded to her mother's few questions, then grabbed her coat and escaped out the door. She tried to forget her mother's stricken face as she raced to the bus stop. Several times she was tempted to run back, to throw her arms around her mother and cry, to beg for understanding, for forgiveness, for protection and advice. But that type of emotional display was not part of her nature. Besides, never once since she had started working had she missed a day, or even been late, so she continued on her way.

Somehow she got through the day. Keeping busy helped. Mr. Howard was preparing for an early morning hearing the next day, so she hurried to prepare the documents he would need. For a few minutes at a time she could almost forget herself. At noon she avoided the staff room, and Agnes and Sandra, by pretending she had an errand and going for a long walk by herself. She'd forgotten her lunch on the kitchen table, but she knew she couldn't eat anyway.

She dreaded going home. She lagged along as she walked from the bus stop knowing, somehow, that everyone would be there. Sure enough, there was Annie's baby stroller in the hallway, and Olive screaming in the livingroom. Annie's visit in itself was insignificant; Annie came over several afternoons a week. But one look at Annie and Miriam knew that their mother had confided in her. Fortunately before anything could be said, Davy came running up the steps, Paul in pursuit, shouting about a broken hockey stick. Johnny arrived and a short time later Charlie strode in and Annie reminded Charlie that they had been invited for supper.

'God,' Miriam thought. 'Why can't they go home for once? The last person I need to sit across from right now is Charlie.'

Then right after supper, as Miriam helped to clean up in the kitchen, she heard Jack and Bill arriving. Any hopes she had that their father hadn't seen them on the docks, and hadn't mentioned anything to them, were lost when she overheard Jack giving his little brothers some money and suggesting that they go to the movies. She saw them looking questioningly at their mother, unable to believe their good fortune, and on a school night too, before they hurried out. Gracie was instructed to take Olive and Amy into the other room and take care of them.

Miriam glanced around. Only Charlie seemed to be oblivious about what was about to happen, as he sat glancing through the sports section of the paper. Then it seemed everybody turned on Miriam at once.

"Miriam, what's this I hear about you?"

"Who did this to you?"

"You've disgraced the family." That was Annie.

"Whatever could you be thinking of?"

"I'll never be able to hold my head up. Mum, didn't you teach her anything? You certainly watched every move I made." Annie shrieked. Miriam thought fleetingly of the six months between Annie's wedding and Olive's birth, but said nothing.

"Who is the father?" Jack was persistent.

"By God, he'll marry you." That was the first that her father had to say.

"Yeh, a shot-gun wedding. No frills. And an eight pound preemie."

"Who was it?" Her father again.

"I don't want to say. I don't want to marry him."

"You should have thought of that before."

"For God sakes, Mum. Listen to her." Who did Annie think she was anyway? If they were alone, Miriam could have stood up to her.

"Miriam, please. You have to tell us who it was." Hannah was the only one who sounded concerned for her well-being, but Bill interrupted before Miriam could form a reply.

"Don't you know??!"

Jack was trying to think. "I'll bet it was that Rob Marshall. Remember he was hanging around last winter. I haven't seen him much lately." .

"Sneaky! Sneaking around behind our backs. A disgrace."

Johnny ignored Bill's outburst as he turned his attention to Jack. "Rob Marshall. Fancy, stuck up Marshall boy. By, God.

This will bring them down a peg. Wait 'til I call on old man Marshall. Always thought he was better than anyone else. Making sure he had a secure job at home when I was off fighting a war."

"Don't worry Miriam. He'll marry you. Just name the day." Jack nodded his agreement.

"But it wasn't Rob! I haven't seen him all year. We never really went out together."

"Yeh, and who else might it be? I've never seen you going out with anybody else."

"I was beginning to worry. No young fellows coming around."

"There's no sense protecting him, Miriam. He's the only one it could have been." Hannah said gently.

"No. No!"

"Who then?"

From where she had first sat down on the ottoman, Miriam looked around the room. Her brothers had taken the chairs by the table but now in their excitement they were up and pacing. Her father was leaning forward in his favourite chair. Her mother and Annie sat together on the old chesterfield, Charlie at the other end, but somehow separate from them, the newspaper forgotten in his hands. For someone who always had plenty to say, he had been strangely quiet, but no one else noticed. Her brothers were talking again about Rob. They were going to go over and confront him. Johnny was going to 'pay a call' on Old Man Marshall.

"But you can't," she cried out. "It wasn't Rob."

Frantically, she tried to think of a way to convince them.

"I tell you, I haven't seen him for ages, and anyway we never did anything like that."

"Well, somebody did."

Her father leaped to his feet.

"Enough of this. By god, I'm the head of this family. Nothing goes on that I don't find out about. Out with it, now!"

Miriam shrank back in alarm. She had seen her father's rages, occasionally seen him strike out at her brothers, once she'd seen him knock Bill down, but she had never defied him before. She had always been able to avoid the worst of his temper. Frantically she looked around for help. Her mother was also on her feet, her soft, "Now, Johnny." was momentarily effective.

Miriam looked to Charlie. Surely he knew whose baby she was carrying. He was the only one who could know. Surely he would speak up. Surely he would take part of the blame. But he seemed to pull back further into the corner. His eyes implored Miriam to say nothing, and as he caught her eye he shook his head ever so slightly.

"Miriam, please. It's not going to help to try to protect the father. You've got to tell us. Was it Sandra's son? I've heard you mention him."

Miriam was shocked. How could they think that she would have anything to do with that pimply-faced sissy who occasionally hung around the office after school waiting for a drive home? God, if he did speak to her for more than two or three seconds Sandra would find some way to separate them.

"No. Of course not. Anyway, do you think his mother would let him have five minutes alone with me?"

Johnny leaped to his feet again, swinging his arm. "By God, listen to her."

Jack took a tentative step forward, but a look from Hannah held him back.

"Miriam, please."

There was no escape. Surely Charlie could see that. Miriam looked at him once more, but he was studying the floor. Obviously he wasn't going to help.

"It was Charlie!" she shouted, and then sobbed. "The baby's Charlie's."

Everybody went quiet. Johnny fell back in his chair. Jack started to ask, "Charlie who?" Then all eyes were on Annie's husband. He seemed to shrink into his chair, hanging his head but saying nothing.

Annie broke the silence. "Mum, did you hear that! Mum! She accused Charlie! My Charlie! Oh, my God," she went from disbelief to realization as she looked at him. "It's true. She's been after my husband. She!!! She!!! She always wanted everything. And now my husband! How could you?" Miriam felt the sting of the slap before she could raise her hands in defense as Annie flew across the room and attacked her. She prepared to block the next blow, but it was unnecessary. Hannah was gently but firmly pulling Annie back.

Jack was almost incoherent as he sputtered at Charlie, "My sister. You and my little sister. I'll kill you."

"Mum, don't let them fight. Don't you dare threaten my husband!"

Then Johnny's voice, quiet rather than the usual booming. "I think you'd better get out of my house."

Charlie seemed to welcome the opportunity. "I'm going. Annie, come on if you've coming."

"Wait. Don't leave me here. You've got to carry Olive. Gracie, come here. Help me get the baby's things. We're going."

Miriam hung her head, in bewilderment and shame. How could this be happening? How had things gotten so out of hand? Neither she nor anyone else thought of accusing Charlie of rape. She had never heard of acquaintance rape, and incest was a word in a dictionary. And this wasn't incest. This hadn't been her brother, but her brother-in-law. The fact that he was almost ten years her senior, and in a position of trust, weren't taken into account. Rape was something that happened when a stranger leaped out of a dark alley. Not among family. And although she had heard the term jail-bait, Charlie had used it more than once in referring to her, she wasn't sure just what it meant. It never occurred to Miriam to claim, "He raped me." Nor did anyone else question her about it.

As Charlie and Annie rushed out with the babies, Hannah hurried Gracie through her bed-time routine as though nothing was wrong. Miriam's brothers turned on her again.

"Why, you little slut. Your own sister's husband."

"He always said you were a tease."

"Frances told me to keep an eye on you. She said that you were as naive as a schoolgirl. But I never expected anything right under our eyes. Your own brother-in-law?"

Johnny roaring again, "What did you think you were doing? You could break up that family? What's going on here anyway? What have you done to us? Have you no shame?"

Miriam was sobbing uncontrollably by the time Paul and Davy arrived back from the movies.

"What's going on? What's all the shouting about? We could hear you out on the street."

"Oh dear, what will the neighbors think! It's all right, kids. We were just having a little disagreement. Do you want something to eat before you go to bed? Can I fix something for everybody?"

But Johnny, Jack and Bill were storming out of the house. Where they went--driving around in the night, or sitting over a beer at the Legion, Miriam didn't know. The children were sent off to bed, wondering what Miriam had done to make everybody so mad; glad that they hadn't been involved, but sorry that they somehow had missed all the excitement; whispering across the room for Gracie to tell them all she had heard.

Hannah passed Miriam a cup of hot tea and tried to comfort her.

"There, there. Don't cry. It will be all right. We'll work something out. They'll calm down. You, just don't provoke your father for the next few days until he gets used to the idea. Just keep out of his way. This is a terrible shock to everyone."

Then, just when Miriam was beginning to think that at least her mother understood, Hannah went on, "Whatever got into you, Miriam. Don't you know that you can't be teasing men, leading them on?"

"But I didn't do anything."

"Miriam, I've seen you flirting with Charlie and others right in this very house."

"I didn't know."

"It's always up to the girl to set limits. Men can't control themselves once they're all worked up."

"But I didn't mean to. I tried to talk him out of it. I tried to push him away. I tried."

"Nice girls don't let themselves get into those awkward positions."

Miriam couldn't believe her ears. How could she tell her mother that she had tried to avoid Charlie, that she hated being anywhere near him, that she had tried to get out of babysitting for Annie because of him? To attempt to explain that to Hannah would be like trying to blame her. To say that Hannah had encouraged, no practically forced, her to go over to Charlie's place, would be accusing her of being at fault as well. No, it wasn't her mother's fault. It couldn't be her mother's fault! No one seemed to really think it was Charlie's. It must be hers alone.

"And to do this to Annie, Miriam. She's always been jealous of you. It always worried me but I tried not to take it too seriously. You had your gifts. She had hers. She just didn't seem to have the confidence to appreciate hers. O dear, I hope she doesn't do anything rash. I hope she doesn't leave Charlie over this. Those two dear babies need a home. Annie needs someone to look after her. Charlie's a good provider. I hope this doesn't ruin their marriage."

As she realized that the attention had turned from her, Miriam felt even more guilty, ashamed and abandoned. Her mother, her only friend, was siding with Annie. Miriam buried her head deeper in her arms. Would it never end? Only when she realized that Hannah was crying too, did she look up in bewilderment. Never before had she seen her mother cry, and this was her fault as well. It never occurred to her to try to comfort her mother, or to mourn together. Instead she leaped to her feet and fled from the scene, throwing herself on the bed so violently that the younger children never dared to question her. Much later she got up, changed to her nightgown and, still sobbing quietly to herself, crawled under the covers beside Gracie.

Chapter Two

If Charlie and Annie ever considered separation, Miriam never heard about it and doubted if they ever discussed it outside their own home.

For the next few weeks they were absent from the Taylor home. Miriam never heard their names mentioned, except occasionally by the little kids: she knew that Gracie was still going over to Annie's after school on the days their mother worked. Except for a few minutes each morning, when the hustle and bustle of getting everybody off to work or school prevented any meaningful conversation, and again at supper time when Miriam managed to avoid confrontation by busying herself helping with the serving and cleaning up, she tried to avoid everyone, spending much of her time lying on her bed staring at the ceiling.

Obviously they weren't going to put her out, at least not right away. If they were, it would have been during that first heated battle, when everybody was surprised, shocked and angry. But what about when she started to show? How would the neighbours react? And how would that affect her family? She was aware that her mother had felt shy about making friends when they first moved to the city. Would those few people that she now gossiped with while hanging out the clothes in the backyard, or going to the corner store, soon start to whisper behind their hands, or cut her dead? Dear knows how much they had overheard that terrible evening; they must already have a poor opinion of the family--all that shouting and swearing.

Maybe, Miriam thought, it just wouldn't happen. Maybe it had been a mistake. Maybe all the worry and tension had made her periods late. But that faint hope was dispelled when Hannah arranged for her to see a doctor. She was pregnant all right;

healthy and well, if a bit young to be expecting. There shouldn't be any problems. Miriam turned away. She hadn't missed the shake of his head.

Maybe she would fall down the stairs. That's what had happened in 'Gone With The Wind'; Scarlett had fallen down stairs and lost a baby. But how could she intentionally do that? Suppose it didn't work! She'd probably break a leg, be more trouble and expense to the family, and still be pregnant. She'd heard rumours about hot mustard baths, knitting needles or coat hangers, but she didn't know how these would work, any more than she knew how to go about obtaining an illegal abortion. Anyway, doing something deliberately to harm the baby would be wrong, terribly wrong. An illegitimate baby was bad enough; getting rid of it was even worse.

Miriam worried during the evenings as she lay on her bed, staring at the ceiling, refusing her mother's entreaties to join the family. She worried at night when Gracie's stirring in her sleep would awaken her, and she would lie there, listening to her little brothers' breathing across the room. At the office she was sometimes able to immerse herself in her work, and forget for a short while, but then it would suddenly hit her again. How much longer would she be able to continue working?

It was three weeks before Miriam ran into Annie again. She arrived home from work early, and there was Annie in the kitchen chatting with their mother; the baby on her knee, Olive playing nearby.

"Hello," she muttered, glad for the distraction when the little girl toddled towards her, with arms stretched out.

"Miriam, Miriam," a wide smile spread over Olive's face.

Annie turned away without acknowledging her. "Goodness, Mum. I didn't realize it was so late. Come on now, Olive. Get your coat. Gracie, bring me the baby's bag."

Before Miriam had her coat off, it seemed Annie was rushing out the door with the babies.

Miriam didn't know whether to breath a sigh of relief, or be hurt and disappointed that her sister hadn't made any effort to build bridges between them. Maybe Annie would never speak to her again. There could be advantages to that, but it would hurt. Obviously, their mother had been glad to have Annie there. Of course, Annie hadn't done anything disgraceful. She was the innocent victim, the betrayed wife and sister. It was Miriam who was on the outside. Probably her family would never forgive her.

In subsequent visits Annie didn't exactly cut Miriam cold. Instead she spoke when necessary, sometimes only after Miriam detected their mother looking at her pointedly, but she kept everything short and distant.

At least they were speaking, and after an initial bit of awkwardness, Jack and Bill were treating her as always once again.

Then came the dreaded night when Charlie dropped in after work to pick up Annie and the babies and met Miriam face to face at the door. She felt herself turning beet-red, and they both tried unsuccessfully to look away.

"Oh, it's you," Miriam stammered.

"Yeah. Annie's here, ain't she?"

She noticed him trying not to, but still glancing down at her stomach; and she put her hands down to hide the little bulge that as yet only she was aware of under her jumper. She detected embarrassment, then anger as he looked back up at her. "You'd better just keep your mouth shut from now on, and stop trying to put the blame on me. Everybody knows what a flirt you are, and how you were always leading me on. You're the one they blame."

Annie and her mother hurried in from the kitchen and he turned quickly away from Miriam.

"Hurry up, Annie. Get the kids and let's get going."

"Just a minute. Gracie, bring the baby. Olive, hurry now."

Previously Miriam had wondered at Annie's complacency, and sometimes wished Annie would show some spunk and tell him to quit bossing her around, but now Miriam was just glad they would be out of the house in a minute. But no, Hannah had stepped in between them.

"Charlie, there's no sense in hurrying them away the minute you step through the door. Come in and show your manners. Annie, there's no need of you rushing off home to cook supper. You saw that big pot of stew on the stove. We might as well all sit down together like family. Annie, you go and get some ready for Olive. Gracie, you set the table. Miriam, come out in the kitchen and help me. And Charlie, you sit right there. Johnny should be home any minute. Boys!" she hollered towards the bedroom. "You two get washed up and out of the way before your father gets here." Miriam could not believe what she was hearing. Never since they had moved in to the city had she heard her mother take charge with so much authority.

Within a short time the family seemed to be back to functioning normally. They had Christmas, and Bill's and Frances' wedding just before New Years, to distract them. Only Miriam held the worry in the pit of her stomach. Soon they wouldn't be able to ignore what was happening to her.

******

The Taylor household had always welcomed guests. There was always somebody dropping by – back home Miriam remembered the crowd of young people gathering on the veranda, neighbours dropping by, family and friends, Johnny's army buddies. In town it was the same – neighbours, people Johnny worked with, family and friends from up-country in town for the day. Hannah cooked big meals: baked beans and coleslaw with brown bread on the side; chicken stew with dumplings; hearty beef vegetable soups; macaroni and tomatoes with hamburger mixed in and a tasty crust of bread crumbs and cheese. There was always room for another chair pulled up, another plate on the table.

After Bill's marriage, Jack came over almost every night.

"I can't cook anything on that stove Mum. I might just as well pitch in on the groceries and eat here."

After supper they would sit around and often Jack would talk about the other men at the rooming house. It was there at the kitchen table when the kids had hurried through their suppers and quickly excused themselves to go off and do their own things while Miriam sat with her parents and brother over a second cup of tea, that she first heard him mention Bruce MacKay.

"There's a new guy moved in the other day--took the little room at the back on our floor."

"From around here?" Johnny wanted to know.

"No. Actually, he's from a farm over near the border. Somewhere around Canterbury; or down by Skiff Lake; I'm not sure. Anyway, he's as green about city life as Bill and I were when we first came here." Miriam, lost in her own thoughts, and barely following the conversation heard Hannah murmur, "Poor boy. Do you know why he came then?"

"We got talking last night. It seems his father died awhile back. He expected that he and his brother would stay on with their mother running the place, but she decided to go off and live with her sister down in Boston. Before she left she explained how their dad had wanted the property divided. The brother, I think his name's Doug, would get the house and farm. Bruce got another piece of property down near the coast in Charlotte County. I guess it used to belong to an old uncle or something. It's kind of isolated, and it's been deserted for years, except perhaps they've gone there hunting or fishing a few times."

"That hardly seems fair," Hannah remarked. Miriam nodded. She knew about fairness. Life wasn't fair. "Bruce must have felt cheated."

"Ya can't judge them that fast," said Johnny. "If Doug was the oldest, maybe he did most of the work on the place. Maybe he earned it. And maybe he was expected to look after his mother and brother. I know that's how I got our place. I was the one who stayed on, and then came back after the war--when all the others took off on their own as soon as they were old enough."

"Anyway," Jack went on as though he hadn't been interrupted. "Bruce didn't seem to be complaining. He says that he loves the property he got, and thinks it might be worth a lot if it wasn't so isolated."

"In the meantime, why didn't he just stay on at the old place and help his brother? Did they have a fight?"

"Nothing like that. I think he meant to stay; but as I understand it almost as soon as their mother was gone, Doug up and sold the place and moved out to British Columbia. He wanted Bruce to go with him but Bruce figured that was a hell of a long way from home, so he came here."

"Poor fellow." Hannah shook her head. "He doesn't have a home. We'll have to have him over for supper sometime soon. How about asking him for Sunday night?"

Miriam reflected that only a few months ago she would have been excited about meeting one of Jack's friends, and worry about how to get him to notice her during the meal. But that was behind her now. She was no longer interested in her brothers' friends. She knew now what could happen when you flirted or teased older guys, and she wanted no part of it. When Bruce came over, she busied herself in the background helping her mother and right after the meal she excused herself to go and help Gracie wash her hair and experiment with hair styles--should she wear her pony-tail high or low? Should she continue to pull all her hair back from her thin face or should she get the front cut shorter? Would she look better with bangs over her forehead or with them brushed over to one side? As a school girl Miriam had never fussed about such things herself, but to Gracie they seemed of utmost importance.

Miriam noticed that her parents took to Bruce, and after that first night, he was frequently at their place dropping in with Jack for supper at least once a week, bringing a basket of apples or chips and pop or other treats for the kids, and staying into the evening to play cards with the adults or just to sit around and talk.

Before long too, it was almost taken for granted that he would join them for their Sunday dinners, when all the family would all be there. Then, partly because of the cramped quarters, and partly out of custom, they would divide themselves into several separate groups with the men congregating in the living room, and Annie settling the baby in her parent's bedroom and sending Olive off with Gracie before she and Frances joined Hannah and Miriam in the kitchen. The children would run around from one room to another until they were ordered into their room to play. Meals were served with the men eating in the livingroom with the big drop-leaf table pulled out from the wall and practically filling the whole room. The children were fed in the kitchen, and the women sat down together after they had cleaned up after the men and shooed the children off again. If Annie and Frances decided to join the men for awhile in the evening, Miriam would stay in the kitchen helping her mother or join the children in the bedroom. She no longer felt comfortable around the older ones and her father.

Chapter Three

It must have been one of the coldest days of the winter when Miriam hurried home from the bus stop. Her legs were freezing when her coat flopped open around her knees and the cold wind blew her dress against her thighs. There was the gap between her girdle and the tops of her nylon stockings that was always cold, and the stockings didn't help much either. The boots that she had been so proud of when she'd picked them up on sale near the end of the season almost a year ago were hurting her feet. High-heels might look sophisticated in the business district if the weather was good and the sidewalks were practically bare, but they weren't very practical on icy or snow-covered sidewalks, and they were pinching her toes. She was sure her feet were swelling a bit toward the end of each day now. She could hardly wait to get her pumps off when she got ready to leave the office, and to put these boots on. And now she could hardly wait to get home and kick them off.

She knew that she'd looked nice today though. Her navy coatdress with the white collar and big white buttons that she'd bought herself in the fall was still loose enough on her--though most of her clothes were starting to feel tight and she'd had to give up wearing anything the least bit fitted. She still had her dark green shift and her plaid jumper and her white blouse, and of course there was the reversible wraparound tartan skirt that she could wear with both her blue and her orange banlon sweater sets. Still the coat-dress was her favorite. Mr. Howard had once mentioned how businesslike it was. There had been so many clients in today it was nice to know that she had presented a professional image. Still with greeting all those clients and serving them coffee she had fallen behind with her work so she that she didn't have the brief ready at 5:00 P.M. and Mr. Howard needed it for the morning. As a result she had worked late and then had to take the 6:00 P.M. bus. Darn it! Jack had taken her mother grocery shopping last Saturday and just this morning Miriam had noticed her mother take a big roast out of the fridge to prepare. That meant Jack, and probably Bruce, would be coming over for supper. They'd arrive before she did; she'd be late to help her mother.

"I'm sorry I'm late, Mum," she apologized as she hurried through the door. "Mr. Howard needed some papers typed for that dispute about the new office building. There were people in all day. He must have changed them two or three times, and I had to type the final copy after closing time. I'll just get changed and help you."

Sure enough, Jack and Bruce were there. Self-consciously she patted her hair. No matter how much she back-combed it, and then pinned it up, it was always coming out by the end of the day. That must be why Bruce was looking at her as though he had never seen her before. She smiled politely and nodded before hurrying across the room and into the bedroom to change. Her old baggy jeans (she had moved the button over as far as it would go at the side and couldn't quite get the zipper up), Jack's old flannelette shirt worn loose, her hair let down and pulled back into a pony tail out of the way, and finally, her feet stuck into a pair of sneakers. That was comfort!

Bruce looked at her again as she emerged.

"God," he remarked. "I hardly recognized you when you first came in. I guess I'd just been thinking of you as one of the kids and hadn't realized how grown-up you are. You work down town?"

"Yes. At a law firm." She ducked her head, embarrassed suddenly by his attention, and hurried to the kitchen. When she returned to set the table, he inquired if she would be sitting down with them and offered to pull up a chair for her.

"Goodness, no. Mum and I will just grab a bite in the kitchen after we get the kids settled."

"Then how about sitting in on a game of cards later."

"Really, I've got other things to do this evening. Besides, you and Jack and the folks can play partners. You don't need an odd one."

From then on, Miriam noticed that any time he was over for a visit he would try to engage her in conversation, and she noticed him watching her as she moved about the room. He seemed to be trying to figure her out, for she was adept at fading into the background, just as Hannah often did, and often too she appeared to be little more than a child helping her mother out and then entertaining herself with the younger ones. But she realized he still remembered her as she had looked that day, a sophisticated legal secretary at the end of a busy and trying day.

She realized too that he was becoming somewhat puzzled about her appearance, and it was only a matter of time until he figured it out. Then one evening as she stood at the sink making sandwiches for the lunch boxes for the next day she overheard him talking to Jack on the back fire-escape.

"Your sister, she seems to be putting on weight. She couldn't be . . . uh . . . uh?"

Miriam felt her face turning red with shame. Thank goodness, they couldn't see her.

"But how? She seems like such a quiet thing. I mean who's the father? Is he going to marry her, or anything?"

"No." There was a long pause. The stairs creaked and Miriam thought they might be moving down the steps, but then she heard Jack again.

"You might as well know. She's named Charlie."

"Charlie?"

"Annie's husband. He hasn't denied it."

"And you're still friends with him!"

"Look, I wanted to kill him." That was the first that Miriam had heard that anyone might have been just a little on her side and she felt relieved; but then Jack went on, "He claims she lead him on. She was quite a tease, but we all thought it was innocent. Anyway we didn't know how far it had gone until it was too late."

"But your whole family accepts him?"

"That was Annie's choice. She stuck with him. I guess he made some promises. Sorry it happened and all that. Anyway he's my sister's husband and part of the family. If Annie and the kids are going to be around, he's going to be around too. I've lost all respect for him, but what can you do?"

They moved down beyond Miriam's hearing before Bruce could reply, and she mechanically finished her task, inwardly dying of shame. How could she ever face him again?.

******

Miriam realized that with each day the time was drawing nearer when she would have to quit work. Already she noticed that Sandra and Agnes looked at her every morning as she took off her coat, checking out what she was wearing, and in the tiny staff room during the lunch break they always seemed to be whispering about this girl or that who had 'gotten herself into trouble'. If Bruce, a man, had figured it out, surely they suspected something? Was this their way of letting her know that they were in on her secret?

Miriam was quietly frantic with worry. What should she do now? These girls that Agnes and Sandra somehow knew so much about all left home. They went off, out west or to the states, to boarding school or to visit some previously unheard of aunt. After it was all over they came home hoping that no one would suspect anything. Miriam knew that neither she nor her family had money for boarding school, and her aunts all had umpteen kids of their own to worry about and had never invited her to visit for longer than a Sunday afternoon.

She vaguely knew too that somewhere there were maternity homes--a recent magazine that Sandra had brought into the office had advertized one down in Nova Scotia. But that one cost money--lots of money Miriam suspected, though she didn't know how much and the ad didn't say. If there were any free ones run by churches or charities, Miriam didn't know about them. She would just have to stay at home and hope that her mother, or more likely her dad, wouldn't put her out on the street. After all, once she lost her job she wouldn't be able to contribute to the family income. Her fears about that subsided a little when she arrived home one day to find Hannah sorting through a box of maternity clothes. If Hannah was arranging for her to have maternity clothes, she must also be accepting the fact that she would be around.

"Where did those come from?" she asked just before she recognized the slightly faded orange and yellow top Hannah was shaking out.

"Annie brought them over for you."

"Annie did that, for me!" Miriam struggled with mixed emotions. She had thought that the days were long passed when she had to wear Annie's hand-me-downs, but still it had to be a gesture of friendship. Then Hannah went on: "I asked her to."

"Oh." Miriam felt deflated. The idea hadn't originated with Annie after all. "I guess some of these will be alright. I'll have to shorten them all though."

"Please be careful. Annie was firm about that. She will want them back."

Miriam sorted through the bundle. The skirts and slacks with cut-out bellies, and the frilly smock topes didn't thrill her much, but she wasn't in a position to complain..

"You'll have to start wearing these soon, Miriam. I've noticed that all your regular clothes are too tight for you."

"I know." Miriam knew what that meant. Tomorrow she would give her notice at work. And then what would happen to her? Miriam wished that she could cry out: 'Mum, I'm so scared. I don't know what to do. I'm so ashamed, so frightened. I feel so disgraced. Tell me that you love me. Tell me that you'll look after me. Tell me what to expect.' But Gracie was sitting at the corner table, half-heartedly doing her homework. The boys were arguing in the other room: something about their hockey cards. And her mother was already turning away, more concerned, it seemed to Miriam, about the beans and the potato scallop baking in the oven than she was about Miriam's whole world.

After she stopped working, Miriam found that she had time on her hands, and even though she started knitting for the baby, she was worried. There were so many preparations to be made and one thing gnawed on her mind more than anything else. Where would she keep the baby? The room she shared with Gracie and her little brothers was already bursting to the seams. How could she find space for the basket or carriage, shelves for the diapers, a draw in the dresser for his things? That left only the front room and kitchen. But the family lived in those two rooms. They were always bustling with activity. How could she keep the baby out of everyone's way, if she didn't even have a place to put it down?

With her worries churning around in her head, Miriam sat in the corner of the living room, with the late afternoon sun from the big window giving just enough light for her to pick up the stitches she had dropped, when she heard Jack come in and as Hannah supervised Gracie setting the table for supper, he casually remarked:

"Mom, what do you say if I asked to move back in with you folks?"

Hannah paused to look him in the face, then slowly, thinking out her words,

"I'd say that would be great, Jack. You know that you are always welcome, but ..."

"You know I'm always over here anyway. And since Bill moved out I'm paying a heck of a lot more than I should for that double room. And be damned if I'm going to take a cramped up single."

"But Jack." Hannah protested. "Where would we put you? We're already over-crowded as it is."

"I know. You'd have to move, of course. In fact, I know of a vacancy. It's only a few blocks from here, and it would be ideal. It's on the second floor, but you'd have the whole floor to yourselves. There's a balcony off the front room where Dad could sit out in the summer, and a back fire-escape off the kitchen. And three big bedrooms. I'd share with Paul and Davy."

Gracie had been listening in growing excitement. "Then Miriam and me could have the other room! We wouldn't have to share with the boys?"

"Sure." Jack reassured her, smiling at her giggles of delight.

"But Jack," Hannah protested. "You'll have to talk this over with your father. There's a lot to think about. A bigger place is bound to cost more."

"But I'd be helping with the rent. Actually you might be better off that way. And I already mentioned it to Dad. He said that it's up to you. If you're agreeable, we can go over in the morning, and if you like it, I'll put a deposit down."

Miriam sat quietly, her head was spinning. She'd actually been afraid that she might be expected to move out, find her own place. Sure, with no money, no job. How could she afford the rent, even on single room. She was sixteen. Maybe she could manage on her own, but not with a baby. But now Jack was offering them a solution. She knew that he was thinking about her and the baby and she would be eternally grateful. She nodded and smiled, but said nothing. If she voiced her relief she might burst into tears, and that was to be avoided. If she thanked him he would be embarrassed. He might deny that he was even thinking about her. He'd already given his explanation. She would accept it on face value but she knew – she knew it was at least in part for her.

The next day when they visited the new apartment, she peeked into the bedrooms. Yes, they were all good sized. The one in front would be for the girls. There was lots of room for her and Gracie to have separate beds, and still room for the baby.

Bruce came over on the weekend to help them move and Miriam didn't know where to hide. This was the first time she had seen him since she'd overheard that incriminating conversation, and now she was in maternity clothes. There was nothing to do but to carry on as usual.

"Hi, Bruce. Nice of you to come and help out."

He smiled broadly. For the first time she noticed that he did have a nice smile. "Think nothing of it. Glad to be of service."

The moment passed. She watched as he turned his attention to the work at hand. Charlie was struggling to balance the fridge on a dolly, but he strode past him, to help Johnny carry the chesterfield out to the rented truck.

Miriam watched as the men and boys did the heavy lifting, and her mother and Annie started in cleaning behind them. She wanted to join in as she always had, but instead Hannah directed her to lighter tasks.

"Don't be stretching and straining yourself now Miriam. Go and box up the stuff from your closet. Remember to put the boys things in separate boxes and it will be easier when we get to the unpacking."

She noticed that, no matter how busy he was with the others, Bruce always seemed to be at hand whenever she went to move a heavy box.

"Here, let me do that for you?"

"For heaven's sake, I'm not an invalid."

"Didn't say you were. But no sense you straining. I can carry that with one hand." he made a joke of it, and Miriam realized that it was nice to have someone watching over her, concerned about her well-being.

At noon they drove over to the new place. Hannah spread out sandwiches that she had prepared the night before, and found the kettle and cups in the boxes marked 'kitchen'. All afternoon, while the men traveled back and forth carrying more stuff than anyone had realized they owned, the women unpacked, organized and put away. By mid afternoon Hannah was preparing a big meal for everyone, and as the men relaxed in the living room after their final trip, she insisted that Miriam go in and rest a bit too. Miriam curled up in the corner chair, as far from Charlie as she could get and listened to the drone of their voices. She was half asleep when supper was announced, and she looked up to see Bruce sitting beside her watching her.

******

Spring breezes blew from the open window above the kitchen sink where Miriam was washing salad greens in the last preparations for her company. Just last week she had run into Sandra on the street on her way back from her doctor's appointment. This morning Sandra had telephoned that she and Agnes were coming over on their lunch hour. Miriam knew they would bring their own sandwiches, but she was determined to entertain properly just as her mother would have done. Salad, tea or coffee, chocolate cake. She would have liked to be able to offer dainty squares, but there wasn't time to make any and Hannah always had cake or cookies available, as long as Paul and Davy hadn't gotten to it first.

Her excitement was mingled with apprehension. Neither of the girls had been overly friendly while she was working; why were they coming now? Just to see her discomfort, or to check out her preparations? She decided to ignore her doubts and enjoy the visit. There, she heard the doorbell.

"Hello, Sandra, Agnes. Thanks for coming over."

"Oh, we had to. We hadn't seen you for so long. And we wanted to bring you this."

Agnes handed over a gift.

"For me?"

"Well, for the --the baby."

"Yes, that's what I meant."

They all laughed nervously.

"I guess I should have told you guys. You must have wondered why I left so suddenly."

"We had our suspicions. Mr. Howard questioned us."

"Oh, what did he say?" God, she hadn't handled things very well, had she?.

"He was sorry to see you go. He said that he had never had such a hard-working and efficient secretary, and that you would be hard to replace."

"Really?"

Sandra made a bit of a face. "You know, you really shouldn't have worked so hard. It made it awkward for the temp they hired until they find somebody."

"Oh, don't worry about that," Agnes tried to cover up, but Miriam hadn't noticed. "Did he say anything else?"

"Something about a very professional letter of resignation, and, oh yes, when we told him we were coming over here today he said to let you know that he hopes that you'll come back some day."

"Really!" Mr. Howard had never said anything like that to her.

"Aren't you going to open your gift?"

"Do you want me to? Right now? I'm dying to see it."

There was a beautiful sweater set, hand knit by Sandra, and three stretchy new sleepers from Agnes, wrapped around a little rattle.

"Oh, beautiful. Come and see what I have ready for him."

"Him, or her? Which do you want?"

Miriam didn't know what to say. Until recently the only honest answer would have been, 'Neither.' She couldn't tell them about the endless nights, lying still in bed, worrying. "Would the baby be alright? What if he wasn't? Babies should be conceived in love. Would it affect him that he wasn't? What if he was born dead? That might be a solution to all her problems. But that was a terrible way to think! Even worse than thinking about giving him up for adoption. But only a bad person would consider giving her own flesh and blood up to strangers. Maybe Annie and Charlie should adopt him--they didn't have any boys. That would be ironic--Charlie adopting his own son. Not to be thought of. But how would she look after a baby? All her life she remembered Gran telling her to leave the baby alone; Annie scolding her whenever she tried to help with Gracie; her mother's non-interference implying agreement. How would she know what to do? The pamphlets she had picked up at the doctor's office and the book she got out of the library hadn't reassured her. There were so many things that could go wrong. What if she didn't love her baby? Would he sense it if she didn't? Did love come naturally? Could she love a baby that had been conceived in fear and hate? Suppose he was like Charlie? Could she love him then? Babies were so sweet and helpless. They should be wanted. Most of the time she felt cold and distant from this baby. Even now, as she showed her friends the baby basket, bath tub, and pile of supplies that Annie had sent over, with the admonition that she was to take good care of them, Annie would want them back some day; and the gifts that neighbours had slipped to Hannah on her behalf, she didn't know whether to give in to the mounting excitement and anticipation, or to the despair that still had her waking at night covered with sweat.

"Come out to the kitchen and we'll have our lunch. And tell me more about the office."

The hour passed quickly, with Miriam hungry for news. She hadn't realized how much she would miss the gossip and excitement of a busy law office: the interesting cases she used to type up; the tension of deadlines; the definitely defined boundaries of who did what; the satisfaction of a job well done; the relief of Friday afternoons.

"Do you know, one of the worst things about not working is not having Fridays to look forward to."

"Really?" They didn't quite understand.

Then before they left the talk turned back to babies.

"I do hope that you will be alright, Miriam. You know my sister had her second one breach. You can't imagine the pain. Twenty-six hours that woman was in labour. They would have both died, but finally the doctor used forceps and pulled the baby out. Then, my God, the stitches. She was torn to pieces."

"My labour was bad enough, but thank goodness in those days they knocked you out for the worst of it. Do you know Miriam, now-a-days they expect a woman to go through it all with practically no medication."

"I read that heavy anaesthetic isn't good for the baby."

"Don't believe everything you read, Miriam. Nor what those doctors tell you either. Like I said, they put me under. And my Stephen wasn't hurt. A teenager now, and he's never given me a moment's trouble."

"My doctor said he would give me Demerol."

"Demerol? That's like giving aspirin for an amputation."

"And you so young. Miriam, you don't know what to expect."

"My neighbour had twins. They didn't know until the last moment. Miriam, you've gotten so big all of a sudden. Are you sure it isn't twins?"

"I don't think so." Miriam whispered, but they paid no attention to her.

"And remember your cousin, Sandra. What she went through!"

"She hemorrhaged right after the baby was born. They were sure she was going to bleed to death. Then they used that as an excuse not to tell her that the baby died. She never saw him. They snatched him away the moment he was born, with her lifeblood pouring out on the delivery table. And afterwards they wouldn't answer any of her questions. She almost went crazy. And no more children either."

"Hush. I think we are scaring Miriam. Don't worry, dear. I'm sure everything will be alright in your case."

"We've got to get back now. I told them we would be late but we can't take advantage."

Miriam shut the door behind them and rushed to her room, throwing herself on the bed. This was horrible! How would she ever live through it? All the horror stories she had ever heard about childbirth, told around the kitchen tables when she had somehow managed not to be noticed, came flooding back. Hours of pain, children born dead or deformed, mothers bleeding to death. Backaches, stitches, problems that never went away. "She's never been well since that last child was born." she'd heard whispered. Where was her mother when she needed her?

But Hannah had taken advantage of her having friends over and had left the house for most of the day. "I'm going to do some last minute shopping, things you'll need for the baby. I'll probably have lunch downtown at Zellers and visit with the girls." (Hannah had recently been laid off during a slow period at the store.) "Then I'll probably drop in on Frances for the afternoon. She wants my advice on the new slipcovers she's making. I may be late, and if I am, try to get supper started for Dad and Jack. There's leftover roast and gravy in the fridge."

Miriam needed her mother now, and she wasn't there.

Before long the boys burst in from school. Miriam heard them shouting for their mother, then rummaging around the kitchen for cookies, before going in and turning on the TV. When Gracie came into the bedroom, tossing her books on the dresser, and kicking her shoes in the direction of the closet, Miriam shouted at her: "Get out.."

Usually Gracie would stop and argue. "It's my room too." but this time she took one glance in Miriam's direction and fled.

By the time she heard Hannah bustling about the kitchen it was almost five and the men would be home hungry within minutes. Miriam slipped into the bathroom, washed her face, and hurried out. "I'm sorry, Mum. I must have fallen asleep. I forgot all about supper."

That night her water broke.

Miriam was terrified. Her mother went with her to the hospital, helped to get her registered, accompanied her to the small, stark room, where a nurse had handed her a johnny shirt and told her curtly, "Put this on." But then her mother left! And so did the nurse! She obediently undressed and climbed onto the hard bed and looked around. This was her first time in a hospital, and she hadn't known what to expect, but this room was stark: no pictures, no radio, no magazines, or pamphlets, nothing but the bare off-white walls and ceiling, and the patch of grey sky that was the only view from the high window. Nothing to distract herself with, nothing to think about except the thousand questions that ran through her mind as her body twisted in pain, and then relaxed.

Finally the nurse was back.

"I'm going to shave you now, and then we'll have our enema."

'What!' Miriam thought, as she spread her legs and closed her eyes in humiliation. Why hadn't her mother prepared her for this?

"Why?" the word must have escaped her because the nurse answered.

"Sanitary. Everything has to be clean and sterile for the doctor to deliver the baby. Now just hold still. You're doing fine. Another cramp? Just breathe through it."

What did she mean, 'breathe through it'? What else could Miriam do? She remembered, all her mother's babies had been born at home. Maybe they did things differently for home deliveries. But she was in the hospital. It should be easier in the hospital where everything was so sterile and there were nurses and doctors to help. But why this shaving of her private parts? And this humiliating enema?

Then the nurse patted her on the thigh.

"Done now. You can relax. The bathroom is in there, but try to hold back as long as you can. After you've had your BM, try to get some rest. You are going to need it." and she was gone.

Rest! How could she rest when a thousand questions were running through her mind, and her body was racked with pains that were increasing in frequency and intensity? She made several trips to the bathroom, then lay back, twisting with each contraction, gripping the sides of the bed, gritting her teeth and tensing her whole body. Then the nurse was back with her doctor. Thank goodness, a familiar face.

He examined her, whistling through his teeth as he did so, and mumbling, either to himself or to the nurse, 'Four centimeters.'

"What does that mean, Doctor?"

"It means that it will be awhile yet."

"Is everything okay?"

"Of course. Don't you worry about a thing. Before long you'll have a beautiful new baby." Then he shook his head and turned to the nurse. Miriam thought she heard a mumble of "And just a child herself." Before she could form questions of the thoughts that were racing through her mind he was gone again, the nurse trailing behind.

This time the wait was longer. The pains were worse. Where was everybody? She wanted her mother. Why couldn't Hannah be with her? Why was there a 'hospital policy' that kept everybody away? She gritted her teeth and held her breath fighting her way through another contraction. God, would they never stop. Suppose the baby was coming now! Suppose she pushed it out with the next big cramp. Alone! She needed help! Somebody should be there! She reached up and pushed the button that the nurse had pointed out to her, and waited.

"Yes. Did you ring?"

"I think--I think my baby's coming."

"Oh, it's too soon yet. Roll over and let me check. Just six centimeters. You'll be awhile yet. Just don't panic. "

"Could you stay with me? Just for a little."

"Heavens, I've got a million things to do. There are three others on this floor who will deliver before you do, including twins. You'll be all right. You can't expect constant attention."

She was gone again, and Miriam fell back on her pillow feeling guilty. She hadn't realized that she was being a bother, demanding more than her share of attention. She was just so frightened; but she would try to bear up. Her mother had had seven kids, surely she could manage this one. If only she wasn't so alone.

The nurse was back in again, then the doctor.

"Eight centimeters. It shouldn't be too much longer." He turned to leave.

"When will you be back?"

"Of course. The nurse will call me when its time. Just let her know."

"How will I know?"

The doctor was out the door, and the nurse answered. "Oh, you'll know. Just ring me when you start bearing down." And she was gone too.

Thank goodness, it would soon be over. She couldn't take much more of this. Somewhere down the hall someone was screaming. Miriam clutched her teeth and tried not to make a sound. Maybe that was the twins coming. Twins probably hurt twice as much. The doctor and nurses would be busy. She just had to lie here and wait her turn. But oh, the pain was so bad. She had a sudden urge to go to the bathroom. She looked around. It was across the room, but with this pain she didn't think that she should get out of bed. She held back, fighting the pain and that terrible urge. If she wasn't careful she was going to soil the bed. She held her breath and grabbed for the sides of the bed, twisting her body, gasping, but holding back, holding back. Total concentration now. Total concentration. Hold back. A sob escaped her, then another.

The nurse was there, patting her shoulder. "There, there, dear. Try not to cry."

"I need to go to the bathroom."

"You must just think that you do. That enema cleaned you out. Now just relax, and I'll check you again. O my God! Why didn't you tell me you were bearing down?"

She rushed out of the room, shouting for the orderly, and the other nurse. "Get the doctor! We've got a delivery, right now!"

Miriam was lost in a sea of pain and fear. Around her people were hustling. Arms lifted her, transferred her from her bed to a gurney, then transferred her again. Bright lights shone in her eyes. Her legs were strapped into stirrups. She couldn't move. She was terrified.

"Push, push!" The nurse by her head, a different one than she had seen before, commanded. Miriam grabbed the nurse's hand and squeezed with all her might, drawing in her breath and pushing. Then she heard the cry.

"A healthy baby boy."

"Can you see him?" The nurse asked, as she freed her hand and shook it, trying to get circulation going again.

Someone was holding him up. Covered with slime, blue, then red in the face. Screaming. Blond hair. And through it all, Miriam saw -- there was no mistaking Charlie's son.

Chapter Four

"Mum, you know I can't go. I can't expect you to look after Albert all day on a holiday, and Bruce says we'll be late getting back."

"Don't be so silly, Miriam. He's no trouble at all. I'm going to be around the house all day anyway, and I'll get Gracie to take him for a walk this afternoon if I need a break. You're the one who needs to get out. A drive in the country will do you good."

"But you take care of him as much as I do."

Miriam felt guilty. Almost from the beginning, certainly since she had gone back to work two days a week, helping out during the summer when the other girls were taking their holidays, Miriam had noticed that Hannah had taken over much of his day to day care. It worried her.

While in the hospital, a few days after Albert's birth, troubled by her ambivalent feelings towards her baby boy, remembering her involuntary turning away when she first saw him in the delivery room, she had asked an older nurse, when would she start loving her baby.

"What do you mean? Surely you love him now. He's such a beautiful baby. All that blond hair, and deep blue eyes."

"Well I'd like to." Miriam tried to explain but it was difficult to put her feelings in words and she was afraid that she was offending this kind woman. "He's nice. He really is. And I guess he's nice looking. I like him, but I don't feel attached to him. You know," she hoped that she was making herself clear. "You know, I don't know if I love him like women are supposed to love their babies."

"That will come, my dear. It's hard here in the hospital, when he's spending most of the time in the nursery. I'm not sure

I agree with all this separating mothers from their babies. It wasn't like that in the old days. But I guess its the modern way. When you get him home and are taking care of him all the time, it will come. Some night when you're getting up to give him his night feedings, or perhaps when he makes his first gassy smile, or reaches out and touches you, you'll suddenly realize that he's just stolen your heart."

But it hadn't happened that way. From the first day they were hardly in the house before Hannah had insisted that Miriam lay down for a rest. Gracie had been waiting to hold him; Hannah had taken over mixing his formula; Jack had hovered in the background; and the little boys had peeked into his basket, promising to teach him to play ball, just as soon as he was older. That evening Johnny had sat rocking him during his fussy spell, and when he noticed Miriam's look of surprise he'd growled, "I know how to settle a baby. I got seven of my own, ain't I?"

Now Hannah was shaking her head against Miriam's protests. "You need to socialize more."

Miriam couldn't understand it. Just a few months ago, when she was pregnant, Hannah encouraged her to stay in the background, helping in the kitchen, entertaining the kids in the bedroom, or just resting quietly in a corner by herself. Now it seemed she was constantly urging Miriam to mix with the other young people when they came over for a visit. 'Go and keep Frances company while I'm finishing up here, now.' she would say. Or 'You sit in on a game of cards tonight. I've got mending to do.' So it seemed that Miriam spent more time than usual sitting in the front room or out on the balcony, and often she realized that she was sitting with Bruce, who came over frequently to spend an evening with the family. Not that she minded. He was pleasant to sit with, or to walk with down to the store to pick up ice-cream for a treat on a hot muggy evening.

Miriam especially enjoyed the times they went for drives in the country. The first had been when a group of them went out to the old place to check for berries and go trout fishing. She'd left Albert behind that time too, and had a wonderful time; she and Bruce going together down the stream, while Jack went up, and Bill and Frances stayed back at the farm house--Frances had grown up in the city and Miriam suspected she was using the excuse that she needed a rest so that she wouldn't be expected to bait a hook or kill a trout. They had had a great time, and Bruce seemed impressed at her skill when she caught more than he did. "I know the brook," she'd explained to him, wiping sweat and fly dope from her forehead. "I love the country." Since then they often took drives together, sometimes stopping somewhere to fish or pick berries, but also just to enjoy getting out of the city. Sometimes they took Albert in his car bed, but more often they left him with Hannah. Then one Sunday they returned from a drive up around Belle Isle Bay to find Charlie and his girls at the apartment. Charlie was rocking Albert, his face buried in the baby's blankets. Miriam had been about to snatch her baby away when Hannah called her out to the kitchen.

"Annie miscarried a baby boy today. The girls are staying here for a awhile, and Charlie just dropped in on his way back from the hospital."

Miriam shivered involuntarily. She remembered how she had almost wished for a miscarriage at times when she was carrying Albert. Now it had happened to her sister, and she felt sorry and somehow guilty. It was all mixed up somehow. She hadn't wanted Charlie's baby, and now Charlie's baby was dead. Was there some way her very wishes had caused that? She shook her head realizing how foolish and superstitious that sounded, but the feeling remained. But still, Charlie had no right to snuggle Albert. Albert was hers, and hers alone.

Even after Annie recovered, it seemed to Miriam that Charlie paid far too much attention to Albert any time they came over. She avoided going out and leaving Albert behind any time she suspected that Charlie might drop in, and always tried to keep

Albert in another room. She only left him with Hannah when she had to go to work and it was safe to leave him then. Charlie had to work weekdays.

Now Bruce wanted her to go for a drive with him out to his property down the coast.

"Pack a big lunch, and maybe something for supper too. It's a fair drive, and we won't be back until late."

"I can't go away for a whole day, Bruce. I've got Albert to look after."

"Can't you just bring him along?"

That was when Hannah had intervened, "He shouldn't be away from home that long. It would throw him way off schedule. I'll watch him. Don't you worry, Miriam. He'll be well looked after."

That wasn't what she'd been worried about - she was sure her mother would take better care of him than she could herself - but she reluctantly agreed. She would enjoy the drive, and even though it was Labour Day, they were still feeling the heat of the summer.

The trip was delightful. Bruce picked Miriam up early in the morning, and drove directly out of town heading down the highway toward St. Stephen. Miriam had never been anywhere in that direction before. It was exciting to catch glimpses of the Bay of Fundy.

"My property isn't right on the bay, but it's on a little river. Really just a stream when the tide is out. But the tide comes in and it's deep and wide. Just a great place. You'll love it, Miriam."

"Did you ever live there?"

"No. Just a few visits when I was really young, and since I got it last year. There's no buildings on it now. Just a few cleared fields. Most of it is forested. A person could make good money cutting firewood and trucking it into town, if it wasn't so far. And logging. There's some trees big enough for logging.

Nobody's lived there for a long time. Any old buildings have fallen in or I tore them down. There's an apple orchard. It needs work of course. The whole place needs work. But it is beautiful."

Miriam had never seen him so animated, so excited about anything. This wasn't her usual picture of Bruce - drinking beer with Jack, complaining about the job on the docks, or about the government. New Brunswick men did love to talk politics. No. This was a different person, one she had just caught glimpses of during the past few months.

They were quiet much of the drive, but there were no uncomfortable silences. Bruce talked about his property, letting her know what to expect. Miriam was surprised at how soon he turned down a dirt road toward the sea, and then off on another with deep ruts and branches brushing up against both sides of the car. Then around a turn and they burst into a field of fall wild flowers, with a view down over the hill to the little bay at the mouth of the stream.

They spent the next couple of hours exploring the property.

"Just look at that fine stand of maple going up that ridge, Miriam. That could be thinned for years, and the lumber sold. Somebody just needs to start up a mill around here. And there's pulp, see along here. And this is where the old shack was - my great uncle's. He's the one that cleared this area and planted the orchard. It's grown pretty wild, but it could be reclaimed. There's a good spring here, and a little freshwater brook for watering the stock. I think that a person could dig out a little pond down here. And build the barns over there." He waved his arms in several directions as he talked.

At low tide they went down to the stream, scrambling over rocks, wading in the ice cold water. Then they climbed up to a point where they could overlook the bay and eat their lunch.

"I've got so many plans for this place, Miriam. Isn't it wonderful? After that stuffy, dirty city. Look at all the space for Albert to run and play and explore as he gets older. He would love it here."

Of course. Miriam remembered growing up in the country, and how her little brothers had resented the move to the city. She hated to think of Albert growing up in the overcrowded flat with the tiny back yard.

"Miriam, I want you to share it with me. You will love it out here. I know you will. I want you and Albert to be my family. Help me to get this place going. Make it our home."

Miriam was flabbergasted. Despite the walks to the store for ice cream, the occasional drives, even this day so far, she had never thought of Bruce as anything more than her brother's friend, a family friend. He was nice, and good looking with his black curly hair and dark complexion, and she enjoyed his company, but they had never been out on a real date. Not to a movie. Not to a dance. In fact Miriam had never been to a dance in her life.

Where was the courtship she had read about in books? Where was the romance? Sure, she liked Bruce, especially now when he was away from the city, excited about his plans. It was impossible not to be caught up in his dreams. But love? She wasn't sure. What was love anyway? Did her mother love her father? Seven kids, and a lifetime together, but Miriam couldn't remember ever seeing any real affection between them. Did Annie love Charlie? Certainly there had been all that giggling and fussing about clothes and hair and where they were going and how much fun they had together while they were going out to a drive-in movie or a dance at the legion or a get-together with other young people; but now they seemed to have settled into a routine much like their parents, except that Annie and Charlie always seemed to be arguing. And Miriam hadn't even experienced that initial infatuation that Annie always had to look back on.

Despite her doubts, within weeks they were arranging for a fall wedding at a nearby church that Bruce suggested. Other than family, there were few guests: Bruce's mother and his aunt from Boston, Miriam's family, a few mutual friends of Bruce's and Jack's. Miriam was pleased that Mr. Howard came, and Sandra and Agnes sent a gift. She didn't wear white. Then they left for a two-week camping trip, their second visit to the property, again leaving Albert behind with the family.

"You don't want a baby on your honeymoon," Hannah insisted.

What a wonderful time they had! The fall weather was gorgeous, a real Indian summer with the leaves at their most colorful. During the first week, the weather was warm and they spent a lot of their time exploring every inch of the property, especially climbing up and down the gorge by the stream. A few hot afternoons they actually went swimming in a sheltered tidal pool, then dried off quickly and cuddled together in the blanket they usually carried with them and Miriam, frightened and tense at first, learned to relax and enjoy their lovemaking, pleasantly surprised at Bruce's gentle concern for her well-being.

The second week a sudden cold front moved in, dropping the temperatures to just above freezing and their attention turned to hunting. Miriam was thrilled that Bruce taught her how to use his second gun and together they traversed the property looking for game. Bruce shot a deer their second day hunting and they dressed it out. Then they concentrated mainly on partridge. "We'll help your father fill the freezer." Then on their final morning, with the air crisp with frost, Bruce lifted the tent flap and signaled for Miriam to crawl over quietly with her gun. A magnificent buck deer was reaching into an apple tree down in the old orchard. Trembling with pride and fear and excitement Miriam took aim. What a beautiful animal! Yet Miriam had been raised in the country until her teens. She well understood the reality. Beautiful animals provide meat. She took aim as she had often seen her father and brothers do, and as Bruce had taught her. She gently squeezed the trigger. The buck sprang into the air and took off.

Bruce started shouting. She hung her head in shame. She had scared him off. But no, Bruce was shouting, "You got him! You got him!" and running out of the tent in his long underwear. She quickly grabbed some sweat pants and a jacket and ran after him. Sure enough, there was the buck down in the corner of the orchard. Bruce went back for his clothes and his knife. They returned from their wedding trip a few days late with slushy snow falling around, and took some ribbing from her brothers. It took awhile to convince people that they were delayed by having to dress down a second deer. Two deer, several dozen partridge - they had enough to give away to family and friends and feed themselves a good part of the winter.

* * *

Although she was caught up in the dream and anxious to get back to the property, Miriam understood that they had to spend the next few months in the city. They would have to build their house before they could winter in the country. So Miriam willingly stayed in the small two-room apartment Bruce had found for them, taking care of Albert and visiting back and forth with her mother and Frances. Occasionally, too, she would spend time with Annie though usually that happened when they ran into each other at their parents' place. They were getting along okay now, but Miriam realized that they would never be as close as society seemed to think sisters should be, or even as close as common interests might have led them.

Bruce didn't want Miriam to go back to her part time job.

"I know we're not rich, but we can manage on what I make. Content yourself with keeping the house and looking after your baby." So she took more interest in Albert and daydreamed about raising a large family on 'the property'. Dreams change. She had given up her hopes for an education and becoming a teacher. Now she put thoughts of a successful office career behind her. She would be a wife and mother - the best wife and mother she could be. Her work would be beside her husband; homemaking, cooking, gardening, helping with the livestock, hunting and fishing, and raising a big family.

Chapter Five

Winter passed slowly. As spring came, whenever the sidewalks were passable, Frances would phone in the early afternoon. "Let's take the babies out for a walk." With Albert dressed in his snowsuit in his second-hand stroller, Frances' daughter wrapped in blankets in her brand new carriage, and Annie's Amy trying to climb out of her stroller to push it, while Olive trailed along, they would walk along the sidewalks enjoying the fresh air, but heading inevitably downtown to the shopping area. Often their only purchases were three cups of coffee at Zellers, where occasionally they would run into Hannah, but they enjoyed 'getting out', 'seeing somebody', and it was good for the kids. Then one of them would glance at her watch. "My goodness, look at the time. I've got to get home and get supper on the table before (Charlie, Bill, Bruce) gets home."

If only a few years before, Miriam had felt envious when, dressed for the office, she would encounter bobby-soxers on their way to school, now she felt a touch of nostalgia any time she encountered one of the girls rushing importantly from the office to the bank or post office on some official errand. But that life was behind her now. She was a wife and mother. Soon they would be living on the property.

Bruce hated living and working in the city. Miriam was neither shocked nor surprised when he announced one Friday night that he had quit his job. Although it would still be cool, she presumed that they would be moving out to the country. But no.

"I'm going over to the mill at St. Thomas, Miriam. I worked there a couple of summers ago. I'm sure I can get on again. You stay here and get things ready to pack. I'll send for you as soon as I find us a place."

"But what about our plans, Bruce. Weren't we going to build a house this summer?"

"Be practical Miriam. Building costs money. Maybe later in the summer we'll have enough to put up a camp, but not now. I'd say that the best we can hope for would be to spend a few weekends there. We'll be closer. We'll pick a few berries, do some fishing. But when we get ahead, then we'll build. I promise you."

It was not what she had planned for, not what she expected, but she couldn't see an alternative. After all, it was Bruce who had to earn a living, and they hoped to have another baby on the way before long. So they spent the summer in St. Thomas..

It was the first time Miriam had been away from her family, and she missed them. No mother living near by to get together and cook big meals, to make preserves and pickles, to ask advice. No little brothers to listen to bragging about their school life and adventures and to run errands. "Paul, would you run down to the store and pick up a can of beans for me. Here's a quarter for a bottle of pop." No Gracie to willingly, even eagerly, to take Albert off her hands. No Frances and Annie to walk with and talk with, and exchange ideas about child rearing and housekeeping.

She made friends. Mrs. Henley next door showed her how to make cheese whiz and asparagus sandwiches and advised her on Albert's rash. There were other young mothers to talk to in back yards after the laundry was hung out, with toddlers playing together in the sandbox or wading pool. There were Tupperware parties, where Miriam soon realized that if she tried she could win most of the silly introductory games, but was smart enough to limit herself to one win an evening. The games were mindless, the friendship and laughter fun, the demonstrations (after the first few times) boring, the lunches sumptuous. "What did you put in these sandwiches? Cream cheese and cherries. That's all. I never would have guessed." And then before the evening was over, the obligation to buy something and decide who would book the next party. "Oh well, it's a cheap evening out." Somehow, Miriam wondered why it never occurred to them that they could get together without a Tupperware demonstrator to direct their 'party'.

Bruce and Miriam spent early evenings sitting out on the doorstep, chatting with any neighbors who passed by, and after Albert went to bed they would go in and watch TV awhile before going to bed themselves. Whenever possible they spent weekends at the property where they would pick wild strawberries, blueberries, raspberries and choke cherries in season. Sometimes they would walk along the stream to its mouth to dig clams, but they didn't even have to leave their property for fishing, and if they followed the stream up beyond the high tide mark they caught excellent pan-sized trout. In the fall they picked apples, and shot another deer and enough partridge to satisfy themselves. But winter came and they hadn't started building, although they had chosen a sight and drawn up their preliminary plans.

Their first anniversary came and went and then another winter. Miriam reflected that while she was often bored, she was also contented. Bruce was good to her. She went home for a few weeks in November when Annie gave birth to her third daughter. Hannah was down with a bad 'flu'. Despite Miriam's reservations about it, she stayed at Annie's to look after Olive and Amy. Charlie seemed to enjoy having Albert there and she tried not to resent the fact that he gave him at least as much attention as he gave his daughters and seemed pleased with his strength and development. "Look how steady he is on his feet, and look at the size of those hands. I've got to hand it to you, Miriam. He'll be quite a man some day." Any interest he had ever had in Miriam was gone. He was charming, friendly and polite to his wife's sister who had come to help out. She remained cool and distant, but polite. After all, he was part of the family and she was staying in his home and eating at his table.

Again in the spring Miriam went home, but this time to be near her mother for the birth of her own baby. She was more knowledgeable now. She stayed home during the early stages of her labour, patiently bore the pain as long as seemed reasonable, asked for Demerol when she needed it, and bore down when the urge came. No false modesty this time. No worry about 'soiling the sheets'. Let the hospital staff look after that. And there was her daughter, Rebecca, Becky — named after Bruce's recently deceased mother.

A second baby is supposed to be easier to care for than the first, but Miriam didn't find it that way. It took her a long while to regain her strength, and Becky was a small, fussy baby.

"She reminds me of Annie," Hannah explained. "She was so colicky, and fussy; I sometimes wondered how I would manage. She cried all the time. And then Annie's second, Amy, was the same. But she'll outgrow it and be a delight. You'll do fine back home with Bruce. Just leave Albert with us. I'm not getting enough time at Zellers lately to make it worthwhile and Gracie can help me. Otherwise she'll be bored with nothing to do. You get rested up, and you and Bruce take time to enjoy the baby."

Good advice perhaps. Miriam knew that she didn't have the energy to chase after an active two-year-old. But it was hard to enjoy a baby that slept fitfully and cried whenever she was awake. Gas? Colic? Not adjusting to the formula?

Perfectly normal, the doctor advised. She'll outgrow it.

All that summer they couldn't get out to the property on a regular basis. Miriam fretted in the heat of St. Thomas. By fall they were able to drive out for a day or two, to pick apples and do some hunting, but it was difficult with a cranky, demanding baby. Then suddenly by the first snow Miriam realized that she had settled down, slept through the night, gulped down her pablum, smiled and cooed at everyone, especially Albert who had finally rejoined them.

They spent the next year in St. Thomas..

Chapter Six

"Ouch!" Miriam felt Albert kick her in the ribs as he turned over and scrambled up on his hands and knees. It seemed only minutes since she had finally closed her eyes. "Maybe if I lie still he'll think I'm sleeping," she thought. "Then, maybe, just maybe, he'll settle down again." She felt the train sway as though it were rounding a bend, and almost immediately sway again. There was a squeal of steel on steel, then the wheels took up their regular clicking rhythm. At her other side, Becky stirred momentarily but settled into her regular breathing again. Deep inside Miriam felt the tiny flutter of life. Albert's threshing about or the change in motion had disturbed the little one.

Albert noticed the faint line of light under the blind and reached up, pushing his head and shoulders under it. No hope that he would settle now.

"Oh, Mummy, wake up. Mummy, look! Mountains!"

She pushed herself up too and lifted the blind. The train was surrounded by mountains--not hills, like in New Brunswick, even the rugged hills near Saint John, nor the big one they called 'The Mountain' near the property. Not even like the big outcroppings of rock that she had marveled at when they passed through Northern Ontario. No, these bore no relation to anything she had ever seen before. In the early light of dawn she looked out across a valley surrounded by mountains, their steep, rock sides reaching up to snow capped peaks breaking the sky. There were a hundred streams cascading down from those mountains, forming a river that twisted its way among the rocks and trees on the valley floor. Never in her life could she remember seeing anything so striking, so dramatic, and so awe inspiring. It was like — she searched for an adequate description and couldn't find the words. It was like being on a movie set. And she was in the center of it.

She crouched on the narrow berth, her arm around her little son, and watched as the train rounded another bend--not so sharp this time; the wheels did not scream--and there was another view--vista after vista opening up beside them. Albert held his breath, silent in amazement.

Should she wake Becky? No, she was too young to appreciate it, and there would be lots of mountains for her to see later. Miriam would share this magic moment with her son.

My, he'd been a trial these last few days: almost four years old, bored with sitting and looking out the window, especially through forests of Northern Ontario, and the endless prairies; bored with the colouring book the conductor gave him, and with the few toys she was able to carry for him. Constantly he'd wanted to run up and down the isles of the train. But she had Becky to watch over. Becky had walked at nine months, awfully early everybody admitted, and at home she was running, trying always to follow Albert, but now, try as she might, she couldn't cope with the swaying of the railway car. And despite her slight appearance, she was solid, heavy. Miriam tired quickly trying to carry her; the early stages of pregnancy always tired her. Only occasionally would Miriam try stretching their legs, guiding her along as they walked the whole length of the train, and only when the conductor announced a long stop would she get off for a bit of fresh air, and maybe a snack at the station restaurant--the food was cheaper there than in the dining car--and the provisions she had brought with her were long since used up. The trip had been a long one. Thank goodness Bruce had insisted, when he phoned and told her that it was time to come, that she take a berth at night. She couldn't imagine how he had sat up night after night, traveling coach. It had been a long trip. But now they were in the mountains. Soon she would be with Bruce again.

She thought back over the past winter, Bruce's restlessness when the mill had cut back earlier than usual in the fall. He hated being laid off, idle around the house. He had no hobbies; he didn't read, except for the newspaper. And even with unemployment insurance, they were constantly worried about how to make ends meet, let alone save for the future. He had gone so far as to inquire about returning to the docks in Saint John, but winter was their slow time too. Then just after Christmas a call had come from his brother in British Columbia. "Come out here. There is plenty of work, and good wages. I can get you on with me. They're hiring all the time."

It was too good an opportunity to pass up. Without much discussion, Bruce had packed his bags.

"I'll go out and look around. If it's as good as Doug says, I'll send for you and the kids."

"But it's so far away. And what about our plans, Bruce? What about your property?"

"We can't build without money. Any there's not going to be any money if I don't find work. That's for damn sure. Be reasonable, Miriam."

That was two months ago, even before Miriam had become aware of the new life growing within her. But maybe this baby would be a good omen. They would be starting a new life in British Columbia.

******

Miriam had to admit that the scenery was beautiful, and the climate agreeable. The children soon settled in: Albert found a group of small children to play with, Becky toddled along. Miriam got to know the mothers. But she was lonesome. Bruce worked long hours, logging at first, and then in the mill. East coast or west, there was always lumbering. She missed her family. True, she had been living out of town for nearly two years now, but what was fifty miles compared to a continent? There were buses and telephones. Visits in to the city. But here there was no one, no relatives except Doug and he was a bachelor, and more quiet even than Bruce. Back home there were people she had known most of her life; here everybody was a stranger. Friendly people, but strangers. And no one seemed to have roots. Everybody came from somewhere else. She was apprehensive about giving birth with no family around. Already knowing it was useless, she phoned Hannah:

"Mum, can you come out and help me when the baby comes?"

"Goodness, Miriam. I shouldn't think so. You know how far it is."

"Yes, Mum. I didn't expect you to walk. But you could take a train. It's only a few days, really. And quite comfortable. We'd pay for you to have a berth. And Mum, the scenery--the geography. Mum, you've always loved geography. Remember the school back home. Everything you taught us about Canadian geography--you could see for yourself. It's true. There's a fairly long stop over in Montreal. I managed to get out of the station and take the children for a walk. You can't imagine Montreal, Mum! There is a big building near the station that's twenty-three stories high, and a park right beside it where people are constantly walking through from every direction, and others sit on the benches and feed the pigeons, and there's a church with the twelve apostles standing guard along the edge of the roof, and even though you're right down town you can see Mount Royal. It was really quite amazing. And you'd never know you were on an island. And Ontario--I remembered all you taught us about the mines and forests of Northern Ontario, and Lake Superior--I never knew that a lake could be so big. Then the prairies--it's all true, Mum, everything you taught us. You should see it for yourself."

"It does sound interesting, Miriam." Was her mother wavering?

"And the mountains. Everybody should see the mountains at least once in their lifetime."

"But you know I can't leave your father and Jack. Who would get their meals when they're out working? And the kids. Gracie is only thirteen. I can't leave her."

'For heavens sakes, she's not a baby.' Miriam thought. 'I was fourteen when you made me quit school. I was expected to be a adult then.' But she couldn't speak to her mother like that.

"It wouldn't be forever, Mum. She could go over to Annie's, or to Bill's. Mum, I need you. The baby's due in a few weeks."

"You'll be fine, Miriam. You've been to a doctor. Everything is going well. And you've already had two babies. It gets easier."

"But I need you."

"Miriam, it's not to be thought of. You'll manage. Just let me know when it comes. I'll be sending something out." She paused, then. "This phone call must be costing you a fortune. Just let me know if there's a problem."

"And who will take care of the kids while I'm in the hospital?" But her mother had already hung up.

The solution came when she least expected it. As they ate their supper together that night, Bruce announced that he had met an old friend of hers at the mill.

"He said that you'd never guess who."

Bewildered, she searched her memory. What 'old friend'? Who did she know who fitted that description? Who did she know in British Columbia?

"He used to live right next door to you."

"In Saint John?" Which of the neighbours had she talked to enough to be considered a friend?

"No. Back at the old place."

"Bruce, who are you talking about?"

"Louie LeBlanc."

"Louie LeBlanc!" She remembered the skinny, sniffling six-year old, and his sister dragging him into the schoolroom. Had she ever spoken more than a sentence or two with him? And then was it on friendly terms? She remembered pokes in the ribs, pushes on the steps, hair pulling when 'Teacher' wasn't looking. Occasional fists flying. Then as they grew older, hostility, resentment, and finally indifference.

"He's been living out here for a couple of years. Hell, I've been working with him. Knew he was from back home, but it wasn't until today that I was talking about Jack and Bill that he suddenly realized who they were, and said he knew your whole family. Anyway, I've invited him and his wife over for a game of cards Saturday night."

"Bruce, you didn't!" Men! They could be so obtuse. She hardly knew Louie, not as an adult, not as someone to invite into her home.

It was awkward at first. Louie seemed momentarily to slip back into his old role, hanging his head and shuffling his feet; and Miriam would have felt superior, but how could she with her big belly, and two children poking their heads around the corner, one who looked so much like Charlie Smart that Louie was sure to notice it sooner or later. Miriam remembered her manners. These people were guests in her home, and were to be greeted hospitably. She reached out and welcomed Louie's wife, Yvonne. Soon they were chatting over the card table.

"Your sisters, Louie? Where are they now?"

"In Moncton. Well no, Claudette's in Shediac. She's got four kids. Susanne working in the hospital in Moncton. You know, a few years after she left home she trained as a practical nurse."

"No, I didn't know." Miriam was impressed. Susanne had been Annie's friend, and certainly Annie had never shown that type of ambition. "And your brothers?"

"Montreal. The young ones went to Montreal. They're both working at a big factory in Outremont. Maurice stayed at the old place. There's just him and papa there now. Mama's gone. You knew that."

"Oh!"

"Cancer, two years ago. Just awhile before Yvonne and I got married and came out here. Susanne came home and nursed her almost to the end. She wouldn't go to the hospital until then. She . . .," Louie hesitated and then went on "She was afraid nobody there would be able to understand her. We told her there were French nurses, nuns even, at the hospital, but she was still afraid."

"She never did learn English?" Miriam was surprised. All those years the LeBlanc's had lived in an English community.

"Oh, she could understand it alright. We kids got assimilated pretty good, and we used to speak it around the house. Of course, she learned. But she wouldn't try to talk. She was afraid people would laugh at her accent." He growled. "The neighbours weren't exactly friendly you remember."

Miriam remembered: her mother forbidding Annie and her to go over to play; her grandmother admonishing that it was no place for a 'decent' girl. And why not? And what should Miriam say now?

Yvonne broke the tension by asking about the children, and the moment passed.

It was Yvonne who came over to watch the children the night Bruce drove Miriam to the hospital. Elizabeth was born within a few hours, much easier than the earlier babies--her mother had been right about that.

But she was lonesome. There was no family to exclaim over this beautiful baby. No one but Bruce to help her to look for family characteristics in the eyes, forehead or chin; to marvel at the head of curly, black hair, the dark eyes, the tiny perfectly formed fingers and toes. Neither Doug who would know the McKay's, nor Louie who remembered the Taylor's seemed much interested in babies, other than to gaze upon her in wonderment.

"She looks like Bruce," Louie finally announced, and Yvonne nodded in agreement. Miriam was delighted.

Breast feeding was the thing to do in British Columbia in the sixties. Back home Miriam hadn't even considered it. Now the British born and trained nurses at the hospital took it for granted. Miriam tried it and liked it.

There were advantages in not having family around. Bruce left baby care almost completely up to Miriam and she could follow her own instincts. Hold the baby as much as she wanted, cuddle her, make all the decisions; feeding her when she was hungry, not according to a schedule; playing with her. And Elizabeth responded. Unlike Becky had been, Elizabeth was a good natured, easy baby to care for. She grew, she cooed little baby sounds, she smiled, she responded to her parents and to her big brother and sister. She reached all the baby milestones: rolling over, sitting up, crawling, attempting to pull herself up as she should. Hannah had been right, Miriam could manage very well on her own.

This was her family now, independent of any other. Her husband, working hard and providing for them; Albert, a sturdy little boy who accepted Bruce as the only father he knew; Becky quickly outgrowing babyhood; and delightful little Elizabeth. Miriam found herself settling into her role as wife and mother, and feeling content. Soon she would have to prepare Albert for school.

Then came the night when Miriam put Elizabeth to bed with a little cold: nothing really, a bit of a runny nose, no fever. In the morning she was gone.

"Crib death." the doctor explained. "We don't understand it. It just happens. Sometimes there is a little cold. Usually no symptoms at all. There was nothing you could have done."

Miriam phoned Hannah and cried out her heartbreak and despair, but there was nothing her mother could do. A continent separated them.

Bruce, more quiet than ever, made the arrangements for the funeral and too soon it was over. Doug came over night after night and sat with them, awkward and uncomfortable, not knowing what to say. Yvonne visited during the days caring for the children and preparing the meals..

"Come home," Hannah pleaded when she phoned back. "Come home and bring Albert and Becky. I miss my grandchildren." Her voice broke, and Miriam knew that she was thinking of the granddaughter she had never seen.

Miriam wanted to crawl into her mother's arms, aware that she needed more comfort than the heartbroken Bruce was able to give. But she didn't know how to say it.

"Mum, I can't travel all that distance on the train by myself with two children. It was hard enough coming out. I can't do it again. Not now."

"I'll send Jack to help you."

But instead, Bruce decided to go back home with his family. Wages were high in British Columbia, but so were living expenses, and it was just too far away. Nothing could make up for family and home at a time like this.

A year and a half after leaving for the west, Bruce and Miriam were home again. He found work at the mill; there was a new, large contract to supply lumber to the States. Things seemed to get back to normal, but they had left a piece of themselves in British Columbia.

There was one other difference too. When they returned from a week's hunting trip to the property that fall, Bruce started talking about church. Over the years he had mentioned it occasionally, usually offhandedly. 'Maybe we should get up Sunday morning and go to church.' or 'Don't you think that Albert should be in Sunday School.' Now he was insistent.

Miriam thought about it. When she was a child living on the farm, her family had never gone to church. The nearest had been too far away for them to walk, and by the time they bought the car they weren't in the habit. Church wasn't something they ever thought about. Certainly when they moved into the city it wasn't a top priority.

Of course, Miriam wasn't a perfect heathen. Hannah always led in Bible reading and the Lord's prayer at school (wasn't it the law?), and some of the books donated for the 'library' book shelf were about religious subjects. Some years there had been Vacation Bible School for a week or two in the summer when enthusiastic young people from the city would borrow the school building and put on a program for the country children. Miriam's family had been indifferent. The children could go if they wanted to and if they weren't needed to help out at home. It was something to do. Songs, games, handicrafts, stories -- a teacher other than their mother. Miriam had always enjoyed it. When she moved into the city, church was only a place to go for Christmas concerts, baptisms, weddings, and funerals. True, the most comfort she had received after Elizabeth's death was from the hospital chaplain. He seemed to genuinely care for her; and in her grief at leaving Elizabeth's grave in B.C. he had promised that it was 'all right', that Elizabeth was with her heavenly father, and that she would be loved and cared for. That must have been what started Bruce on this church kick.

Every Sunday they would dress in their Sunday best and walk down to the nearby United Church. Albert and Becky went to Sunday School. Bruce sat stiffly in the pew, listened to the sermon and shook the minister's hand at the door. "Great message, Reverend."

For Miriam it opened a new horizon. She enjoyed the sermons and tried to talk to Bruce about them, but he never had much to say. She joined the women's group. It gave her an evening out, a chance to meet people, to talk over the little incidents in their lives, problems with husbands and child rearing, something like a Tupperware party without the Tupperware, and with some serious discussion and reflection thrown in, along with a lot of concern for fund-raising. She got more satisfaction from Bible study class, and when she started teaching Sunday School, she began doing some reading to prepare her lessons. This was great! She wasn't a school teacher, but she could teach. Maybe this was her purpose in life. Wife, mother, Sunday School teacher. She devoured the books on the church library shelf, and then started to visit the town library. There was so much she needed to learn, so much she wanted to understand.

Chapter Seven

Two years later, Joshua was born after an easy pregnancy, but a difficult delivery. "No wonder," Hannah remarked. The hour's drive made it possible for her to come up for a few weeks. "Look at the size of his head. He's going to be a genius."

"Just let him live," breathed Miriam.

He proved the perfect boy; and Miriam guarded him protectively. Nothing, nothing would take this baby away from her. All babies are miracles, but, more than any of the others, Joshua was her miracle child. He brought her the reassurance that she was capable of taking care of a baby. Surely God had forgiven her for failing Elizabeth.

Three years later there was David, named after her youngest brother, Davy, who had moved to Ontario and 'made good for himself'.

No longer even talking about developing their property, they bought a house near the mill and settled down. Albert and Becky were in school. The little boys occupied Miriam's time at home, especially Joshua. She found that she was constantly talking to him, playing with him, answering his questions, taking him out to the library or to the park (she worried if he played outside alone for any length of time). Everywhere they went he seemed to draw attention with his curly, black hair and sparkling dark eyes--so much like Elizabeth's had been. He would duck shyly behind her and when she coaxed him out he would flash his brilliant smile. And David, though slightly bigger and heavier for his age, was going to be just like him.

They had a camp on their property now, and spent many weekends, and even weeks, there. Miriam often took the children out for most of the summer, maintaining a small salad garden, teaching them about nature, trees, birds, plants and growing things. They hosted the Sunday School picnic each year, and invited friends out for barbeques and special occasions. But with Albert and Becky in school, and Joshua and David to support and look after, the dream of moving out to the property faded into the background. Only occasionally would they dig out their plans to revise and update them.

Miriam's whole life now revolved around her family.

Albert was growing up. Still looking remarkably like Charlie; he was big, husky, almost as tall as she was. Most people guessed him to be two years older than his eleven years. An indifferent student, he got by on good looks, size and maturity. He was still a favorite with her parents and siblings, often spending time with them when she was busy having babies; and as soon as he was old enough he began taking the bus into Saint John to spend a weekend, or a week or two during school breaks with them. His grandfather and uncles were generous with him, and now he had a paper route to finance his trips.

Miriam heard him bargaining with his sister.

"You deliver my papers this Saturday, Becky, please. I'll pay you double what I would make in a day. Honest."

She readily agreed. At nine she was smart enough to remember his route, his stops, the particular needs of some of his customers. Wiry strength and determination helped her to lug the heavy bag, but with her small stature it looked ridiculous dragging almost to her ankles.

"Albert, that bag's too big for Becky."

"She can manage it. She likes to help me. Don't you, Becky."

"And why can't you do it yourself this weekend?"

"I'm going in to Saint John. Uncle Paul phoned. A crowd's going to the ball game and he asked me if I'd like to come."

"It's just two weeks since you got back from your vacation with them. Your father and I had plans for the family this weekend."

"Mum, you promised. If I could pay my own way, and get somebody to do my paper route, I could go."

She vaguely remembered making the off-hand remark when she was busy thinking of something else. "I didn't mean every few weeks. Aren't you afraid of outwearing your welcome?"

"They like me to come. Gramps is always glad to see me. He keeps peppermints for me as though I was a baby. And all the uncles like me."

She felt caught in a trap. She felt apprehensive about letting him spend so much time with her family, yet she didn't quite know why. After all, she should have been glad they had formed so tight a bond; his own brothers were too young to be companions to him yet. If it was just her family he was visiting, her parents and brothers, she wouldn't have worried, but from occasional remarks he made when he returned from each visit, she knew he was also spending time over at Charlie's and Annie's.

"Don't you find it boring there, with Annie and the girls?"

"Oh, I never go over unless Uncle Charlie's home."

"What do you do?"

"Watch sports on TV. Hang out. Take a walk over to the park and watch a ball game. You know. Guy stuff."

Miriam let him go for another weekend, and lay in bed worrying about it. When she tried to talk it over with Bruce, he was unconcerned.

"You were right to let him go. It's a good thing that he gets along so well with them."

"But I want us to be his family."

"We are his family. He knows that. And we can't hold him, by forcing him to stay with us. Sooner or later, he'll find out where he belongs. Don't force him to make the choice, or you'll drive him away."

So Miriam welcomed him back from his excursions, cooked his meals, washed his clothes, worried about his schooling, and found her satisfaction in mothering the little ones. Bruce tried to spend more time with him, and to interest himself in television sports, and in the fall he drove him to hockey practices; but at home Bruce's favourite was his little daughter, Becky.

There was never enough money to do the things they wanted, even to go to an occasional movie or concert. When Francis phoned, excitedly planning a trip to Moncton for the Ice Capades, Miriam had to decline.

"Awe, Miriam. It would be so much fun. Annie and Charlie are coming along with Bill and me. But I'd like you to come too. Please."

"I don't think Bruce would be interested."

"Men aren't, until you get them there. But then he'd be happy he'd come along."

It was tempting, but even as the idea came into her head, she was turning it down.

"We'd have to stay overnight at a motel. That costs money. And a baby sitter besides. What are you doing with your little girl?"

"She's staying with my mother. Couldn't you bring your kids in to your folks?"

"I've got four of them. Anyway, I imagine Annie has already asked Mum if the girls can stay there."

Life was hard at times like this, but most of the time Miriam realized that she was contented. Bruce wasn't much for company in many ways. He seldom talked much, but he was companionable, hardworking, kind and a good husband and father. If they didn't go to parties, dancing, or visiting, or take trips, or share discussions around books, they made up for it in their love for the outdoors. Camping, hunting, fishing, gardening were their common interests.

* * *

It seemed strange that it took them so long to discover ice fishing. They had long since realized that they couldn't afford a snowmobile and the noisy mechanical things were not especially to their liking, so usually they had found the winters long and tedious. Things were often slow at the mill during the winter and during long layoffs they had time to spend together. Their camp wasn't winterized so they seldom visited it, and there was no place on their property for ice fishing. Between the tides and the swift current the stream never froze solidly.

Then Bruce went ice fishing with one of the guys from work, visiting a lake not too far out of town and just a few hours walk from the road, and he came back full of enthusiasm. Within weeks Bruce and Miriam put up their own shack, took out a little homemade stove, a drill and a few other necessities or comforts and went out for a day as often as possible, usually taking the children with them, although it was difficult with David still in diapers, and not able to run around enough to keep warm. Miriam was grateful that Mrs. Henley was often willing to keep him.

They were disappointed when an early thaw threatened to put an end to ice fishing near the beginning of March. For several days there was warm rain. Bruce even wondered how he would get the shack off the ice and onto the shore. But then Thursday and Friday were cold and Saturday morning proved bright and crisp.

"I'm going out to check it out, Miriam. If the ice looks good, we might get in another week or two fishing."

"We might as well come with you. It's going to be a beautiful day, even just for the drive."

"Well, I'm not going," Albert interjected. "I promised my friends we'd play road hockey, and I've got my paper route and I don't want people complaining."

"Albert, we might be gone most of the day. I don't like to leave you alone that long."

"He'll be all right. Leave him a sandwich when you make up ours, and we'll be back for a late supper."

"I think I'll get Mrs. Henley to keep David. The damp weather started up his sniffles again. Maybe she'll keep an eye on Albert."

"Mum! For Heaven's sake. You'd think I was a baby. I'm not going over there and sit around her place all day."

"You won't have to. I'll just tell her that you're staying here, and you only need to go over if you need something."

"What do you think I'm going to do, burn the house down, or something?"

"No. But just in case."

The drive out was beautiful with the sun glistening on the crusty snow. Even the two-mile hike along the snowmobile trail, from where they left the plowed road in to the lake, was pleasantly invigorating. A quick check of the ice proved that whatever had thawed on the surface had frozen solid again. Bruce pronounced it safe. They gathered some boughs and branches from the pile they kept gathered on the shore, walked out to their shack, started a fire and re-drilled their fishing holes, while waiting for the kettle to boil. Soon the shack was reasonably warm inside. Another couple arrived to fish nearby and dropped in for a 'cuppa'. Despite the warmth of the sun everybody was sure that the ice was thick. "It takes a long while for the ice to melt on these lakes. Look, you've drilled through a foot or more here."

No one minded that the fish weren't biting. Fishing is a game of patience, and the catch only a part of the pleasure. However Joshua was excited that he was the first to catch one small trout. Their company returned to their own shack. They heated a can of beans to go with their sandwiches and Miriam cooked Josh's fish for him. The children grew bored, and went out to run around for a while and to build a snowman with the packing snow. They came back later their mittens dripping wet and reported that there were puddles of water. Bruce went out and checked. A bit of melt water from the hot sun on top of the ice he reassured Miriam. Nothing to worry about. In the next hour they caught two good sized trout. Then the other couple stopped by to report that they were heading back home.

"Jesus, Bruce. It's really getting warm. Must be ten degrees above freezing. Maybe you'd better think about leaving."

"No, not quite yet. We're just starting to get some fish. Don't worry. We'll be going soon."

"Keep an eye on it then."

During the next half hour they caught two more fish. By then the kids were whining. They couldn't go out to run around. It was too wet. Their snowman was melting.

"Come on, Bruce. Let's go."

"Okay. Help me get the lines in. And I want to take as much of this stuff back today as I can. Tomorrow I'll try to arrange to haul the shack in." He began loading the sled. Miriam helped the kids find their mittens and hats. They objected. 'It's too hot.' It was another fifteen minutes before they started for shore. Becky was ahead, anxious now to get back home; Joshua, tired, was dragging a little, hanging onto Miriam's hand. Bruce brought up the rear, pulling the sled.

Miriam had always thought that there would be some warning, some movement of the ice, some sound of cracking; something; but there was none. Suddenly the ice shifted under her feet. Behind her Bruce yelled, was it "Run"? Ahead, Becky took a quick step, fell and scrambled forward on her hands and knees.

Then Miriam was in the water. It closed over her head. Joshua's hand was wrenched from hers. She struggled and surfaced, her jacket still buoyant with trapped air. Splashing and grabbing, she closed her fingers around the hood of Josh's parka. She pulled him toward her, trying to keep his head above water.

Ahead she saw Becky standing up on firm ice, running back toward the hole.

"Stay back! Stay back Becky, or you'll fall in!"

Behind her she could hear Bruce shouting and splashing.

With one arm she grabbed what seemed like solid ice and tried to heave Joshua out on it. She almost succeeded when it broke away, tilted and they went under again. This time she didn't let go. They struggled to the surface again, it was harder this time - her clothes were dragging her down, but her thrashing feet touched something--a rock or sunken tree stump. Again she was clinging to the solid ice, her balance precarious, while trying to get Joshua out. She could hear Bruce thrashing behind her. Joshua was so heavy in his sodden clothes. Why didn't Bruce come and help her? She struggled, and heaved Joshua up. Then the ice crumpled again, and she almost lost her footing as she struggled — fearing to lose him under the ice. Should she try again? She was too cold and weak. Should she call Becky to come closer to pull him out? Becky was running back and forth shrieking, just a few feet away. No, she couldn't risk having the ice break under Becky. She couldn't save both children then. Think!

"Becky! Run, run to the shore. Get a branch. The biggest one you can find and bring it back."

"I don't want to go."

"Becky, please. It's the only way. Go now. Get a big stick."

'Where's Bruce?' Again she thought, 'Why isn't he helping us?' By hanging onto the edge of the ice with one hand, and holding Joshua with the other, she was just able to keep their heads above water, while her toes slipped on her foothold, but at least the ice wasn't breaking any more. Then Becky was back dragging a big spruce bough from the brush pile.

"Good, Becky. Now don't come any closer. Push it out to me."

Somehow Miriam maneuvered the bough into position, and heaved Joshua out on it. "Crawl, Joshua. Crawl to Becky. Becky, keep him away."

Then Miriam rearranged the bough and using strength that she didn't know she had, she managed to crawl out on it and roll quickly away from the black gapping hole. She lay for a moment, gasping and choking on swallowed water. Only the children's screams brought her around.

"Daddy! Daddy! Mummy, you've got to help Daddy."

She struggled to her feet and looked back. Behind her was a large, black hole, twelve or fifteen feet across. A few ice chunks and slush floated on it; the water was still. There was no sign of Bruce.

"Mummy, where's Daddy?"

"Quick, Becky. Take Joshua to shore."

"I don't want to. I want to stay with you. We've got to find Daddy."

"Do as I say. Oh God, Becky. Just take him. Do you want the ice to break again?"

With the children heading for solid ground, Miriam retrieved her branch and using it for balance she circled the hole, yelling Bruce's name. Calling, calling. And then listening. But there was no sound but the echo of her shouts and the pounding of her heart. She followed the children to the shore.

Miriam became aware that a breeze had sprung up. The temperature seemed to have dropped in minutes. Or was it just because of these heavy, freezing, wet clothes. What to do? The books she had read offered no answers. Jack London would have had his heroes building a fire, setting up camp, drying their clothes, and there would have been a big super-intelligent dog to help them. But how could she do that? Everything they had with them was on their backs. She and Joshua were soaked to the skin, from head to foot. Becky was not much better off. She couldn't strip them all naked and wait for their clothes to dry while night set in. Besides where would she find a dry match to set the brush pile on fire?

"Come on, kids. We'll have to walk back to the truck."

"What about Daddy?"

"Mummy, we can't leave Daddy behind. We've got to find him."

"Mummy, where's Daddy? Daddy will help us."

She realized then that they had not understood what her numbed brain had not yet fully comprehended.

"No, Daddy can't help us. And we can't help him. We've just got to keep walking."

How she would manage, Miriam didn't know. Joshua didn't walk more than a hundred yards. She had to pick him up and carry him; cradling him close, trying to shelter him with her body. Becky kept whining and lagging. She would fall behind, then Miriam would have to coax her forward. Finally Miriam insisted that Becky walk ahead.

"I can't, Mummy. I can't walk any further. I'm too tired." With Becky ahead, Miriam could see how often she fell. But she had to keep on. Miriam was falling too, almost dropping Joshua. Would it be easier to crawl? No, she struggled to her feet, reached down and shook Becky, forcing her forward, and shifted Joshua in her arms. He had stopped whimpering. Was he actually falling asleep? Should she wake him, perhaps force him to walk to keep his blood flowing? She knew this would be impossible.

The breeze behind them had changed to a stiff wind. The shadows were long across the trail. It would be dark soon. And colder! How long had they been walking? It had been late afternoon when they left the fishing shack. How long had they been in the water? How long on shore? How far had they come? When would they reach the truck?

Becky fell again and Miriam almost stumbled over her.

"Come on, Becky. Get up."

"I can't, Mummy. Can't we just stop and rest awhile?"

"No Becky. We'd freeze to death. We'll rest when we get to the truck."

"Then carry me."

"I can't."

They stumbled onward. How much further? How many times did they fall?

Miriam didn't hear the noisy machines coming up behind her, but there were two men on snowmobiles. They were shouting at her and one of them was trying to pull Joshua from her arms. She fought him feebly. But then she saw that he'd stripped down his snowmobile suit and taken off his down vest. He wanted to wrap it around Joshua. The other man was doing the same for Becky. Hats and scarves were being distributed. Then they were opening a thermos of coffee and holding the cup to her lips. Joshua was crying.

"Goodness, woman. Are you alone?"

"Where's my Daddy? Did you see my Daddy?"

"My husband? Did you find him? We broke through the ice. We almost drowned. I can't find my husband. Did you see him?" Hope, without reason, struggled to the surface of Miriam's mind.

"We found the hole and figured out what must have happened. God, woman, what were you doing out on that ice? With all this rain earlier, it's badly undercut - then with this hot sun ...." his voice trailed off, and the other man spoke,

"We couldn't see any sign of life. We were afraid everyone must have gone under. Then we found your tracks, and we've been following them. You say your husband was with you? Where is he?"

"I don't know. I couldn't find him. Didn't you see him?"

The two men questioned Miriam and even Becky, but soon determined that no one had seen Bruce after they got out of the water.

"You'll have to go back and look for him," Miriam insisted. "Aren't there air pockets under the ice? Or maybe he got out. Maybe in the confusion we were separated. He may be hunting for us. You have to go back."

The two men exchanged glances. "We will, but first we have to get you and these kids to safety. Then we'll get help and go back."

They climbed on the snow machines. One man took Becky between his arms, the other took Joshua, and helped Miriam on behind him. Somehow she managed to cling to his waist. She could never quite remember the next few hours. She didn't know if they stopped at the truck at all, but there was a strange house, strangers offering warm dry clothes and blankets and warm drinks, phone calls being made, people coming and going. Finally she was back in her own house. Albert was asking, "Where's Dad?" And Becky's reply, whether it was an accusation or simply a statement of fact. "Mummy left him in the water."

PART THREE

Chapter One

    Miriam lived in a fog for the next few months. Surely she went about the day to day motions of living; surely she looked after her children, prepared meals, returned phone calls, made decisions, signed documents, but later she had no memory of the details. The minister, the church people, the neighbors were wonderful. Her family arrived to help with the necessary arrangements. Mr. Howard came up for a morning to see her through the inquest, and wouldn't hear of her paying him for his services. Everybody was helpful. Everybody offered advice. Before she even got over the initial shock, Miriam found that she had sold her house and moved her children back to Saint John, taking a small apartment just a few blocks from her parents. Mr. Howard helped her to invest the insurance settlement and the proceeds from the sale of the house 'for the children's future', and to apply for death benefits and survivors' benefits. Because Bruce had never formerly adopted Albert, even though he had always called him his son and Albert used his name, there were no benefits for the boy and Miriam had to make do supporting four children on benefits intended for three. Help from her parents or her brothers was sometimes generous, but always irregular. Sometimes $5, sometimes $20, would be stuffed into her pocket at the end of a visit. At least she and the kids would never go hungry when they could show up at her parents at any mealtime and be sure to sit down to a hearty feed--stew on Friday, baked beans on Saturday, and roast beef on Sunday, with beef hash and other hardy 'meat and potatoes' meals on weekdays. Hannah enjoyed cooking for a family and the type of meals she prepared could always be stretched to feed anyone who showed up: doughboys in the stew, cornbread with the beans, a few extra potatoes always ready for extra people, or to be fried up the next day. Johnny liked to have a crowd around.

Help from Charlie was even more sporadic and completely unpredictable.

She was sitting at the kitchen table patching Albert's worn jeans, and wondering how she would get him to wear them without a fight, not because of the patches but because he was growing so fast they were short at his ankles. She could imagine his protests, 'Mum, the kids call them 'Floods'. I'll be the laughing stock of the whole damn school.' As she pondered how she could explain that she just couldn't afford to buy him new jeans every few months, he spun into the yard under the fire escape with a brand-new bicycle.

"Where did you get that?"

"I can't tell."

Until a few months ago she had confidence in her parenting ability and trusted her instincts to know if something were wrong. "Albert, I have to know. You didn't steal it did you?" My God, what would she do if he was a thief, or a bully - maybe he had taken it from a smaller child. Somehow she could imagine his father taking anything he wanted.

"No. Of course not. But I'm not supposed to tell."

Suddenly she understood. "Did your Uncle Charlie buy it for you?"

"Yes. I saw him on my way home from school. I think he was waiting for me. He wanted me to go downtown with him, and he bought me this. He said every boy deserves a decent bicycle and he'd noticed that my old one is practically falling apart. Then he made me promise not to tell anyone. He got me a lock too. See, it's a combination. I worked it out with my birthday so I'll remember it."

Miriam remembered Annie mentioning that Charlie had recently bought bicycles for Olive and Amy. Had he felt guilty that his son didn't have as much? Did he even think of Albert as his son? Did she want him to? She felt ambivalent. Certainly she should appreciate anything Charlie was able and willing to do for Albert. Surely he had some moral responsibility. But did he have the right to have anything to do with this child? So many things were never talked about in her family.

She searched Albert's face to see how much he understood but saw nothing. He had always believed Bruce to be his dad and he gave no sign that he thought of Charlie as any more than a kind and generous uncle. All of his uncles occasionally slipped him a few dollars for no reason at all, or hired him to do some chore for them and paid him well. Birthday and Christmas gifts for Albert were almost taken for granted although with the expanding list of third generation Taylors, not all nieces and nephews were remembered by everyone every year. No, Albert didn't realize there was any difference in his relationship with Charlie.

Miriam knew that some time in the future he would find out and she recoiled at the thought. She hoped that he would be old enough to understand and forgive her before that happened. It never occurred to her that perhaps she should explain it, the sooner the better. She had too many other things urgently pressing on her mind right now, when all she wanted to do was to lay her head on someone's shoulder and go to sleep.

Becky would be clamoring for a bike now. Albert's old one was still much too big for her, and she would have to agree with him it was in poor shape. How could she manage a safe and decent bike for Becky? Maybe Jack would help out. But she hated going to anyone for help. It was bad enough to be in the position she had to accept all offers that came her way, without having to ask specifically. She understood now that it was more blessed to give than to receive. She hated being on the receiving end of anybody's charity. Still, she was grateful.

Mr. Howard offered her a job explaining that they could always use her skills, but she turned him down. She had no energy or ambition. The children needed her. They had lost their father, and moved from their home. Albert was surly, putting on a show of maturity and independence that Miriam was sure he didn't feel. Becky seemed fine at times, but then when she had to have her hair washed she screamed bloody murder as the water poured over her face. That puzzled Miriam because, as she remembered it, Becky had never been completely under water at the lake. Becky had nightmares too, and would wake up screaming so that Miriam had to run to her and hold her and comfort her, so that neither of them was getting a full night's sleep very often.

Joshua and David seemed unusually quiet. Of course, David knew and understood nothing of what had happened. He only knew that changes had taken place in his family. Joshua seemed somehow to have blocked it all out. He never mentioned the lake, the water, his father, the men who had rescued them, the snowmobiles, anything. Miriam thought it best not to bring it up. Somehow it seemed strange to hear him tell a neighbour, "I caught a fish in the ice once, and Becky and me made a snowman," as though they were the most important events of that day. Miriam was thankful but a bit uneasy. Maybe it would be better to talk about it more, but she couldn't bring herself to.

Of all her children, Miriam felt that it was Joshua who kept her sane. After Albert and Becky left for school each morning, she would talk to him and David while she tidied the apartment and did the dishes, then she would take them out with her, to the grocery story, the park, or just for a walk. Often they stopped at the library where she would help him choose books for himself and his little brother. Then in the afternoon while David napped she would read to him, or play games, unintentionally giving him the kindergarten education that she could not otherwise afford.

This was the child born so soon after she lost Elizabeth. This was the child that she had pulled from the lake and carried to safety. He was beautiful with his dark curly hair – so much like Bruce's – and he was intelligent, full of questions and quickly catching on to her answers. If he was also a bit shy and withdrawn among strangers, that was all right. After all he was only five, and he was loving with his siblings and cousins.

By the time David would wake from his nap, Becky and then Albert would be home from school. Supper would have to be prepared, homework supervised, bedtime routines followed. Finally they would all be tucked in.

Then came the lonely time in the evenings when Miriam sat alone. She tried to find an interest. She borrowed books from the library that she visited with the children, but she found she couldn't follow their stories. She would read a page and realize that she had no idea what she had read. If she didn't use a bookmark she might reread an entire chapter before an incident or a turn of a phrase would remind her that she had read the same chapter the night before. Once she was about to sign a library card when she noticed her name on the line above and realized that she had just returned that same book. Watching television was the same. She couldn't concentrate. She didn't know what was going on. She never knew if a show was a new one or a rerun, and sometimes when she visited at home and heard Jack and her father discussing an item in the news she would wonder vaguely where she had heard it before and realize that it must have been when she was sitting staring blankly at the screen the night before.

She gave up trying to read or watch television. Then in the evenings when the children were asleep she would sit out on the back fire escape and watch the leaves of the old poplar tree twisting against the sky. She vaguely remembered someone explaining to her sometime long in the past that each poplar leaf had a twisted stem that made it turn in the slightest breeze, so that even on an almost calm night the poplar trees would be whispering. Watching them made more sense to her than all the books or magazines she could read or television programs she could watch.

Chapter Two

Guy Harris lived in the small apartment next to hers: she'd seen his name on the mail slot. She vaguely recognized that he was the same person who ran the small corner grocery store where she shopped almost every day, when he climbed over the fire escape one evening and introduced himself.

"Mind if I sit down? I've been watching you sit out here every night and you look so lonely, I decided that maybe you would like some company. I'm not a stranger, you know. You bought pork chops from me this morning."

She was indifferent to his visit. He could sit if he wanted to; the fire escape was common property. It was okay if he wanted to talk too, as long as he didn't expect her to entertain him. She didn't feel up to witty or amusing remarks or intellectual conversation. He didn't seem to mind.

"I'm from Nova Scotia. My parents run a big store down there in the valley. I grew up in the business, and when it came time to start out on my own, I bought this little store. You like it don't you? I notice you in often. I know it's small, but I plan to expand when the market is right. In the meantime I try to stock everything my clients need. If anyone asks for anything, I make a decision right away. I think, 'Is there a demand for that product?' If so, I order a few. If they sell I start carrying it regularly. That's the way to do business - be sensitive to the market. Is there anything that you would like that I don't carry? Just speak up, let me know."

"Not that I can think of, right off."

"Good. But if there is you know who to come to. Just think how convenient, living right next door to the proprietor. Those must be your two little boys that I see with you. Cute little rascals aren't they. You hardly look old enough to have two kids."

"I feel old enough. And I have two older ones."

"Oh, yes. I've seen them coming and going. Tall boy, small girl - but quick and smart. I guess I didn't realize they were yours. You can't be that old."

"I married young."

"Yes, you must of. Oh, of course." Could it just have occurred to him? "I heard that you're a widow. Your husband was killed in an accident."

"He drowned while ice fishing last winter. I don't want to talk about it."

They sat in an uncomfortable silence for awhile. Then he looked up through the leaves of the tree and remarked at what a nice night it was. "But I must be going in. I have to open the store tomorrow. Mostly I let my help open, but tomorrow she asked to come in late. Night, now."

Miriam sat out for a few more hours until common sense rather than fatigue drove her to bed for another restless night. She wouldn't have believed that she slept at all if it wasn't for Becky's screams startling her out of deep unconsciousness.

"Mummy, Mummy! Help me, Mummy!"

"There, there, Becky. I'm here. Shhhh, shhhh, now. Let's try not to wake the others."

"Don't bother," Albert growled. "I'm already awake. Does she have to do that every damn night? How is a person supposed to get any rest in this house?"

"Shhhh, shhhhh. Don't wake Joshua and David now. You go back to sleep, Albert. Becky, please stop crying. You're all right. Let's go to the bathroom and then get a glass of water. Now I'll sit by you until you fall back to sleep. It will be morning soon."

God, how was she supposed to manage? How could she look after these four kids, when she couldn't even think for herself? She certainly didn't need a boring, inquisitive neighbour on top of everything else.

Nevertheless she was almost glad when he came over a few nights later and again sat on the steps with her. Maybe it was better than sitting alone.

It became a regular pattern for Miriam. As she sat out each night after the kids went to bed she would find herself listening for him to come home after closing the store at nine o'clock and waiting for him to join her on the steps. Sometimes she brought out a cup of coffee and some home baking; sometimes he brought something from the store - ice-cream or muffins or whatever. As fall progressed and the nights grew chilly, Guy would sometimes join her in the kitchen for their snack. He would talk on and on. She had never known a man to talk so much, unless he was talking to another man about politics, war stories, sports, cars or hunting, subjects Guy never mentioned.

Miriam wasn't sure just how it happened but by winter Guy was coming over in the mornings for toast and coffee before he left for the store. He was there one day when Annie dropped in with some clothes her girls had outgrown. 'Could Becky use them?'

It didn't take long for the word to get around. The next time Miriam visited her home, Hannah remarked:

"Annie tells me that you have a gentleman friend."

Miriam was bewildered. "What does she mean? Gentleman friend? I never go out anywhere."

"She said that she met somebody - a Guy Harris - at your place one morning."

"Oh Mum. He's not that. He's just a neighbour and he's trying to keep me company. He thinks I'm lonely."

"Is he a nice man, Miriam? Do you like him? Does he like the children?"

"I guess so. Albert and Becky are in school almost every time he comes over, so there's just the little ones. I guess he likes them. Sometimes he brings cookies and chocolate milk for them." Miriam couldn't understand her mother's interest.

"A storekeeper you say. Miriam you could do worse. A widow with four kids doesn't have a lot of prospects."

"For heaven sakes, Mum, I'm not looking for a husband. And I'm not going to marry Guy Harris. Nothing could be further from our minds."

******

In the spring, hardly more than a year after Bruce had died, Miriam married Guy Harris. Her parents hosted a small reception for them at the Legion Hall and his parents visited from Nova Scotia.

"Our only child and his lovely bride," his mother cooed.

"With a ready-made family," remarked his father.

"Oh, dear. But such lovely children. Becky is so nice and helpful, and the boys so polite and mannerly. But I do hope for grandchildren of my own someday."

"Mother Harris (as she insisted Miriam call her), we haven't even thought about that yet."

"Yes, Mother," Miriam had noticed that her father-in-law always addressed his wife as 'Mother'. "Let them get back from their honeymoon first, before you start pushing them to have children."

"Oh, no rush. No rush at all, but I just don't want any misunderstandings. And where are you going on your honeymoon?"

"Not far, mother dear, and just for a few days." Guy came up behind his mother and gave her a hug. "You know I can't leave the store now that I'm in the middle of an expansion."

Miriam was thankful that he didn't mention the fact that she couldn't leave the kids. Despite everyone's congratulations, and the unspoken relief that Miriam had married again, no one had offered to take four kids. Gracie and a girl friend were coming over to spend the weekend. They would see the kids off to school on Monday and drop off Joshua and David with Hannah, but then they had to go to their own classes. Miriam didn't even think of the irony of Hannah fussing that Gracie couldn't miss even one day of her classes at the community college where she was studying hairdressing, despite Gracie's nonchalant attitude towards school that had already put her several years behind, when Miriam hadn't been permitted to go to high school at all despite her pleas. Anyway she and Guy had better be back from their 'honeymoon' by the time the kids came home from school for lunch on Monday.

Of course they had to move almost immediately. Neither of their apartments were big enough for a family of six. But Guy found a decent apartment not far from the store and set about furnishing it.

Miriam didn't know what to think. Never before had she known a man to take an interest in home furnishings. Both Frances and Annie fussed about curtains and lamps and toss cushions, paint and wallpaper and generally fixing things up as best they could. But nobody they knew had money to redecorate their whole place at one time. Furniture and fixings were bought hap-hazardly, as needed – but with an effort any woman could make her place seem homey.

Guy had different ideas. While he had a few nice pieces, he decided that most of the rest was not worth keeping. The almost new daybed that served her as a couch could go into Becky's room. Maybe Paul and Susan could use some, they were just setting up housekeeping. What they didn't want could go to the Salvation Army.

Mornings Guy would pour over decorating magazines (he never liked to work mornings). At first Miriam was interested, but before long she realized how ignorant she was of furniture styles and decorating ideas and she left it up to him, busying herself as usual with household chores and child care. Didn't he know that the children needed her attention.

When it came time to do some actual shopping, he encouraged Miriam to drop the kids at her mother's place and to go with him, but Miriam let him make all the choices. Soon he had found a matching chesterfield and chair in a green brocade, a comfortable lounge chair in a brown leather-look vinyl, drapes that picked up the colour of the chesterfield, a neutral rug, a few toss cushions and lamps to complete the look. Never before had Miriam had a living room that looked like a picture from a magazine, even down to the magazine rack that sat beside the lounge chair. She was almost afraid to relax in it, or to let the children rough-house.

Guy did almost the same with their bedroom, except now he agreed to keep more of her original furniture and concentrated on choosing bedspread, drapes, and lamps. Her extra dresser, he preferred his own 'highboy', could go into the boys' room.

The children's bedrooms he left up to Miriam, paying for the bunks that she needed for Joshua and David. She picked out serviceable yard goods and made curtains for both of the children's rooms.

By the time the hot weather of the summer set in they had a beautiful apartment.

Chapter Three

Miriam knew Guy hated the big family get-together that the Taylors seemed to hold at least once a month, for any excuse they could think of. Before they had married he had accompanied Miriam to a few, but afterwards he always made excuses. Now she had to insist.

"It's Dad's birthday. He'll expect all his family to drop around. Mum's worked all week preparing a feast. They'll be disappointed if we don't show up."

"What about the store?"

"Goodness, Guy. You're the boss. Get one of your helpers to run it for an evening."

"Wages cost money, you know."

"He only has a birthday once a year and he likes us to make a big deal of it. I tell you what. The kids and I will go over early in the afternoon, and you can work til five or so. Then you'll only need someone for the evening. We can be back before closing time at ten to pick up the receipts."

"Saturday is so busy I'll need Albert to help through the afternoon. The customers want him there to pack their groceries and carry them out."

"Okay. Dad will be disappointed. I'm sure Albert is his favourite grandson. But okay. I'll tell them that you both will be there for supper."

So it was, twenty or more people crowded into the duplex that Johnny had bought when he sold the farm. Kids and grandkids were everywhere. Men gathering in the front room to talk incessantly about politics - God, they kept track of everything: municipal, provincial and federal with more than a little interest in what was going on in the 'States'. The women hustling in and out of the kitchen. Guy wondered what the big deal was about everybody being there. They never sat down together for a meal. The kids got served in the kitchen first. Then a long table was set up in the livingroom, and the men were served - Albert priding himself that recently his place was set at this table. Once the kids were finished, and the men were taken care of, the women would gather around the kitchen table, though Hannah and her daughters never seemed to take much time to sit down. Only when Johnny was presented with the huge birthday cake to blow out the candles did everybody crowd together into the livingroom, or stand on the stairs or in the doorways, to sing happy birthday. The whole day seemed to be bedlam.

Had Miriam not been so busy herself she might have noticed that the separation of men and women bothered Guy. He generally worked with women at the store and was more used to talking to them. He would have liked to sit down with Paul's Susan and have a chat with her. She seemed a nice girl, as did Frances, but they hardly paused in the living room. When he wandered out to the kitchen, he soon found that he felt like an intruder. The women obviously felt uncomfortable with him there. Back in the living room he looked around at the other in-laws. Charlie obviously fitted right in. Gracie's 'boyfriend' seemed a bit out of place but he was making an effort, talking first with Paul and then giving his attention to Albert. Albert, just thirteen but looking fifteen, was as relaxed as any of them. It was Guy who felt out of place. As soon as he got the chance he signaled to Miriam.

"Isn't it time to be going now?"

"I can't leave Mum with all this mess. Just give me another half hour and then I'll round up the kids. David's fallen asleep on Paul's old bed. I'm going to leave him over-night and pick him up in the morning."

It was almost ten when they left Miriam's folks' place. Then they drove the kids home, directing Becky to take Josh in and put him to bed, while they went on to the store to let the 'help' leave and then to pick up the cash and paper work. Miriam talked excitedly about the party and how much her father had enjoyed it.

"I hope that you had a good time, too. Are you getting everybody sorted out yet?"

"Mostly I guess," then he thought of something that had been bothering him vaguely all evening.

"Were your first husband and your sister's pretty closely related? Cousins, maybe?"

"Not at all. Why do you ask?"

"Then I can't figure it out. I tried to put together the family connections. You, of course, look like your father. Annie and Gracie look more like their mother, kind of tall and willowy. And Becky looks just like you must have at that age."

"She's slighter. She's got my height, or lack of it, and my colouring, but her father's more slender build."

"But Albert? Miriam I can't figure it out. If your husband wasn't closely related to Charlie, how come Albert is the picture of him?"

"Oh, Guy. I thought you knew. Bruce wasn't Albert's real father. Charlie is."

Miriam saw the look of shock and surprise on Guy's face but couldn't read his thoughts. Like that. No shame, no apology. Just 'I thought you knew.' It took Miriam a minute to realize that Guy hadn't been around thirteen years ago, and he didn't hang out with any of the Taylors or their friends. Too late she realized that he wouldn't have known unless she told him. So now she tried to explain matter-of-factly something that had happened in the past and no longer had much importance. And he listened to her confess some sordid story about an affair she had had with her sister's husband when she was a teenager. She tried to blame it on Charlie, but of course she would want to show herself in a good light. Why hadn't she told him before they were married?

Guy didn't know what to think. Wasn't it normal for any man to want to be the first and only man his wife had been intimate with? But Guy hadn't rushed into marriage in his twenties when the young people he had grown up with were dating and choosing their partners. When in his thirties he had met a suitable woman to choose to be his wife, she was a widow with children, and he realized that his expectations of marrying a virgin were futile. But was he wrong to assume that there had only Bruce before him? God, what other surprises did Miriam have for him.

Guy was already starting to realize that her children came first for Miriam. He ran a pretty poor second there. She hadn't shown much enthusiasm in setting up their home. She'd expected him to make all the decisions about the main rooms, the living room and master bedroom, but then she'd expected him to pay for things for the children's rooms. Nor did she take much interest in his store. Sure, she was a good listener when he talked about his plans, but by now he realized that she wasn't really devoted to it. She was willing to give him a few hours each day, but her real abiding interest was in her children. And now this surprise for him! What more could he expect?

****

How long it took for Miriam to realize that the marriage had been a mistake, she didn't know. She had never fooled herself into thinking that she loved Guy. She had been lonely and in shock from losing Bruce. Guy was there, company during the long evenings. Everybody thought he was a 'good catch'. She needed security for her children. At the same time she realized that Guy didn't love her. Although in his thirties, he was living away from his home and parents for the first time and he too had been lonely. He wanted a home, someone to talk to when he came in from the store, someone to cook his meals and look after his clothes, and take an interest in his business.

The fact that it was a mistake from the beginning didn't necessarily mean it couldn't work, Miriam realized. Many married couples didn't seem to have any more going for them than she and Guy had. At least she knew the terms. She could make it work. Marriage was a lifetime commitment, for better and for worse. She wasn't a starry-eyed school girl, but a mature adult, willing to make a trade-off. She would be a good wife and manage a comfortable home in exchange for the security Guy had to offer.

She only wished that he would take more interest in the children. It was more a disappointment than a surprise to Miriam to realize that Guy didn't care much for children. Almost from the beginning he treated them either with cold indifference or impatience. Too late, Miriam remembered that often the treats that he had brought home were stale-dated; still good but not the best. He had little time for Joshua and David, though sometimes he would ruffle their hair absent-mindedly as he walked by - didn't he know that Joshua hated having his head touched? It was to Becky that his indifference almost bordered on cruelty.

From the first night back from their brief honeymoon Guy couldn't understand why a big girl like Becky had to have her mother get up to comfort her at night. Within a week he refused to have Miriam go to her, but went himself, shaking her awake and scolding her. Miriam was shocked! Didn't he know that Becky was frightened? But he wouldn't be reasoned with, so the next day Miriam tried to talk to Becky.

"Guy is right, you know. You are a big girl. Everybody has bad dreams once in awhile. Why don't you try getting yourself a drink and going back to sleep? I'll leave a light on in the bathroom."

Becky never got them up again and Guy was sure that he had solved the problem. "You've spoiled them terribly you know."

Didn't he know, as Miriam did, that for several nights in a row Albert got up when he heard his little sister, and calmed her down with a drink and a few kind words as he had heard his mother do so often. But gradually, Becky learned to sob quietly to herself, and finally she was sleeping through the night, and Miriam was too. Perhaps Guy had been right.

Chapter Four

The store was thriving. By fall, with the new expansion completed, it was more than twice as big as when Miriam had met Guy. Mrs. Muggins, the middle aged women who was his 'help', continued coming in mornings. Miriam sent the children's lunches to school with them, and took David with her, so that she could help during the busy noon-hour and afternoon shift, and continue until the older children came home. Then Albert would help out in the store or make deliveries. Despite Guy's protests, Miriam always went home.

"David is tired and should be home. And Joshua needs me to be there for him."

"Can't Becky watch them? I really need an extra pair of hands. We always get a rush when the shifts end at the dock."

"Becky is too young. She shouldn't even be alone herself. You'll have to hire a teenager if its too busy for you and Albert."

Miriam enjoyed being home to greet Becky and Joshua. Joshua was always so affectionate and eager to share his experiences.

"Mum, I'm so glad to see you. Look at my paper. See what we did today. I got it all right. The teacher says I'm a smart boy. Look, a gold star."

"Very good, Joshua. Tell me about it."

He would talk excitedly about his day, his classmates, his teacher, his adventures, and all the new experiences he was having and the new things he was learning. He would still be waving his hands with enthusiasm while she and Becky started peeling the potatoes for supper, and they would eat. By six Albert would be home to take a lunch down to Guy before sitting down alone to his supper, while Miriam helped Becky and Joshua with their lessons and read to the younger children before putting them to bed. Then she would ask Albert about his homework but he would complain that he was too tired, and would obviously rather watch TV than apply himself to his studies. She managed to coax him to do just enough that he didn't often get into trouble with his teachers, and somehow each year he passed his exams by the skin of his teeth.

Albert was the only one of her children with whom Guy had formed any relationship at all. Albert was a dedicated hard-worker, strong enough to lift heavy boxes of cans or produce, tireless in stocking shelves, quick and friendly with the customers, accurate in filling orders and making change. Albert never complained to Guy. Only occasionally Miriam would hear him grumble about not having time for friends and on Sundays, his only day off, he would leave the house early, sometimes before anyone else was up. If asked where he was going he would grumble 'Out.' Miriam didn't push. From casual remarks that Hannah would drop, Miriam knew that he was spending a lot of time with her family and, she suspected, with Charlie. Although she felt the old uncomfortable feeling in the pit of her stomach whenever she thought about the attention Charlie gave to Albert, she didn't know if, or how, she should stop it. She reminded herself again that she would have to have a talk with Albert some time in the future.

Sunday was the only day the store was closed. Miriam discovered that Guy liked to sleep in, have a leisurely brunch, and then spend the afternoon going over the books, writing up orders and otherwise doing his paperwork. He liked to have the house quiet and Miriam to be there to talk things over.

That left Becky to entertain the younger children – keeping them quiet in their room, or taking them out. She complained but Guy insisted, and Miriam didn't interfere. Her mother had never argued with her father. She wouldn't fight with her husband over the children but tried to smooth things over, and if Becky wasn't happy she would learn to accept it. After all,

Miriam reasoned, she and Annie had spent a lot of time watching the little ones back on the farm. That was the way with families.

They settled into a routine. In a few years David started school and life became smoother and her schedule easier to juggle. Then Miriam started opening the store and working with Mrs. Muggins in the mornings, and Guy started having Albert watch the store so that he could take a bit of time off for supper. That meant that Albert missed out on the family meal, but it couldn't be helped. Miriam could keep something hot for him. The store was thriving. Guy began paying Albert for his help and Miriam gave Becky an allowance from her housekeeping money. After all, Becky's help around the home was valuable too.

Chapter Four

Knowing how little patience or interest Guy had with children, Miriam didn't really think that he would want another, but each year after his mother's regular visit and a barrage of hints, he started bringing it up.

"She's getting old, Miriam, and she would like to have grandchildren."

"We've got four to look after. She could be a grandmother to them."

"It's not the same. Anyway they're your kids, and your mother is their grandmother."

"I've been helping more in the store. Didn't you want that?"

"I can hire help. I can't hire someone to have my child."

The logic of that argument got to Miriam. She had always wanted a big family; perhaps if Bruce had lived they would have had more children by now. Surely Guy deserved at least one child of his own. Against her better judgement, but not entirely against her wishes, Miriam stopped taking 'the pill'. Chelsea was born less than a year later.

Miriam couldn't get over how Guy acted around this baby. He was absolutely fascinated by her. From the beginning he held her, playing with her fingers and toes. When she was sleeping he listened to her breathing. He insisted on helping with her care, holding her, feeding her, burping her. He almost neglected the store for her, and accused Miriam of neglecting her when he came home early one day and found her crying while Miriam was busy putting a bandaid on David's skinned knee.

Mother Harris came for a prolonged visit. She almost fought with Guy for the privilege of caring for the baby, ecstatic in her pride and joy in her granddaughter.

"My Granddaughter." "Guy's daughter." Sometimes Miriam wanted to shout, "I had the baby. Isn't she mine, too?"

But she tried to be reasonable. She had other children, this was Guy's first. Maybe the novelty would wear off. Certainly her mother didn't make the fuss over her many grandchildren that she had over Albert.

When Mother Harris offered to help decorate the girls' room, Miriam was a bit surprised. She'd thought it was adequate, with a dresser and bed for Becky, temporarily given up for Mother Harris while Becky bunked in with the boys. Right now the baby slept in a bassinet that she had borrowed from Paul's wife, but soon they would need a crib and perhaps some shelving for diapers and such.

Within a few days, Miriam realized where Guy had gotten his flair for decorating. When Mother Harris took on a project, she took it seriously. Mother Harris was horrified by the hand-me-downs. Surely her only granddaughter deserved new things. Soon she and Guy were pouring over decorating magazines and wallpaper samples.

"But I wallpapered that room just a few years ago. It's still good."

"I know, dear. But do you really think it's suitable. Isn't it rather busy with all those bright colours?"

"I let Becky have her choice."

"I see." Mother Harris shook her head. It would be like Miriam to let a mere child decide on something so important. "But it's hardly suitable for a baby. Look, Miriam dear. I'm leaning towards this pastel with the bunnies. It's got flowers too, since you and Becky seem partial to flowers."

"But that won't go with the curtains I made."

"Oh, but I've already picked out some white islet curtains, dear. They'll match the bedding I've picked for the crib. And oh, did you see in this catalogue. I think that this crib and dresser would be just perfect." Miriam involuntarily drew a breath when she saw the price and hoped that she wouldn't be expected to pay for everything out of her housekeeping money.

"It will be my gift, Miriam."

"Oh, no. We couldn't allow it. You've already done enough. Hasn't she, Guy?"

"But I want to. Nothing is too good for my grandchild. But only with your approval, Miriam dear."

Somehow it just didn't seem right to Miriam, but when she looked to Guy he was nodding:

"Of course she approves. Mother you always did have such good taste. Chelsea will love her room when its finished."

It was perfect, or almost so, for the effect Mother Harris was aiming for was somewhat spoiled by the fact that Becky's bed and dresser still occupied one whole wall. She hadn't solved that problem when it came time for her to go home again.

Miriam's whole life was tied up with homemaking and child care now. With the baby at home and the older children coming home from school each day, she hardly ever went down to the store. Albert became Guy's main helper

Chapter Five

Guy was the one experienced in running a business, who supposedly understood demographics and could read trends, but Miriam was the one who sensed trouble as soon as the Supermarket opened up almost across the street from their store. At first they hung on. Guy was adaptable and he made changes. They opened earlier in the mornings to catch people before they left for work. They stayed open later in the evenings. They changed some of their merchandise. Unable to compete directly, they tried to supplement the services offered by the Supermarket - longer hours and fast, personal service; delivery if necessary. Joshua started going in after school with his wagon. Sometimes David would help too, working for tips.

They had always offered credit to their regular customers. A child could show up after school with a hand-written note for two cans of beans, a loaf of bread, a quart of milk and a package of cigarettes and Guy or his helper would put together the order and send it home with her, charged on the 'bill'. Pay day at the mill or down on the docks was always a busy day when the men came in to settle their accounts.

For several years after Chelsea was born they managed to hang on. But times were changing and finally Guy too could see the writing on the wall.

They had lived a comfortable life from the proceeds of the store. They were well fed, at wholesale prices, and well dressed. Their apartment was comfortable. Several times they had looked into purchasing a home but Guy could never find one he liked at a price he could afford. They occasionally went out to movies. They owned a station wagon that doubled as a delivery van. They went on vacation. That is, once every year Guy and Miriam took Chelsea to visit his parents, while the other children visited various cousins - now that Albert was older he slept at Hannah's but showed up at the store every afternoon to work his shift and keep an eye on the help.

Every year, sometime in July or August, Miriam would take the family out to the property for absolute freedom. They would open the stuffy camp and air it out; prime the hand pump; get a little fire going; and race down to the stream to check on the tide and see whether it was time for swimming. For the next two weeks they would lounge around, fixing things up, fishing, soaking up the sun, enjoying the outdoors. They always kept a stack of old books and magazines at the camp so they could look up information about tides or osprey (there was a nest in the old pine tree down by the point) or pond life in fresh water as opposed to tidal pools. One year they studied the stars, staying up late every evening, and then finding the Big Dipper, the Little Dipper, the North Star, and comparing them to the pictures in a book. They caught frogs which they played with for awhile and then let go. Frogs are good for the environment. They eat insects. Then they walked down the stream to the bay and dug clams which Miriam steamed for supper.

Guy wouldn't join them, but he did spend a day when he drove them up, helping them to get settled in and making sure they had everything they needed.

"You're going to be okay now? Do you have everything you need? Are you sure it's safe here in the woods?"

"For heavens sake, Guy, we've been coming for years."

"What about Chelsea? She's only a baby. How are you going to protect her from insects? There's mosquitoes around."

"The others were babies once too. I've got the mosquito netting for the crib. Don't worry. We're all going to be fine. You'll be surprised at how healthy and tanned we'll be when you come for us next week."

"Don't let Chelsea get too much sun."

"I've looked after a baby before. You worry too much. Bye, now. And don't work too hard. We'll be looking forward to seeing you again."

******

The solution to their problems with the store hit Guy when he least expected it. Just a few months after returning from their annual visit to Nova Scotia, this year at apple blossom time when the neat little farms and villages in the valley had been decorated with a mass of pink and white flowers, and two-year-old Chelsea had clapped her hands in delight at the parade during the festival, Miriam insisted that the whole family take their 'vacation' in the country. That meant he would not only lose their help--he especially would miss Albert, and he had to admit Becky and the boys were contributing towards the family business too--but he would have to take a day off to drive them out and make sure the camp was opened up safely so they could manage on their own until he again took a day off to come back and get them. They were all crowded into the station wagon, with Chelsea in the front seat on Miriam's knee and the others in the back with duffle-bags and pillows and books and boxes of food and supplies piled around them.

Becky was arguing with the two younger boys, "Stop leaning up against me. You're getting me all sweaty."

"I'm not. You're crowding me. Get over."

"Stop shoving. Mum, Josh's pushing me."

"Am not. Am not. Get your elbow out of my ribs. That hurts."

Then Albert, in his superior 'almost grown-up' voice growled, "Quit all that squirming around. And quit bumping into me. Can't you kids sit still for two minutes."

"You're hogging the window. You're always hogging the window."

"I warned you, Josh. Quit touching me."

"Mum, Becky's patting me on the head. Cut that out, Becky."

Much to Guy's annoyance, Miriam was completely oblivious to the children's arguments, which she considered quite normal in a hot crowded car on a long drive. He blamed her for never disciplining the kids. She was sitting there now checking off in her head a list of the things she had packed.

"Oh dear. Guy, we're going to have to stop in St. George. I forgot to buy film for the camera."

"Good grief, all I want to do was get there, Miriam. I've got to get out of this hot, sticky, noisy car and let these kids run off their energy. You know that if we stop they'll all want drinks or ice cream. I know what that will cost." Miriam nodded, knowing that he would be upset about the delay, and he was always complaining about the kids eating in the car and getting it all sticky. But they were just kids. A person couldn't be saying 'No' to them all the time.

"Miriam, can't it wait until we get there and get unpacked? Then one of us can run to the nearest store."

"Guy, the nearest store is St. George. You're not going to want to drive back there. Anything we want we have to take with us, or do without until you come again. I'd like to get some pictures this year."

She explained it then. There wasn't a store within twenty miles of the camp. Not a gas station, not a convenience store, nothing. There was no village to speak of anywhere near but, in the years since Bruce had first shown Miriam the property, people had started moving to the area. Besides the few old ramshackle farms, with their greying barns and unpainted houses showing signs of recent improvements, every so often scattered along the road there would be a modern looking bungalow or new mobile home. There were gravel roads leading off on both sides of the highway and more houses down those roads.. Just a bit beyond their farm there was a little cove off the bay ringed with summer cottages. Besides that, the highway was fairly busy, with lots of traffic between the States and Saint John, especially during the summer.

As they approached the farm Guy remarked: "Miriam, maybe we've been overlooking something. Could this be the place to open a store. I would imagine there are lots of potential customers - no competition at all."

Miriam couldn't believe her ears. Guy was suggesting that they move out to the property and open a store there. She was immediately enthusiastic about the idea. For years she had dreamed about living in the country again.

"Guy, do you mean it? Really! I'd love to bring the family out here and live on the property. Do you really think that we could make a go of it? As soon as we get settled in we could drive around and assess the potential."

From then on Miriam never looked back.

As soon as Guy stopped the car they all spilled out and began haphazardly dragging things into the camp. Albert hurried around opening all the windows, Becky was unpacking her things in 'her' room. Josh and David were climbing up to the loft to check out what they had left behind from last year. Miriam was trying to get some order in the confusion.

"Boys, somebody has to go down to the well for some water to prime the pump, and somebody has to fetch some kindling so I can start a fire. Becky, leave that for now and help Guy carry in the bedding. Chelsea, you stay close by now. Just play with your doll on the veranda."

"For heavens sake, Miriam. Somebody has to watch her."

"We all will. She won't wander very far."

Out of chaos there eventually came order. In a surprisingly short time their supplies were unpacked and stowed away, sleeping bags were spread out on beds and Miriam had lunch heating over the wood stove. As soon as they had eaten and cleared the dishes away, the kids began clambering to go exploring. With a minimum of instructions, mainly limited to "Albert will be in charge. Becky, you help him. Josh, David, obey your brother and sister and everybody stick together," they set out for the stream. Then Guy and Miriam took Chelsea for a drive around the immediate area with Miriam pointing out all the advantages.

"It sure looks like there is a demand for our services, Miriam. We'll have to look into it further."

Miriam was delighted at the prospects. She couldn't stop talking, making plans as though it was already decided.

"Miriam, a lot of our success will depend on location. We have to be on the main road. Does the property run out that far?"

"Of course. This is a big place, Guy. Just a minute until I call the kids back and get Chelsea settled for her nap." She pulled out a whistle and blew three sharp blasts and a few minutes later the children were heading back up the hill from the stream. "Becky, please watch Chelsea while I show Guy around the property."

Within minutes she had him traipsing out over the farm -- across the clearing to the spring, up to the highest point of land, then down to the stream and climbing over rocks and jumping tidal pools, down almost to the bay where she pointed out an iron marker. They left the stream, climbing the embankment, ducking under overhanging boughs to the foot of the old pine tree with the Osprey nest, to where she waved her arm towards the side road to point out that the property line followed it back towards the camp site. They walked back, passing the driveway and finally ducking down through another seldom-used path and coming out near the main road where she pointed out the markers defining her property as running from the road allowance of the little side road several hundred yards to the gully of the stream.

"You own all this, free and clear?"

"Of course. Guy, it has such potential. I fell in love with it the moment I saw it."

"The corner where the roads meet would be the perfect place for the store. I can't understand why you didn't build your cabin out here." Miriam shook her head. Surely it was obvious.

"Bruce's uncle had cut the trail in to the clearing from the side. Besides that's where the spring is -- and the best view. And we don't have to worry about traffic all the time."

"We'll need traffic for the store."

Guy went back to his store in Saint John still unsure of what he should do. He felt overwhelmed by Miriam's enthusiasm. He hadn't had time to think things out.

The supermarket across the street was having a mid-summer sale that week. There was no way Guy could match their prices. Maybe, just maybe the time had come to sell. When he went back two weeks later for his family they could talk about nothing else.

"Mum says that we're moving out here. Gee, that will be great."

"How soon can we get started?"

"Not this very minute."

In fact not until the next spring. Miriam pointed out that there was school to think of first. In the meantime they had to prepare and put the store up for sale. By mid winter they had a potential buyer -- an Italian immigrant who wanted to turn it into a specialty store for the ethnic market. And there was no end to plans to be made.

Guy came home from the store one night to find Miriam with papers and drawings spread out over the whole kitchen table.

"What's this?"

"My dream home! Actually, plans for the house I've always wanted to build on the property. I haven't looked at them or dared to think about them since Bruce died. But this is the house I want. Look, it will have a bedroom for each child -- that will give them each a space to call their own."

"And hopefully cut down on their continual bickering."

She was in too good a mood to be annoyed by his attitude.

"And I'd like it all open on the main floor. See, I've planned it with the fireplace and stairs partially separating the kitchen/eating area from the living room. Then we can talk back and forth while we're preparing meals and eating or doing homework or balancing the books."

"What about the store, Miriam? I thought probably we would build our living quarters at the back of, or above the store."

"But Guy, as you said, it will have to be out by the road."

"I presumed we'd live out there too."

"Oh no! Guy. That wouldn't be suitable."

Guy couldn't understand why not. He had grown up in an apartment above his parents' store, handy for security purposes and for after hours customers. But ever since he had first mentioned the possibility of moving he felt that everything was out of his hands.

"I have it all worked out." Miriam continued, as though he didn't have any say in the matter. "This is where the house should be on the highest point of land." She pointed with her finger to near where the cabin was now, close to the spring, and just up the slope from the barns.

"The barns?" Was there no end to surprises?

"Of course. We'll need barns and a big garden. We'll sell eggs and produce at the store. Many of the local people will have their own, but in the summer we can put up a big sign on the highway 'Stop for FRESH VEGETABLES and EGGS, 1000 Yards ahead' or something like that. It would be a waste not to grow our own food. We'll need a couple of cows, and I'd like to try raising goats. I've heard that they aren't much bother and their milk is richer than cow's milk. Some pigs to raise through the summer when they can eat table scraps, and old stuff from the store -- then in the winter we'll eat them. And some ducks and hens. See here," she pulled a piece of paper towards her and began drawing a map. "The house will be here. The septic tank should go over on this side. The well is here. It's spring fed and never goes dry not even in August. It runs down to that wet area that we should dig out to make a pond. The barns will be over here."

Miriam suddenly realized that she hadn't really explained all this to Guy. But it was just common sense. She remembered that Guy had never lived out in the country and realized that he probably didn't know much about planning around the lay of the land, prevailing winds, and the all important drainage patterns. His expertise lay in the store. She would leave that up to him.

She drew his attention to the plans for the house, explaining in detail how the fireplace would be built of stones gathered from a crumpled old stone wall that had been built a century or so ago, and how the veranda would wrap around three sides of the building.

"Holly cow, Miriam. I can't afford to build this place."

Miriam had another surprise for him. From the time Guy had met her he had presumed that she was barely struggling along, just managing on Canada Pension Survivors' benefits and the children's allowances. Since they'd been married he had supported her and contributed towards her children. Oh, occasionally she had mentioned something about the 'bonds' for the kids future, but he had assumed that these were a few Canada Savings Bonds she and Bruce had managed to purchase each year. Now she was talking about cashing in on her investments to build the house for the children. It turned out that her former husband had life insurance and a partially paid-for home which she had sold. Not a fortune, but with compound interest that she had never touched during the hard times, a tidy sum had grown and she was now willing to cash in to put towards building, and still leave enough for emergencies. "It was for the children's future" she explained. "But what could be more important to the children than a home of their own, on their property. It would still be an investment."

It certainly would be one less worry. However, Guy found that instead of being relieved he was resenting that all these years since they had been married Miriam had continued to go for advice to the lawyer she had once worked for instead of talking it over with him. After all, he did have some education and managed his own business, including investments. How many more secrets did she have?

By spring everything was ready. The Italian was anxious to buy the store. Guy, Miriam, and family began going out to the property on weekends. They had the camp moved out to the road . Again Miriam had looked after the details. She talked to a neighbour up the road and next thing Guy knew a crew of men was jacking up the building, putting it on skids, widening the trail, and towing it out, while Miriam and even Albert talked knowledgeably with them about how it should be done and what to watch out for, and Guy stood around feeling useless and in the way.

All spring they visited the site on weekends, managing to live in the camp and sleep up in the loft while walls were moved, shelves were put up, counters built and merchandise brought in. When Guy wanted to discuss plans for opening day, Miriam was busy arranging to have the ground ploughed up so that she and the children could begin planting. In the evenings, when he asked her opinion, she was more interested in making arrangements to get the house started.

Finally school was over. They gave up their apartment, put most of their furniture into storage, and moved out to the property, setting up two tents for living quarters now that the camp was converted into a store full of groceries and supplies and customers were coming in. It was time to build.

Miriam had originally taken it for granted that they would do most of the building themselves. That was how she remembered her father and brothers adding rooms to the old farm house, and extra buildings around the farm. That was how she and

Bruce had built their camp. It took Guy a while to convince her that would be false economy. He would be busy with the store - and he didn't know a thing about building. Miriam finally agreed it made sense to have the house built by experts. They would hire a contractor to worry about the plumbing, the electricity, the carpentry. Nevertheless, Miriam spent much of her summer checking on work on the house, and at the same time she and the kids got their share of hands-on building by helping the neighbour she hired to put up the barn.

It seemed almost impossible but by fall, less than a year from the first suggestion, Guy had his country store with no local competition, and Miriam was living in her dream-house on her farm.

She couldn't have been happier. Since the day she first saw it sixteen years ago, Miriam had longed to live on the property. It had been hers and Bruce's dream, continuously put off for another year or so, but always there. She had been sure that at some time it would happen. Even after Bruce's death, when she had realistically pushed that dream to the back of her mind, it wasn't quite forgotten. Then Guy had never had the least interest in the property, except once or twice to suggest that she sell it. Now she wondered what they had put it off so long. They had a little store and regular cash income. They could develop the property, clear the pasture, put up some fences and buy some stock. Next year they would plough up a bigger vegetable garden and sell farm produce to the travelers. The orchard would need to be cleared-out, the old trees trimmed and a few more apple trees planted.

Of course there were sacrifices in leaving the city.

Albert didn't come with them. Almost from the beginning he hadn't shared her enthusiasm. There was no changing his mind. Miriam tried without success to coax him, but he was practically an adult now and he was stubborn.

"Where will you stay?"

"With Gram and Gramps of course."

"Do they know?" Thank God Albert had her folks to depend on.

"They're always glad to have me."

"What about school? Will you promise to finish your final year at school?"

"Yeh. I'll finish. But I wouldn't out here in the sticks." He seemed to realize that he would win his argument if he agreed to continue his education. Mum always made such a big deal about it. Now she looked at Guy, trying to read his opinion, but his body language told her that it was her problem, that he wouldn't interfere between her and her children. Finally, against her better judgment, Miriam agreed.

"Just another example of how you spoil these kids." Guy complained later. "He's the only one old enough to be much help to us. I've spent years training him to the business, and you say he doesn't owe us anything--not even one year to get us started, while we provide him with a home."

"I can't force a seventeen year old. If he insists, then there's not much we can do about it."

Becky had waited until Guy left the room and then she too surprisingly also put up a fight.

"If Albert isn't moving, I'm not either."

"But Becky, you've always loved the property."

"To visit, maybe. But not to live there. What about my school? I don't want to change schools. And what about my friends? You can't make me."

Miriam couldn't take her seriously. "Don't be silly, Becky. You're only a child – much too young to live with your grandparents. You'll still go to school. We've checked and the bus goes right by the road. You and Joshua and David will be going to school in St. George, that's the nearest town." When she saw the look of disappointment on her daughter's face Miriam softened. "I had to move when I was just about your age and I didn't like it either. Then I wasn't able to go to school. I promise you, you'll be able to go to school."

"Yeh, and come home and work. Without Albert, I'll be expected to do everything on my own. I know."

It was disappointing that everyone didn't share her dream. After all, the property was for the children. They were a family. Miriam started to explain that everybody worked together for the benefit of the family, but Guy had returned to the room and he cut her off.

"Don't let her talk back to you like that, Miriam. There's nothing to discuss. We've made the decisions. That's it."

Becky darted him a look, shrugged her shoulders and stomped from the room. She knew that she wouldn't win this one.

They built lavishly. Miriam was tired of being cooped up in a city apartment. Nor did she want a sprawling farm house like the one she had grown up in, with new wings and small rooms added on to the original with no overall plan. Guy agreed. Do it all at once, do it right. They made a few changes to the plans -- a small den or office at the back of the large open room which Guy called the "Great Room", a balcony off the master bedroom Because of the slope of the land they would be able to drive right into the basement at the back. They could use it for storage both for the home and for the store. They would make do with the camp converted into a store until they built up their business and were ready to expand. Then they would build something worthy of their ambition.

Dreams and reality were not the same. Guy knew nothing about country living. Miriam was surprised at his awkwardness handling an axe or hammer and his lack of understanding or interest in the garden or the livestock. He passion was for the store. Miriam sometimes wondered if he realized how much her contribution, and that of the children, went towards supporting the family. By late fall they finished harvesting their vegetable garden, and arranged for the pig to be slaughtered. Then one cool autumn morning Miriam stepped out onto the balcony off the bedroom and shot a deer in the orchard. She remembered the joy and excitement of the first one she had shot so many years ago and could not understand Guy's look of disgust.

"Do we have to act like hill-billies?"

"But it's food Guy. You have no idea how good a venison stew will taste? Come and help me haul it up the hill."

"Are you crazy? I've got to get breakfast and out to the store. Do what you want with that beast."

"Suit yourself." She was disappointed that Guy wouldn't share her happiness, but it would be his loss so she called to the boys: "Come on Joshua, David. I'm going to show you how to dress out a deer." She'd helped Bruce many times in the past. Surely she would remember something and be able to figure out the rest herself.

Together with clams, trout, partridge, three different types of wild berries, and apples, all obtained in season, they had their freezer and basement shelves almost full for that first winter. They could snare some rabbits. Through the fall they gathered deadwood and dragged it into the basement for burning in the fireplace. They would neither freeze nor starve. Next year they would have a real garden, a horse, some cows and more pigs and chickens, and of course the store would be paying for itself by then.

Despite the hard work over the next few years, Miriam had to admit that she was happy. The store never took off as well as Guy seemed to expect it should, but some money came in, and they had few needs that they couldn't provide from the abundance on their own property. She didn't even experience Guy's acute disappointment when the government, upgrading the roads, decided that the particular stretch near their property needed to be straightened and that the new highway would by-pass them by several miles. Gone with that decision were Guy's plans for the drive-by trade. He would only attract those who chose the 'scenic route'. Miriam sold excess firewood and lumber as they cleared more land for the farm. They got by, with plans for rebuilding the store constantly put off until 'next year'.

Becky finished high school and Miriam burst with pride as she attended the graduation ceremonies. Despite his promises Albert had never gone back to school but was now working full time on the docks with her brothers. Now Becky had accomplished Miriam's old dream. To her mother's disappointment, but as expected, Becky could hardly wait to get away from the farm and back to civilization. "Like I said, Mum, it's great in the summertime, but there's no future for me here. I've got to get a job, and the jobs are all in town."

The following winter business was so slow at the store that Guy closed it for a few weeks to take Chelsea to visit her grandparents. Miriam didn't go. Joshua and David were in school, the stock need to be cared for, and the house couldn't be left alone in winter without draining the pipes and closing it up. No, she hadn't accompanied him on his trips home since they moved to the property. He came back all enthused. His parents had converted their store to a 7 - 11 franchise. That was the way to go. Profit by volume purchasing and advertising. A little research showed him that it wouldn't work on the back roads of rural New Brunswick.

Becky came back the following summer, but only on weekends, to help fix up the house and prepare for her wedding. She brought Carl O'Donnell with her, a handsome man, twice her size and fifteen years her senior, but apparently settled in his job and devoted to her. Many times later Miriam got out the pictures, hardly believing the joy of that day. There was Becky in the floor length white dress that Miriam had made for her, glad that although she had never worn white her daughter would. Chelsea was a precious flower-girl, just the right age to follow directions and do things properly but young enough to be adorable. It would have been hard to choose a bridesmaid from among her many cousins, and Miriam felt the old regret. Becky had had a sister; they should have grown up together. Elizabeth would be the perfect choice as bridesmaid. Instead Becky asked Carl's sister, and he had Albert as best man and Joshua and David as ushers. The 'great room' overflowed with guests spilling out into the dining area, and as soon as the ceremonies were over, out onto the large wide deck and down into the door yard. Hannah, Annie, Frances, Grace, Susan helped out in the kitchen area, passing plates piled high with food out to the dining area. Davy and his wife Verna came from their home in Ontario. Miriam's whole family was there. Mother Harris had come too. "I couldn't miss my granddaughter's wedding, Miriam Dear, even though Dad couldn't leave. I just had to be here for this happy occasion."

That was the first time Miriam had ever heard her refer to any of the older ones as her grandchildren, but perhaps she meant that she couldn't miss seeing her granddaughter dressed up in her fancy flower girl dress taking part in a wedding.

Miriam couldn't let that put a damper on her feelings. She was filled with pride. She had done it. She had almost single-handedly raised her daughter to be this beautiful bride. Her sons were all there with her. Albert looked so handsome, and Joshua and David so sharp, and her brothers and other guests couldn't get over the property.

"Nice place you have here." She heard over and over again.

Even Johnny seemed impressed, "Sure looks well built. I like a big house myself. You've done okay for yourself, girl. You and Guy. I'm proud of you."

It was to be the first and last time she was hostess to all her family and friends at a celebration of joy and happiness.

Chapter Six

A few weeks later came the jarring telephone call advising that Dad Harris had died suddenly of a massive heart attack. Guy must come home immediately. Although she had never left the farm for more than a days' shopping trip and visit to her family in Saint John, Miriam knew that her place was by his side.

"Of course, Mother Harris, we'll be there as soon as possible."

"Hurry, hurry. I don't know what to do. I need Guy."

"Don't feel pressured into making any decisions. We'll be there to help as soon as possible." Miriam tried to remember arrangements for Bruce's funeral. It would have been different, with the recovery of the body, the autopsy and the inquest, but certain basic things would be the same. "Have you called an undertaker yet?"

"No, I told you, I'm still at the hospital. I don't know what to do. Guy has got to come."

"He will. I'll go right over to the store and tell him. Give me a number where we can reach you."

"Miriam, aren't you listening? I told you. I'm at the hospital. I don't know the number."

"Listen, Mother Harris. Ask one of the nurses or the ward clerk. She's the one working at the nurses' desk. They will tell you a number where you can be reached. I'll have Guy phone in less than fifteen minutes. He'll help you decide which undertaker to call, and you won't have to do anything else until we get there. While you're waiting you might want to call a friend or neighbour."

"I don't need a friend. I need Guy."

"I know. We're coming."

Miriam went over to the store to tell Guy. Then, while he was calling his mother, she tried to think what to do. They would have to close the store for awhile. A few things like fresh milk would spoil and the baked goods would go stale, but it couldn't be helped. Joshua and David would be home from school in less than a hour. There was no reason to take them out of school and down to Nova Scotia. They had only seen Dad Harris a couple of times, and never formed a relationship with him. They would be better off in school, but they were too young to leave alone, and then there was stock to look after every day. Should she call her family? No, Johnny would never come and Hannah wouldn't come without him; everyone else worked. When Guy finally calmed his mother down enough to get off the phone, Miriam called the Foxes across the main road.

"Of course, the boys can take their meals and sleep here. My husband's brother, Eddy, is staying with us. I'll send him over with them every morning before school and again after supper to feed the stock and do the milking. We'll keep an eye on things too. Don't you worry. What about Chelsea? I don't know . . ."

"Oh, we'll take her with us. Mother Harris would never forgive us if we didn't. But, thanks. Thanks a million."

"That's what neighbours are for."

Quickly now, decide what to take: Guy's suit, her best dress. The suit she had made for Mother-of-the-Bride was pale pink, not suitable, but her navy from last year would be okay. More clothes for each of them - how long would they be gone? She decided to pack for a week. Chelsea's things. A few toys. Guy was down at the store, closing it up. The boys came running down the lane from the bus, and she quickly explained to them what was happening.

"Run upstairs and get a few things together - your toothbrushes and pyjamas and some clothes for tomorrow. You don't need to pack a lot. You'll be coming by the house everyday. Now are you sure you're going to be okay? Do you want me to call Grandma Taylor? We could drop you off in Saint John until we get back. You'd have to miss school."

She saw David's eyes light up and he grinned but Joshua answered:

"Oh, Mum. We'll be fine. We'll stay here and keep an eye on things."

Less than two hours from the initial phone call Guy, Miriam and Chelsea were in their car heading out the driveway. Less than a week later Miriam took the train home.

At first they kept up the pretense to themselves as well as to everybody else that it was temporary. It was so logical. Miriam had to get back to the property, the boys and the livestock. Of course Guy had to stay behind to help his mother with a myriad of tasks she faced following so sudden a death. Miriam's mistake was in leaving Chelsea behind, but even that had seemed logical at the time. Almost since her infancy the little girl had made the trip every winter to spend a few weeks with her 'Granny'. How was this so different?

"Leave her with me, Miriam Dear. She'll be company for me. I'm so lonely and Guy will be busy. I don't know what I'm going to do. There's so much to worry about. Thank heavens Guy is staying to help out. But don't deprive me of my grandchild so soon."

Before Miriam could think of an answer, Guy had interjected. "Of course Chelsea will stay with us, Mother. I can't think of any reason for buying her a train ticket, just so she can go home a few weeks early. She'll be perfectly fine here with us."

Guy never spent a penny without careful consideration. Surely even a half-fare ticket would be a waste to send a little girl home with her mother. But the days grew to weeks and the weeks extended past a month. Despite the expense, Miriam tried to call frequently. Her first premonition came when Chelsea mentioned that she had started kindergarten.

"Mummy, it's so much fun. Daddy takes me every morning. I get to play and sing and make things. I'm going to send you a picture I made with finger paints."

"That's nice, dear. I'm glad you're having fun. Now let me speak to Daddy." Then, "Guy, what's going on down there? When are you bringing Chelsea home? She tells me that she's started kindergarten."

Oh, he reassured her. It didn't mean anything really. Kindergarten was part of the public school system in Nova Scotia. It wasn't costing anything. It gave Mother time to look after a few things in the morning, and Chelsea a chance to meet other children. She was lonesome.

"Lonesome for me and her brothers."

"Of course she misses you. But it's just for the term."

"What do you mean? For the term? When are you bringing her home? When are you coming home?" A chill went down Miriam's spine and her heart started to race.

"Not before Christmas, I'm afraid. I can't leave Mother now. There's far more to do than I ever imagined. The store keeps me busy from morning to night."

******

So it was that Guy sent Miriam money for her and the boys to join him at his mother's for Christmas. "I can't leave her alone."

"Why not bring her back here with you?"

"I couldn't do that. She misses Dad so much. We (at least he was still saying we) can't expect her to leave her home the first Christmas after she's lost her husband. And I can't leave the store. Surely after all these years, you know that this is the busiest time of year."

"You've got a store here at home and it's going to pot without you. The boys and I have been selling the merchandise from the shelves but we haven't been reordering much."

"That little place! More like a hobby than anything. It hasn't made money in the winter for years. Miriam, you might as well close it. This place down here is a real business. I can see lots of potential. If you want us to spend Christmas together, you'll have to come down."

So Miriam asked around and found that her neighbour's brother, Eddy Fox, was still with them. He would willingly stay at her place for the holidays, keep the heat on in the house and look after the animals. So she and the boys were reunited with Guy and Chelsea, spending Christmas in a strange house that the boys had never visited before, with a step-grandmother they hardly knew. They missed their home, and especially they missed Becky. They had looked so forward to her bringing Carl to spend Christmas with them, and having Albert drive up for a day or two.

They stayed until after New Year's. Then it stormed. Miriam was frantic to get back home. She had sensed that Eddy Fox was a bit slow and she worried about him staying alone for an extended period, but more importantly, she had to get the boys back to school. Chelsea was whining with an ear infection.

The weather cleared some but was still unpredictable when they packed the car to return. And only then did Guy tell Miriam that he had decided that it would be best to leave Chelsea with his mother. No argument could shake him. Chelsea wasn't well. She shouldn't be traveling in this weather. She'd be better off with her grandmother where she was already settled and happy. Miriam was being selfish, as always, wanting to put the baby at risk. Miriam was arguing and shouting, almost hysterical. Her voice was breaking as she fought for control.

"Don't be crazy, Guy. She's my daughter! Surely I have some say in this. She belongs with us! We're her family."

Then she saw the boys, standing together warily, not knowing what to expect; and Chelsea curled up in the corner of the chesterfield next to Granny, her big eyes looking from her father to her mother, frightened of whatever the outcome would be. Don't fight in front of the children, the child guidance books all advised. Don't make a scene in front of outsiders, her family had always cautioned. Miriam would always wonder what would have happened if she had walked over, wrenched Chelsea from her grandmother and wrestled her into the car. Would Guy have fought her physically? Would he have torn Chelsea from her arms and returned her to the house? Or would he have simply refused to get into the car and drive it home? If so, what would he have done if she had gotten behind the wheel and driven away with all three of the children. But she couldn't risk upsetting them all by trying. It might scar them for life. Guy sensed her hesitation.

"I don't know why you are making such a fuss. I'm going to have to be back and forth all winter getting things settled. I can bring her home when she's feeling better and the roads are cleared. It would be ludicrous to set out with a sick child in this weather." He was so controlled, so logical, while she was almost crazy with emotion. Did he actually wink at his mother as he herded them out the door while Chelsea cried and the boys, bewildered, waved and threw kisses to her.

"Goodby, my precious girl." She had left Elizabeth alone in British Columbia. Now she was leaving Chelsea in Nova Scotia. But only temporarily, she reminded herself.

Chapter Seven

The next month was a nightmare. It soon became obvious that Guy had no intention of staying away from his mother and his 'home'. His idea of settling things was to tie up loose ends in New Brunswick. He wasn't deserting his family. He begged Miriam to put the property up for sale and move down with him. Joshua and David were welcome to come too, of course. Weren't they all a family?

It was out of the question for Miriam. She could not even consider leaving her home.

"Miriam you are the most unreasonable woman I have ever met. I'm the breadwinner in this family, and I decide where we will live. This is the perfect opportunity for us and my God, I can't make a living here. The store is never going to pay for itself this far off the highway."

"But the farm. We can live off the farm and wood lot."

"Don't be silly. Miriam, you're so delusional. Even Bruce knew better than to move his family out here. He must have realized that it was all a dream. It's a hobby farm. And I can make a good living for us in Nova Scotia. I inherited the store. We'll live with Mother. It's a big house. She'd love to have you. She needs us. Don't be so stubborn. We have to put the house and property up for sale, and decide what to take with us."

Miriam couldn't even consider it. How could he ask her to move away from her home and her family. Joshua and David would hate living with his mother. And Albert and Becky would be so far away.

"No. I won't sell my property."

Sick from longing for Chelsea, unable to understand Guy's attitude, worried about her future, Miriam was desperate to have someone to talk to, someone who cared. She wanted her mother. Guy was traveling back and forth to Saint John every few days to "look after details". What details she couldn't imagine. Guy, who had talked incessantly ever since they had met on the fire escape, had stopped talking to her, other than the casual comments about the weather and pass the potatoes. When she told him she wanted to go to town he put her off. He wasn't going again for awhile.

She kept after him until finally he agreed. He would drop her off for a few hours at her folks place. It was a silent drive through the winter landscape.

She sensed that her parents were uncomfortable almost from the beginning, and when after a cup of tea and an oversized ginger cookie she tried to explain what was going on in her life they already knew. What's more, they agreed with Guy.

"He's been here off and on these last few weeks. He wants us to persuade you to be reasonable. He can't understand why you are doing this to him."

"What!" Miriam couldn't believe it. Guy never wanted to visit her family. Now he had been coming alone, and trying to turn them against her.

"What does he mean – doing this to him? It's Guy that wants to leave. Not me."

"A woman's place is with her husband." Hannah explained. "Didn't I move in to Saint John with your father?"

"I thought you both agreed on it."

"We did. That is, I guess we did. Anyway, whatever he decided, we did. Families have to be supportive. Hasn't Guy always been a good husband? Hasn't he always supported you well?"

"Yes, I guess he has."

"And he's been so good to the children. Remember, Miriam, he took on four children that weren't his own. Hasn't he been good to them?"

"Yeh. In a way."

"Then what is the problem? Support him in his decisions. It's Guy who has to make the living."

"But Mum, Dad! We've been so happy out at the farm! How can I leave it? I'll never be happy at his mother's place. It's difficult enough visiting there. You can't imagine what it might be like to live there, in her house."

"What do you mean, I can't imagine? Miriam, don't you remember what it was like out at the old place while you were growing up? Who's place did you think that was?"

"Ours. Well, yours and Dad's, I guess."

"It was, and it wasn't. It was your grandparents first. It was only after we were married and after Jack was born that your grandparents built themselves a separate house up on the corner of the place. But your grandmother was always coming over. It had been her home; she didn't even knock on the door, but just walked in whenever she felt like it."

"She had every right," Johnny interjected. "It was her home first. My mother was always welcome to come over any time she wanted."

"Yes, it was her home first. And your folks were certainly helpful all the while you were off to the war. I'm not saying I didn't appreciate that. But don't you see, Miriam. I could never call my home my own. I could never call my children my own. Gran was always there."

"I thought that she came over to help out while you were teaching."

"Yes, and I'm thankful for that. But the point is she was there everyday anyway so we made the best of it. We appreciated her help. My goodness, I never could have taught school if it wasn't for her. Miriam, a woman has to make the best of things. Count your blessings."

"I don't want to move to a strange place and start over. I don't want to disrupt my life and my children's."

"You were willing to move all the way to the west coast to be with Bruce."

"That was different. We were younger then. It felt like the right thing to do. But look what happened. We lost Elizabeth."

Had she not been so upset herself, Miriam might have noticed the look of anguish and pity that crossed her mother's face, but Hannah quickly regained control. Long years of practice had taught her how to hide her emotions until she usually succeeded in denying them even to herself. "Miriam, the doctors told you there was nothing to be done, no matter where you lived."

"I could have visited her grave."

Her mother was trying to be reasonable, but her father was losing patience. Calmly talking things over had never been his way and some things were best forgotten. His only recourse was blustering: "I've heard enough of this. Even running down my mother now, and her in her grave. I would think that you'd be happy wherever your family is. I've never been able to figure out what's wrong with you anyway, girl. Do you think you're better than the rest of us? So high and mighty. Always with your head in the clouds. Always dreaming big dreams, and never a thought to what's best. Who's going to support you if you don't go with Guy? He's going. You can be sure of that. He's been here almost every second day it seems, begging us to persuade you to go with him. God, what's the problem? Be grateful that he wants you."

Guy had been there before her. Somehow he had turned her family against her. Or had they always been that way. Everything was okay as long as she went along with whatever they expected of her. Don't expect anything for yourself. Don't rock the boat. Don't ask for anything.

Hannah reached out and touched her arm. "Miriam, if you don't go, just what do you think you are going to do?" she asked gently.

"I don't know. Get a divorce, I suppose."

"Divorce?" Her father practically shouted.. "Just listen to her, Hannah. No one in this family has ever been divorced. We stick together. Marriage is a lifetime commitment. A woman sticks by her husband."

"Yes, Miriam. Look, even Annie stuck it out when things looked so bad for her. Surely I don't have to remind you of that. They've raised a lovely family, and they treat Albert like one of their own. He's over there all the time. Goodness, girl, that's what's expected."

Miriam thought of her sisters. Would they give her any support? Not likely. Certainly not Annie, and Gracie was so much younger they had never even talked except on a very superficial level. And no doubt Guy had already talked to her brothers. She couldn't rely on her family.

She went out for a walk and when she returned and things had quieted down she made a quick phone call to set up an appointment with Mr. Howard for the following week.

She didn't ask Guy to drive her to town, or to let her have the car for the day. She took the bus.

Chapter Eight

At last Miriam had someone to talk to who seemed willing to listen to her point of view, which was a relief even though his information agreed closely with that of her family. Domicile was established by the husband. He was not deserting her. He was willing to move his family and to provide for them. From what Miriam had told him, Mr. Howard concluded that financially they would probably be better off relocating since their store was hovering just above bankruptcy and his parents' store in Nova Scotia, which he now claimed that he owned, was doing well. That was a strong argument in his favor. If Miriam refused to move with him, he could charge her with desertion, not the other way around. However, Mr. Howard attached no moral judgement on Miriam's refusal to go. In fact, he seemed to understand.

"I see a lot of unhappy couples in my practice, Miriam. They've made me change my opinions since I was a brash young lawyer just out of college. Usually there's no right or wrong, no black or white. Oh, sometimes the husband is a brute, and sometimes the wife is a money-hungry shrew; but usually they are just two unhappy people seeing their lives going off in different directions and trying to make the best decisions for themselves. Think things over very carefully. Consider the facts. Guy is determined to move down to his mother's. You're determined not to go. Have you considered what you might be giving up by your refusal? Divorce is almost always final, and despite the best of intentions on both sides its usually not very pleasant."

"All I want is my home and my children."

"There shouldn't be any problem with the children. Let's see. Albert is of legal age, and Becky's married, so they wouldn't even be considered. Then you have two, no three, little ones."

"Two boys of Bruce's. Then Guy and I have a little girl."

"Did Guy adopt the boys?"

"Not legally, but they call him 'Dad'."

"And the little girl? How old is she?"

"Five, almost six."

"The Courts almost always award custody of young children to the mother, especially in the case of a little girl. I'll tell you what, Miriam. If you are sure, and only if you are sure, I'll start proceedings. Let me know who Guy's lawyer is and try not to worry. We'll try to act like mature adults and work something out. I'll be in touch or call me if you have any questions."

Their next visit didn't go so smoothly. Guy was charging her with desertion. He wanted the property sold and everything split half-and-half. What was more he wanted sole custody of Chelsea. "Miriam, why didn't you tell me that she was living with Guy's mother?"

"It never came up. I didn't think to mention it. I don't consider her 'living' there. She's just visiting until we bring her home. Is it important?"

"Very. She's enrolled in school there. That's her home now."

"No!" Miriam felt her knees going weak. Was this what she had suspected all along, but never faced? Guy and his mother were taking Chelsea from her. "No! Not my baby! You can't let them keep my baby! Don't tell me I've lost her!"

"We'll do our best, but it does complicate matters. And it looks like they are going to play hard ball. Now, be honest with me and tell me everything, even if it doesn't seem important to you. Tell me what is the best you hope for, and the least you're willing to settle for, and we'll try to reach a compromise."

"My children and my property."

"Nothing more. No alimony. No child support."

"My children and my property. Nothing else matters."

The next visit the news was worse.

"Miriam, if you're going to fight for custody for Chelsea, Guy is asking for custody for all three minor children."

"What? What do you mean? My boys! How can he do that? They aren't even his kids, he never adopted them, and he doesn't really like them. He's never shown any interest in them. He's never given them any affection. He just tolerates them because he knows he's supposed to. How can he even consider taking my boys?"

"It's probably just a power play. I can't see the judge taking his claim seriously, but he claims that he supported them and considered them his sons all these years. Tell me, has he ever abused them?"

"What do you mean?"

"Hit them. Deprived them of necessities. Punished them harshly."

"I told you. He ignores them most of the time. When they need discipline, I'm expected to do it. Sure he shouts at them sometimes, and occasionally sends them away from the table if they're acting up. No, I can't say he's cruel, not physically at least."

"This is bad. He's accused you of being an unfit mother. I know it sounds ridiculous. Anyone who knows you, knows that you are the exact opposite. We'll just have to get a few character witnesses."

Miriam couldn't believe her ears. Guy accusing her! Saying that she was an unfit mother! Where was he coming from?

"What does he say?"

There was a whole list of charges beginning with the circumstances of Albert's birth. She had been promiscuous. She had actually been a threat to her own sister's marriage. She had born an illegitimate child. Then rather than caring for Albert herself she had let others take over the job. She had left him with others (they were his grandparents, for God's sake) for months at a time. Then there was the baby who had died mysteriously in British Columbia. Crib death always leaves unanswered questions. Worse, she had put two young children at risk by taking them out ice-fishing in uncertain conditions. She was very lucky they hadn't drowned or died of exposure then. She had kept her children in poverty while investing the proceeds of their father's life insurance, surely meant for their well being. Only after she married Guy had they had financial security. And after Chelsea was born he had to take over much of her care. There was an incident when he came home from work and heard her screaming all the way down on the street. When he came in she was lying in her own filth with Miriam totally ignoring her.

"What? What?" Miriam couldn't remember.

"He said that after that his mother came and stayed a few months, looking after the baby and getting things organized so that you wouldn't be so overwhelmed."

"What??? A few months? Was it that long? It seemed like years. And I didn't see it that way." Miriam was flabbergasted. The only thing that had overwhelmed her was Mother Harris taking over, as though she and the other children didn't matter.

Mr. Howard nodded, taking notes.

He skipped over the next few years to when Guy had returned after attending to matters following his father's death only to find that Miriam had a strange man living on the property. "What? Who?"

"Let's see. I have it here. Edward Fox."

"Eddy Fox? He's just a neighbour I had helping out while Guy was away."

It certainly raised a lot of questions. Whether or not there was anything between Miriam and this Eddy Fox, it was questionable whether he was a fit companion and role model for her boys.

Miriam tried to argue, tried to explain.

"I know Miriam. I know you, and I know some of the circumstances he's talking about, and I can't believe the twist that he's put on things. I don't believe any of it. But these are serious charges. Guy claims that he once caught Mr. Fox exposing himself to the children. Do you know anything about that?"

She searched her mind. Where was Guy getting these ridiculous ideas? Mr. Howard went on:

"Guy is obviously going to play dirty. It could get very unpleasant. Go talk to your parents, and other people you know. Get all the support you can. Round up some character witnesses. There was that minister I met when Bruce died. He should be a good witness."

"He's dead. I read his obituary in the paper last fall. And I haven't been to church in years."

Miriam returned home with her head full of questions and struggled through the week to keep from bringing anything up with Guy. It was in the lawyers' hands now. She returned to the city again the following week.

She felt discouraged even before she reached her parents' place. Things hadn't been going well all day. From the time she'd seen the boys off on the school bus that morning and told Guy that she was catching the bus in to town to do some shopping and look after a few things, she'd simply been feeling that she was fighting an up-hill battle. First there had been that long walk out to the highway, the road slushy and dirty from an unexpected early thaw. Years ago there had been an early thaw – and she remembered this was the very date that Bruce had died. She tried to put it out of her mind. Just put one foot ahead of the other, keep going. There were things that had to be done, her children who had to be fought for. Then there was the long bus ride to the city.

She'd met with Frances for lunch. She always enjoyed Frances' company, more so than either of her sisters', but when she mentioned that she might need someone to speak for her, a character witness, Frances put up her hands.

"Uh-uh. Bill and I anticipated something like this when you called. Please, just leave us out of it. We're sorry that Guy is giving you a hard time, but Bill tends to agree with him. Anyway, we don't want to get involved."

"Frances, I thought we were friends."

"We are, and I'd like to keep it that way. But I don't want to fight with my husband either, so don't try to get me involved."

Nothing could persuade her, and Miriam had considered her to be her last hope. She knew that she couldn't count on the rest of her family. She'd already approached them with the same request and they'd flatly refused.

"I told you from the beginning that you were making a mistake," her father explained. "I never much took to Guy but he's provided for you. You knew what you were doing. You made your bed . . ."

Annie agreeing with their father, always on his good side: "Dad, she's always thought she knew more than the rest of us. So independent. No sense of family values. But then she's always running back here for help."

Hannah trying to avoid conflict: "Miriam, don't you think that you should try to work things out? You know, talk things over with Guy."

But still Miriam hoped that when the chips were down she would be able to change their minds. Her older kids should be a big help too. She didn't argue further and her mother welcomed her as warmly as always when she knocked and walked in.

"Miriam, in town again so soon?"

"I had some things that I had to take care of."

"Well, you picked a good day to come. I just baked today, and goodness with just Dad and Jack living here now, there's nobody to eat them up."

"Mum, I've never known anyone to have more company than you. You've always got kids and grandkids gobbling up everything as fast as you cook it."

She sat down to a cup of tea, and considered her choices: big soft molasses cookies, moist oatmeal drop cookies; and her favourites — dated-filled sugar cookies. Her mother must have worked all morning, mixing and rolling the dough, cutting them out with her largest cookie cutter, placing a daub of stewed dates in the centers, folding them over, pressing them down. They were still hot from the oven. Delicious!

Miriam leaned back and relaxed. She had a good hour before she would have to leave to catch her bus, and it was nice to be pampered for a change.

"Thanks, Mum."

She was disappointed when she heard footsteps on the porch, and the door banged open. She could tell in a minute that Annie was furious, but she didn't let it bother her. Annie was always getting upset up about something: Charlie's extravagance, the girls' teachers, the line-ups in the grocery stores, a rude neighbour. She could make a mountain out of a mole hill, and, Miriam suspected, she found meaning in her rather dull existence by exaggerating everything out of proportion. But now she seemed especially worked up, and as she struggled out of her jacket, she turned angrily towards Miriam:

"How could you? How could you do this to Albert?"

"What! What are you talking about? I haven't seen Albert in weeks."

"I know. We all know that you never go out of your way to look him up. You never explained anything to

Albert! He's just found out that he's a bastard! Guy had to tell him everything. Such a shock to the poor boy, to find out his mother's a tramp. You can't imagine how upset he is, and him thinking all along that Bruce was his father, but wondering why you never loved him like the others, why you always treated him different."

"My God, Annie. When? When did Guy tell him all this?"

"Just today. He met with him at lunch time. Albert took the afternoon off work to come over and ask me about it."

"Guy's in town?"

"Yeh. He's talking to everybody who knows you, trying to figure out what's going on, why you're doing this to him. I guess he thought if he talked to Albert, Albert might be able to help him. But Albert was just devastated. The shock . . . "

"Guy is the bastard. He had no business . . . But Annie, where is Albert now? I have to explain."

"I don't think he wants to hear anything from you, now or ever. Don't bother to call. Charlie and I told him that he's always welcome at our place, that we'll be a family to him. After all we've done our best by him all along. He doesn't want anything to do with you."

All fight went out of Miriam. Some of the accusations were true. She had never felt about Albert as she did about the others, but that didn't mean she didn't love him. He refused to meet with her. He sent word through Annie that if necessary he would testify on Guy's behalf. She was a cold, devious, self-centered woman, who always had to have her own way regardless of who suffered for it. Deflated, deserted by her family whom she had always thought she could depend on even if they criticized her, Miriam was willing to give up.

"Just get me my children and let me keep my property," she told Mr. Howard.

"I'll do my best."

In the end Guy dropped his claim for Joshua and David, in return for her dropping her claim for Chelsea. Miriam was given generous visitation rights. Chelsea would make her home with Guy and his mother and attend school there, but she would visit Miriam several times during the year for a week or two, and for a month in the summer. Guy didn't even ask for visitation for Joshua and David, much to their relief. What was more, Guy suddenly and unexpectedly agreed that she could keep her property. It wasn't in joint ownership, something Guy had neglected to look into when the house was built. It belonged partially to Miriam and partially held by her in trust for Becky, Joshua and David. She in turn had no claim on Guy's property in Nova Scotia - it belonged to him and his mother. She didn't ask for or receive any support.

Miriam felt that she had lost her reputation amid rumour, innuendo and hints of scandal. She avoided most of her neighbours realizing that they would think there must be something wrong with a woman who could have her child taken away from her. She lost her right to raise her little daughter, to be with her day by day, to enjoy her childhood and influence her development. It hurt, almost worse than losing Elizabeth, because there was no malice involved in losing Elizabeth, just a cruel trick of fate.

She lost Albert too. Never again did he come out to the property to see her or to visit his younger 'half'-brothers. If she ran into him in town, at first he cut her dead; and as years went by and he realized that was putting him in the wrong, he mellowed enough to treat her with cold politeness. She never had an opportunity to talk with him, to try to explain all those years away.

She almost lost Becky, as Becky sided with her brother, and Miriam remembered back to that day long ago when Albert had asked, 'Where's Dad?' and Becky had replied, 'Mummy left Daddy in the water.' Somehow Becky was still accusing her of failing them.

She lost too her sense of family, her belief that her parents and siblings would always be there for her. Oh, she was still welcome at her parents home, but she didn't feel like visiting. Frances was still friendly, but over the years they had grown apart and they had little in common anymore. She was on her own. Miriam and her boys on their property.

PART FOUR

Chapter One

Miriam found herself mourning Bruce all over again. It was strange that while Bruce had been quiet, hardly ever taking an active part in a conversation, and Guy had talked continuously, it was Bruce Miriam missed the most. During the first few months after Guy finally did his damage and left for his new life at his mother's home and store, Miriam found herself mourning Bruce. She felt abandoned, deserted. She was living on the property they had long dreamed about, and she missed him. It was with Bruce that she had shared dreams, hopes, and the mutual interest in raising their children. She realized as she looked back that she had never shared anything with Guy. Despite his incessant talking, they had not communicated. They had lived together, worked together, eaten together, slept together, conceived a child together and they had never shared anything. They hadn't even shared their love for Chelsea, for she had never felt included in Guy's love for the child which seemed to her to be part of his selfish, self-serving nature. It was as though he, and he alone, had produced this friendly, attractive child. No, she never mourned Guy. After the bitterness of the divorce, she lost all affection and respect she ever had for him. For the first time in her life Miriam felt free.

Even during that long winter and spring when everything was up in the air, and nothing settled, she had begun the process of regrouping, planning for a future for herself and her boys on their own with very little cash income or financial security.

The store was gone. That was one of the things Guy had taken care of during those few months after New Years--selling off whatever merchandise remained in the store and then closing it down. As soon as possible she put it up for sale, knowing that it would not bring in much, but also knowing that she had to sell it and the building lot beside it on the main road. She needed the cash to cover her expenses and to buy a second-hand truck. Gone were the days when a family could consider living in the country without transportation. She also considered how they could cut expenses to a minimum and depend on the property to supply as many of their needs as possible. She and the boys followed the little river upstream, beyond the reaches of the highest tides to where it narrowed and divided into several small brooks, and there they found early spring fiddleheads. They were not as large or as plentiful as those that would be found a few weeks later in the northern parts of the province but they provided a welcome taste of fresh greens. Their second trip up, they took along their fishing rods and caught a mess of pan sized trout, and ate like royalty the next day. When the gaspereau were coming up the stream and she and Joshua rigged a net and caught a few -- delicious after you picked out the bones. The rhubarb patch in the sunny corner beside the house provided stewed rhubarb for their breakfasts, and with the promise of warm weather, she began preparing the garden.

It was backbreaking work for a woman putting in a garden, repairing fences and expanding the pasture land, caring for the animals, and cutting a little firewood even with her two boys working beside her after school and on weekends. When dark drove them inside, there was still homework to supervise. She usually followed the boys to bed exhausted, but arose early the next morning to cook up a pot of oatmeal, and prepare their sandwiches, before sending them off to the school bus.

One evening Eddy Fox showed up on the veranda. Could she use some help? At first she didn't understand what he meant. He was inarticulate, not used to explaining himself. But finally she put his few words and gestures together. He would be working at the nearby sawmill through the summer and he needed a place to stay. Of course, he could stay at his brother's, that's where he was now, but they didn't need him. If she would put him up, he would be glad to help around the barn or whatever she wanted him to do. Miriam put him off that evening, saying she would think about it.

He'd looked after the place at Christmas, proudly responsible for feeding the livestock, milking the three cows and the goats, cleaning the barn, keeping the fires going in the house and the snow shoveled away from the steps. She'd been relieved to have him there and she couldn't understand the fuss Guy had made when they had come back after New Year's unless perhaps he was trying to pick a fight. The idea of an affair was the furthest thing from her mind and, if she had considered one, it wouldn't be with Eddy Fox. Certainly she wasn't attracted to him, nor did she believe he ever thought of her as anything but his brother's neighbour. Then a chill ran down her spine. Among Guy's accusations, was the one that Eddy wasn't fit to be around young children. Didn't her lawyer say that Guy had claimed Eddy had exposed himself to the boys?

She couldn't have him around them, and Chelsea would be coming home for the summer. Then Miriam remembered Guy had made a lot of accusations that didn't make a lot of sense. Some of them, such as the innuendo that she and Eddy were having an affair and the suggestion that he was perverted seemed contradictory to her. She remembered some literature David had brought home from school.

"We had an assembly today. The lady told us to take this stuff home for our parents to read."

<u>Street proof your child. Warn your children - A Stranger May Mean Danger!</u>

She hadn't paid much attention to it at the time. There weren't many streets around the farm or in the little town where they went to school. As for a stranger being dangerous; it hadn't been a stranger who had raped her, but a member of her family. Now, however, it seemed to make sense. She called the boys to her and began awkwardly, "You know Eddy Fox?"

"Yeh."

"Of course. Why?"

"Do you like him?"

Joshua nodded. "He's okay."

"What's there to like?" David wanted to know.

"Uh, uh." this was hard to put into words. "Has he ever done anything he shouldn't?"

"What do you mean? Like stealing or something?"

"He swears, Mum. I heard him saying words he shouldn't. Like when he hit his thumb with the hammer, he really swore. Do you want to know what he said?"

"No, David. That isn't necessary. But . . . but Guy said that you boys told him that, uh, Eddy exposed himself to you."

"What!" from Joshua.

"What does that mean?" from David.

"We saw him going to the bathroom in the barn once."

David, remembering, started to giggle. "Yeh. We thought it was funny. We laughed at him."

"What did he do then?"

Joshua was beginning to understand her line of questioning. "He acted real embarrassed. Like, I'd yelled in a real deep voice 'What's going on here?' and he turned real startled like, and then when he saw us he turned his back and told us to get out."

"Yeh. And he shouted at us. Remember Joshua. He said, 'Go away and leave me alone. I need my privacy.'"

"We hadn't realized that Guy was around. You know he hardly ever went near the barn. But suddenly he shouted at Eddy, real mean. Old Eddy just started stuttering, and we got out real fast before Guy would start yelling at us too. He always was getting mad about nothing."

"Are you sure that's all that happened? He didn't try to . . . uh, he didn't try to touch you or anything?"

Suddenly Joshua began to understand. "You mean like that woman at the school was talking about. No, Mum, nothing like that. Eddy wouldn't do anything like that. He was so embarrassed Mum. He was just answering a call of nature. You don't have to worry about old Eddy."

"Yeh, when you gotta go, you gotta go."

That evening Miriam walked over to the neighbour's and told Eddy that she would be glad to have him sleep in the little bedroom on the ground floor in return for his help around the place. He would take most of his meals at the cookhouse at the mill, but on weekends she would be glad to feed him, and do his laundry. Two weeks later he shyly passed her a handful of bills.

"What's this, Eddy?"

"My board money. Ain't it enough?"

"I didn't expect you to pay board. I thought you were working for your room."

"I always pay my board. Every pay day. I ain't no bum. You got expenses, you know."

If she hadn't needed it so desperately, she would have argued, but she had a feeling that it wouldn't do any good. Eddy wasn't very bright, but he was a hard and willing worker and he always paid his way. For the next few years, whenever he was working in the vicinity, or between jobs, Eddy came and stayed at the farm.

****

Chelsea came for the month of July. Miriam and the boys delighted in her, enjoying every minute as she reacquainted herself with the house and yard. Becky came out for a visit, to see her little sister and to discuss her first pregnancy with Miriam, and the hard feelings of a few months before were buried in the past. Only when Miriam asked about Albert did Becky freeze up.

"He's really bitter, Mum. You never treated him right. You should have told him. He's working with Charlie and he's okay now but he doesn't want to see you. Now let's drop the subject and go down to the stream to cool off."

When it came time to send Chelsea back it hurt like a part of her was being torn away all over again. David wanted to hide her in the barn, and Joshua couldn't understand why they couldn't just keep her, especially when she didn't want to go back to Grandmother, but the court order was to be respected and Miriam wasn't ready to reopen the fight.

The summer passed quickly and fall came, with it the time for picking apples, harvesting the last of the garden, arranging for the pigs to be slaughtered, filling the corner of the basement with firewood for the winter, and of course getting the boys back in school: Joshua entering high school, David starting junior high. As always Miriam took a keen interest in their studies, always making time in the early evening for reading, homework and discussion. Their efforts paid off, and when she went in for the first parent-teacher interviews she was pleased to learn that both her sons were performing at or near the top of their classes. Joshua's teacher especially raved about his dedication, his performance and his ability to discern and to focus on what was important. Her only concerns were in his social development. He still seemed shy and ill at ease with his contemporaries - maybe it was because he lived so far out of town. However she was pleased to report that he was taking an active interest in the science club.

David's teacher, on the other hand, was somewhat disappointed to report that while David did well, he was not the scholar Joshua had been when she taught him. She wasn't sure that David always worked up to his full potential. While no, he wasn't failing - far from it - he occasionally passed in a B paper when she was sure he was capable of an A. Joshua had never given less than his best. On the other hand, David was well liked by his peers. His Phys-Ed teacher reported that he might develop into quite a basketball player. 'He's taller than Joshua was at that age, isn't he?' He enjoyed playing in the school band, and hadn't she overheard him mention that he was in Boy Scouts. In short, he was a well rounded student; if only he would apply himself to his studies a bit more.

Miriam went home feeling good about her sons and affirmed as a mother. Surely she was doing something right. They had been through a lot but they were okay. She would encourage David to study harder, but unlike the teacher, she tried not to compare her children. She remembered how jealous Annie had been about her academic successes, while she had envied Annie her homemaking skills. Now she and Annie barely spoke to each other. She was proud of both Joshua and David. Funny though, at home Joshua who had been described as somewhat of an introvert, was the talkative one, always explaining something to her, excited about an experiment he had done in biology or physics, or something he had read in history or geography. David, on the other hand, was quiet at home; almost surly at times, as Albert had often been, when she questioned him about his work.

Of course she had to drive David in to Scouts once a week. Then she usually would do some shopping, and end up waiting for him in the parking lot of the United Church where they met. It was there that she met the young minister of that church and, after chatting briefly about weather and teenagers and what not, he invited her to attend worship services on Sundays. Goodness, it had been years since she had attended church. True, Bruce had been keen on it, especially after Elizabeth's death, and she had gone and taken an interest while he was alive. She had expected to continue, but with Guy's disinterest, and the paperwork from the store to do on Sunday mornings, she had stopped going, and before long the children had stopped too, other than Becky attending CGIT with some neighbourhood girls, and David of course involved in Cubs, but even with her limited experience Miriam realized that that wasn't church. No, she probably wouldn't have even thought of going back, if she hadn't received a direct invitation from the minister. Then she thought, 'Why not?'

Sunday was usually a lonely day for her. Traditionally it was a day for families, for visiting or receiving visitors, especially those of the extended family. But she seldom went in to Saint John, and if she did it was through the week when stores and businesses were open. And none of her family had been out to the property since Abby's wedding. She didn't visit her neighbours much either; she still wondered if they believed any of the scandal about her that Guy had hinted at. Had she been inclined to visit, she wouldn't on Sundays when they were probably busy with family. Church, she decided, would give her and the boys something they could do together. She would give it a try.

Miriam was surprised when Joshua absolutely refused to go.

"It's up to you, Mum. Go if you want to. But don't expect me to tag along. I've got better things to do. I'm working on a project and I have to go down to the beach at low tide to gather some specimens."

She might have given up on the idea but David was willing. "Yeh, it might be worth giving it a try. One of the scout leaders goes, he wants us all to get our _Religion in Life Badges_ , and some of the guys say they have a youth class that isn't too bad. I'll go with you."

That first Sunday, however, Miriam wished that she had tried harder to persuade Joshua to come with her. She felt certain that he would have enjoyed the experience.

Later, as she got to know the people and involved in church activities, she heard lots of criticism of the new minister. He was too young. 'They're always sending us young, inexperienced ministers.' He had too many high-faluting ideas. He didn't run the service the way they were used to. He used too many big words. He didn't preach the Bible. But Miriam was impressed from that first week.

There was a baptism early in the service and his meditation was about 'water'. She heard him talking about water in a general way, and then something about water from a rock in the desert. Then he was back to baptism, and being washed. Her mind drifted a bit, thinking about the little river and the bay. The minister was going on about water being necessary for life. When he mentioned science, Miriam thought , 'Josh would like this. He's always interested in anything scientific.'

"We know," the young minister was saying, "that all matter is made up of molecules, and that as matter passes from the gas to a liquid to a solid, the molecules get closer and closer together and the matter becomes more dense - heavier. Except for water. The molecules H_2O behave properly at first, following all the 'rules' of science. As water vapour cools and becomes water, and even as water cools, it becomes more compact, denser. Except just before the moment of freezing. Then suddenly the molecules expand. As water freezes to a solid it expands, it becomes less dense. It pushes up the caps on milk-bottles. It breaks bottles. Ice floats! And because ice floats, life as we know it on this planet is possible. Because ice does not sink to the bottom of the lakes and ponds and oceans, and lie there in a solid mass, the water is continually turned over. Warm currents and cold currents are created. And because of this, life was able to develop -- algae evolving into green plants, tiny single celled creatures evolving into fishes, amphibians, animals, primates and humans. Life in all its variety and all its abundance is possible because of that miracle of nature. The fact that the molecules of water do not obey the rules of science, makes life possible, and that to me is all the proof I need of an intelligence behind the universe."

While Miriam was mulling this over, wondering how she would explain it to Joshua, wishing that she had paid more attention to the science books she had read, wishing that David was here beside her instead of down in a basement room with his Youth class, the minister changed direction and suddenly it seemed that he was talking to her alone.

"And this Intelligence that seems so far off, so distant and unknowable, has revealed its very nature to us. This Intelligence that we call God, came and lived among us and taught us. And what was the central message He brought? It's this, that in this vast and magnificent universe, each one of us is important. Each one matters. Each one is loved. Each one of you is important for your own self. And if there is one message I want you to take away with you this morning, it is the simple one that I want you to say over and over to yourselves, 'I am important. God loves me.'"

Suddenly Miriam felt that her life was changed. Her whole life mattered. She was not just Johnny Taylor's daughter, the middle girl in a large family, the one who did well at school and somehow was accused of thinking herself better than the others, the wayward one, the one who had disgraced the family and had an illegitimate child. She was not just somebody's wife, or somebody's mother. She was not that divorcee who had lost custody of her youngest daughter - there has to be something wrong for a mother to lose custody. She was important just because of herself.

At home over dinner she tried to explain all this to Joshua, but he couldn't understand.

"So, he told you a scientific fact, Mum. What does that mean? Surely you remember, I explained all that to you not long ago. About water and ice and currents, I mean. And as for you being important - of course you are. You're our mother." And Dave shrugged. His class had been talking about peer pressure. He wasn't sure what they were getting at. You played your sports, and your trumpet, and did what you must to keep up at school and you didn't hang around with losers. So what? Nevertheless, the guys were all right, and when one of the girls had asked him, he had told them that he would be back.

Chapter Two

That winter Johnny Taylor died after a lingering illness of which Miriam had only been vaguely aware. A few times when she was in town she had thought he seemed quiet, not his old self, but when she asked he had claimed it was nothing to worry about. True, her mother had mentioned a few times that Dad seemed poorly, but no one had ever indicated to Miriam that it was anything more than an extra bad case of the flu that just hung on.

Leaving Eddy Fox to take care of the farm, she took the boys home for a few days for the funeral, and a brief visit with the family.

At the funeral home she looked around, not certain what was expected of her, not certain what to expect of herself. Her mother, of course, was doing all the proper things, though she seemed a bit vague and occasionally repeated herself as she accepted condolences from neighbours and friends. Miriam had expected everyone to be sad, she was herself, but as she looked around at her siblings she realized that both Jack and Annie seemed devastated. Jack was in shock, sitting with his head in his hands, shaking off her hand as she patted his shoulder, rejecting any words of comfort from anyone. Annie was red-faced from crying, and even Charlie looking as though he had been kicked in the ribs.

Johnny lay in his casket, surrounded by flowers: from the family of course, the Legion, the dock-yard, the neighbours. Shrunken from his illness, but also smaller than she remembered him; he was clean-shaven and dressed in a suit for probably the first time since Becky's wedding.

Miriam found herself wondering as she looked down on him, 'Who was this man?' She could remember once as a small child sitting on his knee feeling warm and secure as he swapped war stories, but mainly she could remember being somewhat afraid of him. She couldn't remember him ever striking her, yet she had always suspected he might, almost to the point where she was prepared to duck the blows. Always it seemed the whole household had walked around him on tiptoes, trying not to set off a tirade. He had ruled his family with an iron hand, but had supported them to the best of his ability. He had not turned her out when she was pregnant, and he had accepted and made a place for Albert in his home. He had welcomed her and her family back for visits, and during that year after Bruce died, he had provided for them better than mere custom required. He had even shown pride in her home in the country and congratulated her on her success. She shivered as she remembered this. But then she remembered, at the time when she needed him most, when Guy had threatened to take her children from her, and ruin her life, Johnny had let her down. No, she did not particularly mourn Johnny Taylor.

She did mourn Albert. Visibly shaken by his grandfather's death, he was there at the house from time to time, and at the funeral home. She tried to find an opportunity to speak to him, to offer some words of comfort about his grandfather, to open some communication between them that might be widened in time until they could talk things out, but he was very obvious in trying to avoid her. As she entered the funeral parlor he was going out the side door to the little room set aside for coffee. When she made her way to it he was just leaving by another door. When they met face to face in the hallway, he ignored her outstretched hands, swerving around her, and that cut like a knife.

Back at the house he was barely civil to Joshua and David, but talked animatedly with Becky or with his uncles and aunts whenever Miriam was around. Becky, just nicely over the birth of her daughter, was torn between love for her mother, and loyalty to the big brother she had always adored. Always one to avoid a confrontation and sensing that he was upset about his grandfather, Miriam decided to leave things as they were. Surely time would help.

Miriam would have liked to stay a few days after the funeral to be with her mother and to visit her siblings and try to rekindle relationships. She especially wanted to talk with her youngest brother Davy, home from Ontario with his attractive and stylish wife and two children, but he had to return almost immediately and she had to get back. The boys were missing school, and she didn't want to leave Eddy solely responsible for the place any longer than necessary.

Whenever she phoned she found her mother in reasonably good spirits, a fact confirmed by Frances when Miriam had to go in to Saint John to see the dentist and arranged to meet her sister-in-law for coffee.

"We're all amazed with Mum. Bill can't get over her. We expected her to be completely lost. You know how she always just seemed to live for Johnny; this past winter she hardly left the house because she wouldn't leave him alone. We didn't know how she would manage without him. But honestly, Miriam, she's a different person. She's on the go all the time. Out visiting at Annie's or Gracie's, or with me or even all the way out to Paul and Susan's place, or going down town shopping. You know she never went out unless she had to. We always had to go there. And she spends money. Goodness, when Johnny was alive I'll swear he pinched every penny twice, and she had to account for every dime she spent. Now she buys things - did you notice the new curtains and slip covers - she's buying things for herself too, and for the grandchildren. You wouldn't believe it."

But when Miriam invited her mother up for an extended visit that summer, Hannah declined. "But why not, Mum. I know you couldn't come before and leave Dad, but surely Jack can manage for himself. The boys and I would love to have you. It's so lonely since Chelsea went back after her break."

"You don't understand, Miriam. It's not that I don't want to visit you. It's just that I've got other plans."

"What?"

"Davy sent me a plane ticket. I'm flying to Toronto to spend some time with his family."

Her mother! Flying to Toronto! Miriam couldn't believe it. Hannah had never been more than two hundred miles from her birthplace in her whole life. The few trips to St. Thomas to see Miriam when the children were small, and the trip out to the property for Becky's wedding were the extent of her travels. At one time, while living on the old place, a trip to Saint John had been considered an adventure. Now she was casually talking about flying to Toronto. After all these years it seemed that Hannah was going to have a life of her own. She was taking control, and if she could surely Miriam could too.

Chapter Three

That summer, after Chelsea's visit, Miriam worked as a waitress at a restaurant in St. Andrews. Though running the farm was a full time job, she needed cash she brought home. With it she could pay the insurance and the up-keep on the truck.

That fall Miriam decided to sell the larger animals, the horse and the cows. They were too much work for her and the boys and two expensive to feed through the winter. Anyway, her family actually preferred goats' milk for their own use, and the horse had always been a luxury. The goats, the chickens and ducks were much easier to look after through the winter and she would continue to get a couple of pigs each spring.

She was offered the same job again the next summer but had to turn it down to be home when Chelsea came for her visit. When Chelsea went back in August she was only able to get occasional work. Fortunately Joshua had worked through the summer and was able to help out by buying his own clothes and supplies for school that fall. If she was able to keep the old truck running they would just barely be able to manage. She checked the property and discovered a few young fir that they could sell for Christmas trees, and she decided to transplant more to the lower field that she wouldn't need for pasture any longer. They could be harvested in a few years when the boys would need money for college.

Then shortly after Christmas and a brief visit from Chelsea, she was able to find work as a housekeeper for a lawyer in St. George, and again she was able to meet expenses and manage to hold on to her property. And when Chelsea came again that summer she was able to take the little girl to work with her and keep her job.

Chelsea was adjusting well. She went to the playground and the swimming pool with the lawyer's girls, and hung around the house just as though she were one of them. Miriam marveled at what a cheerful, adaptable girl she was, but realized how much Chelsea enjoyed the casual freedom she experienced during her visits with her Mum.

"Grammy is so strict, Mum. Would you believe that she still picks out my clothes? I'm not allowed to wear jeans to school and almost all the other kids do."

"Did you explain that to your father?"

"I tried. He says that Grammy loves me and wants me to look good, to be a credit to the family. Sometimes I think that he understands, just a little, cause he says that Grammy has old fashion values. But he won't stand up to her."

"Then I guess you'll have to make the best of it, and let your hair down when you're here."

"Yeh. This is great. Grammy wouldn't let me go hardly anywhere without checking with her first. And I'm only allowed one friend."

"That sounds a bit harsh. Can't you play with the other kids at school?"

"Well, at school. But I'm only allowed to bring one friend home with me. And I can only go to her house."

"Well, here you can make as many friends as you want in town, but there's no one to play with at home."

"That's o'kay. I've got you and Josh and Dave. And all this space. I can run, and swim, and get dirty, and make noise. You never seem to mind."

"I guess I'm used to it with the boys. At home when I was growing up the boys got dirty and made noise all the time. But Annie and I were expected to keep quiet. Around here, boys and girls can both enjoy themselves. Just try to act a little bit like a little lady in town."

"Now you sound just like Grammy. 'Act like a lady.'"

"Then Grammy and I agree on something."

Chapter Four

Before she knew it Joshua was graduating from high-school. This was the payoff for all her hard work. This was what made it all worthwhile. He had the highest marks in his class, some of the highest that school had ever boasted about. He won a four-year scholarship to attend university, but he turned down the opportunity to be class valedictorian.

"Mum, I'm not going to get up in front of all those people and give a speech."

Miriam realized that he was still very shy.

Becky came out to spend a few days and attend the ceremony. Hannah and Jack sent a cheque, as did Davy from Toronto. Miriam swelled with pride as she watched him receive his diploma. Maybe she had never had the opportunity, maybe her first two children weren't interested, but by God this son would attend university.

The thought of him leaving filled her with anguish. Joshua was her special child: her second chance after Elizabeth had died. And he had been given back to her again from the dark cold water that had claimed his father.

They enjoyed the summer as a family.

Then Chelsea was gone. A few weeks later she was driving Joshua to Fredericton and getting him settled in the apartment he would share with three other boys.

She had cried the night before Albert's birth, and again when Elizabeth died, but never since then. Not when Bruce died; not when Guy left and took Chelsea from her; not when her father died. But now, after leaving her son at university where she wanted him to be, on the way home she could barely see to drive, as the tears spilled from her eyes. 'This,' she told herself over and over, 'is what I wanted for Joshua all along. He is too bright, too intelligent, he has too much potential to stay buried on the farm.' She was more proud of his accomplishments than she would have been of her own.

Then came the lonely time. True, she still had David. Now it was his turn to be treated like an only child. She could heap her love and attention on him. However, he had grown up independent. He had never been chatty at home; had never shared his thoughts, his hopes and dreams as Joshua had done. He was busy with school and sports and music and his friends. He didn't need her attention.

Joshua was home for Christmas. He was thin and exhausted. Miriam tried to fatten him up, as she divided her attention between him and Chelsea, and prepared for Becky's short visit with her little ones. Goodness, this must have been what it had been like for her mother, trying to divide herself among her seven kids, and still keep Johnny happy. Miriam should be relieved that she only had five, and no husband to cater to.

In the summer when he came back to his home and his previous job, Josh spent the evenings and weekends roaming over the property regaining his strength, while Miriam rejoiced in having him back with her again. She had kept the goats, mainly for him, but as he prepared to go back to University that fall she explained to him they were too much work for her through the winter. Eddy Fox hadn't been around for a year or so now, and David was busy and not very interested in the stock. She would keep the ducks and hens for another year and see how that worked out, but the goats should be sold. He reluctantly agreed. He couldn't do otherwise. He wouldn't be around to help her.

The next year Joshua did better at University and Miriam didn't worry about him. But she was still lonely. A brief relationship with a fisherman from down the bay was a pleasant diversion - she especially enjoyed going out in his boat - but she wasn't ready for a serious commitment, nor was David. He appeared to be so independent, hardly needing her at all, so she was surprised by his jealousy. He needn't have worried. It didn't last long.

Another summer, with Josh and Chelsea home, and Becky coming to visit. Such a busy time of year, and so delightful to have family around. When he went back for his third year Joshua had moved again but finally found a house where he was treated like one of the family. By then he had made friends, and was coming into his own, and Miriam realized that he didn't need her to worry about him anymore.

It was Miriam who needed something more. Housekeeping and child care was all right. The lawyer and his wife were good people to work for. The pay was adequate and there were the perks, such as being able to have Chelsea with her during visits, and having David drop in after school on the days he had nothing else to do, to wait for his drive home. Miriam realized that she needed some adult contact.

Sometimes the breaks seem to go against a person, sometimes they turn and things go her way. Mr. Brown's secretary was leaving. Her husband had been transferred to Ontario; they would be moving soon. Miriam hesitantly talked to him about the job.

"I used to be a legal secretary. I know I'm rusty, and it might take me a bit to get up my speed, my shorthand has always been my bugbear, and I'd have to get used to your methods, but I'd like to be considered for the job. Could we arrange an interview at your convenience?"

"Miriam, why didn't you mention it before. I never knew you had worked in an office or I would have had you in here lots of times. Don't worry about an interview. The job is yours if you want it. But tell me, who did you work for? What all did you do? We'll start training you on the new computer tomorrow. And don't worry about your shorthand. I do almost all my work by dictaphone."

Like that, she moved from the kitchen to the front office. She was able to dress up every day. She typed letters and documents, answered the phone and greeted clients. Now she was thankful for those years at Business College and working for Mr. Howard. They had prepared her for making a living and building a life for herself.

She needed a life for herself. David graduated from high school and was off to university. His scholarship wasn't as large or impressive as Joshua's had been, but he had more in savings from more lucrative summer jobs. Nevertheless, she realized that she would have to help him out.

He adjusted well to university, perhaps because he had socialized more in highschool. He knew his classmates better and was more aware of which ones would take their studies seriously once they got away from the watchful eyes of their parents.

She was alone now on the property. Each day she got up to an empty house, fed the dog and cat and left for work. They were the only ones who welcomed her back in the early evening to a chilly, empty house. It was lonely. The house had been built for a big family - six bedrooms, and the large open living area. All she needed was a couple of rooms. She moved down to the small den off the great room, making it into her bedroom, and shut off the upstairs rooms.

The barns looked empty and deserted, even the ducks and chickens gone now. If it wasn't for the dog and cat she wouldn't have any reason to go home. David was home for a few days at Thanksgiving. She visited Josh when she drove up, but he was too busy to come. She was alone again until Christmas, and for a couple of weeks the house was full with noise and confusion. She almost wished that Carl and Becky and the kids would visit at some other time, so she could enjoy each one separately, but it was natural that they wanted to come and see Chelsea and the boys. There was a distance between her and Becky that she couldn't quite explain but it seemed that Becky preferred to visit when there were others around so she could hold her mother at arm's length, so they wouldn't get too close. 'You're imagining things,' Miriam told herself, but it was there: that distance. Did Becky still blame her for failing to rescue Bruce? Or for the way Guy had treated her? Or was it over Albert? Or was she just jealous of the younger boys, as she had been when they were little? Or maybe mothers and daughters were naturally wary of intimacy. After all, Miriam wasn't particularly close to her own mother any more.

She rested up from their visit during the first week in January and then began looking forward to spring break. Some years the boys' university break coincided with the school break in Nova Scotia. This was one of those years and again the boys and Chelsea were home. Once again the house was full of activity. Toward the end of their visit, Miriam approached the subject that had been on her mind all winter. Perhaps she should sell the property and move into town. They all looked at her as though she had gone mad.

David actually put it to words, "Mum, have you gone crazy?"

Joshua tried to be reasonable, "Dave, you know how hard it must be for her out here alone."

"But Josh, think of all we've sacrificed for this place. You remember how hard you and I worked. I thought you loved it here. I suppose you'll be going on for your Masters and your PhD. You won't need your old home."

"Of course, I love it. I don't mean that Mum should sell. Mum, we've got to think of something else. Becky was just saying the other day when she came out how much she always enjoys it here; how she has always appreciated having a home to come back to, even just to visit; and how much her kids enjoy a visit with Grandma."

"For heaven's sake. I'll still be their Grandma. They can visit me wherever I live."

"It wouldn't be the same. It wouldn't be 'home'."

Chelsea butted in, "What about me, Mum? Before long I'll be sixteen. Dad says then I can decide where I want to live and I've already told him that I'm thinking about going to high school here."

"Your father actually said that?"

"Yes. He's not as bad as you think, Mum. He knows that Grammy is too strict, too fussy. I don't know what all went on between you, or what went wrong, but he's not a bad person. And he wants me to be happy."

"You never told me before."

"I hadn't decided yet for sure. But I'm thinking about it. Don't you want me?"

"Of course, I want you. Chelsea that would be a dream come true. All I've ever wanted is you kids and my home."

"Then why are you talking about selling?"

"There's got to be a way."

"But Joshua. If you're considering more study, then you'll be moving away for good."

"Not for sure Mum. I'm going to be a marine biologist remember. I'll always have to live near the ocean. What better place to build my home, even if its mainly a summer home, than on that bluff overlooking the bay where I've always planned to. And Dave, didn't you have a spot picked out?"

"Yeh, up nearer the road."

Miriam had her answer. She knew now how her family felt about the property - just the same as she did - they loved it. She couldn't take it from them. She had been wrong about Becky. Becky did love her. Even though she had only lived here for a few years, she wanted her children to share in her old home. The boys had helped her develop it and considered it part of their lives. Chelsea, who had only spent vacations there since she was five years old, wanted to make it her home again. Only Albert wasn't there to make his opinion known, and Albert had never lived on the property. No, she couldn't part with it.

She would find a way to cope with the loneliness. At least she no longer felt deserted and abandoned as she had many times in the past. Her faith that she had developed over the last few years gave her the affirmation she needed that she was important in her own right. It also confirmed her belief that there was something beyond her understanding, a purpose. She remembered her near-death experience that she had pushed to the background after Bruce's death - no one she had tried to explain it to had taken it seriously - and realized that at some time she would be rejoined with Bruce and Elizabeth, but not until she had lived out her life in whatever direction it might take. She would manage.

The only question remaining was, 'How'? How would she manage physically and financially to keep up the property?

Chapter Five

None of Miriam's brothers or sisters from Saint John had ever been out to her property for more than just a day trip. Now occasionally they would telephone on a Sunday morning.

"Hi, Miriam. Are you going to be home today?"

"After church, I will be. I don't have any plans. Can you come out?"

"Oh yeh. You go to church. But that's all right. We wouldn't be there before two or so. It's such a nice day, we thought we'd go for a drive."

"I'll be expecting you. I'll get an early dinner ready."

"Don't go to any bother. We won't be staying long."

Only her mother ever stayed overnight, but she got restless after just a few days. "Goodness, Miriam. I had enough of the country when I was younger. I don't know how you can stand it. It's so isolated out here. Almost worse than the old place."

"Mum, its less than half a mile to the highway and there's a bus goes by to the city every day. And I have a car. I get out to work."

"But you look out in any direction and you don't see your closest neighbour."

"But I know they're there. I keep the trees around on purpose. I like my privacy. But there's the two houses up on the main road, that used to be part of the property. I've let the cedars grow up between us, but the boys kept a path tramped down until recent years. And there's the Foxes just across the road from there, and Greys own the property across the stream."

"I can't see their house."

"No, they built up closer to the road. But sometimes you'll see their kids down by the stream. They stick to their own side most of the time."

"That's just the point, Miriam. No near neighbours."

"It's not like the olden days, Mum. With a car and a telephone I can be in touch in a minute. True, it's lonely without the kids, but when they come home we appreciate it. Really we do."

That spring her brother Davy surprised her with a phone call.

"I'm bringing the family down for a few weeks vacation this summer in August. Of course, Mum will want us to stay with her, and I'll want to spend some time visiting around but I don't want the kids cooped up in the city the whole time. That's part of the reason to get away. So, if it's okay with you, we'd like to come out and spend a week at your place. I want the kids to experience some real country living. They've lived in Toronto all their lives. When I tell them about how we grew up, or about what farms are like now, I think they get completely confused between pioneer days and the big mechanical farms they see on TV. I want them to run in the grass, to catch frogs, to climb trees; to pick their supper from the garden and the berry patch; and swim in water that isn't poluted or chlorinated or both. Please say that you'll have us."

"Davy nothing could please me more. I'll love having Verna and the kids. I hardly know them. How old are they now?"

"Raymond's twelve. Jesse's ten. It'll be great for them to get to know my side of the family."

"The only thing, Davy. I'll have to work. You're welcome to be here. But Joshua, David and I will all have jobs. We'll be home on evenings and weekends, and my boss is good. He'll probably let me leave early a couple of times, but mostly you'll be on your own."

"That's okay. In a way that's how we want it. Anyway, knowing Mum, she'll want to come out with us. She just smothers me whenever I get home. Gee, I'm looking forward to this summer. Miriam, it'll be great! Old times. Remember when . . . but this is a long distance call. We'll save our remembering for the summer."

Miriam couldn't believe it - Davy, the youngest brother, the one who hated moving to Saint John so badly, the one who was so lost and nervous in the big school that he pee'd his pants, and who had to be taught to defend himself against the teasing, but the one who finished high school and went to Toronto and 'did good for himself', was coming to visit.

It was just like she had imagined it would be. Davy got up and had breakfast with her and the boys before she left for work. Joshua was working shift work at the Marina and often didn't leave until noon, or was back for the afternoon, so they weren't alone much. But even when one of her family wasn't at home, Davy remembered how to entertain himself and his family in the country. And Hannah was with them. Usually they would have supper ready when Miriam got home. Then down to the stream for a quick swim or just to sit and watch the water. Later they would sit around on the deck and reminisce.

"Remember when . . ."

"Remember when we used to go fishing in the brook, how I used to get my line tangled in the alders."

"Fish hanging in trees. Yes, I remember."

"You always had so much patience to help me work it loose. And remember when I fell in during the spring run-off and you had to come in after me, clothes and all. I was so scared."

"Remember when we used to go sliding on the hill behind the barn. One year we hit a tree with Jack's old toboggan and almost killed ourselves. Then we had to be careful that Mum and Dad wouldn't find out. We hid the toboggan, and our bruises."

"Remember when you made the fudge and it turned out hard as a rock. No wonder Annie hardly ever let you in the kitchen. Paul and I teased you something merciful. Now I tell

Verna what good cooks New Brunswick women are. And I mean all my sisters."

"Remember when Paul and I got into trouble and were going to run away."

"Remember when . . ."

Miriam was surprised at how often Davy's stories mentioned fear of their father, and how he had worried about hiding his fears and weaknesses from him. She had so often thought that she was the only one afraid of him. It surprised her to hear Davy talking about it as though she should have known all along. He must have been better at hiding his feelings than he realized.

Near the end of the visit, Davy was sitting with Miriam's family on the upper deck one evening having drinks and watching the sun set, while Verna and the children played monopoly in one of the bedrooms, Verna trying to keep the sibling bickering to a minimum. Davy was going on again about what a great time they had had.

"I've just got to get down more often, Miriam. In Ontario they call us 'Down-Homers' because we Maritimers talk so much about 'Down Home'. This to me is 'roots', this is what it's all about. My God, Miriam. You're sitting on a gold mine here!"

"Well, it is beautiful, Davy! I love this place - my children do to - but I certainly couldn't call it a gold mine. It's more like a White Elephant I'd say. I've almost considered selling it more than once. It's so big, and it needs up-keep. There are so many repairs to be made, some of them urgent, like replacing the windows on the north side. I'm getting a bad draft whenever the wind blows up from the bay, and it's so expensive to heat. When we were all here we burned wood but now I have to depend on electricity. It's a big place to heat all winter."

Both Joshua and David looked at her with mouths agape, "Mum, I thought we'd decided that we can't sell, that we've got to manage somehow."

"Yeh, I thought it was settled."

"I thought so too, but I just don't know how I'll manage."

Davy butted in, "Miriam, you've got to be kidding. You'd never get what it's worth. Look, Dad sold the old place for a fraction of its value. We could never buy it back now. And if you let this place go now, its gone forever. Miriam, you've never seen my home. It's tripled in value since I bought it. It's worth almost a quarter of a million now. Real estate prices sky-rocketed in the eighties. It's a good thing I got in when I did, or I'd never be able to swing it on my salary now. But I could stand on either side of my house and stretch out my arms and almost touch the houses in either direction. The garage takes up half the front lawn, and the back yard is just a little square. I shouldn't complain because newer houses are being built on even smaller lots. People in Toronto would never believe this much space."

"I know. You live in a whole different world."

"That's just the point, Miriam. Look how much we've enjoyed this vacation. Part of it was getting to know you again, and rehashing old times, but Verna and the kids think its heaven too. Like I say, you're sitting on a gold mine."

"More like an empty shaft to dump money down. You don't know the worry and expense. Except for the garden, and I've let some of that go back to nature, I don't have time to keep it up. It's not producing."

"Miriam, look to the future. People I know spend thousands of dollars on their vacations. Last year we drove down to Florida. That cost a pretty penny. By the way, I plan to give you a little something for having us here - maybe you can put it towards those windows."

"Davy, you're family! I don't charge family for visiting me."

"That's my point. Look, I've already got the envelope ready. I was going to leave it under my pillow or something. I'd be spending more if we went anywhere else. But do you know how many people would pay for a vacation like this?"

Joshua suddenly was beginning to catch on. "You mean, like a farm vacation."

"Yes. Or a 'Bed & Breakfast'. Look how many rooms you have - six bedrooms."

Hannah butted in, "We always wondered why they had built so big."

"I wanted a separate room for each of the kids, so they'd have their own space. I didn't want them to feel cramped."

"Miriam, during the tourist season you could rent out all those rooms. Overnight or by the week. City people would love to have a place like this to relax in."

Joshua and David both were getting excited.

"Just think, Mum. We could get some animals again. Tourists would like that."

"And not just for summer, Mum. Think ! Cross country skiing is a big thing now. We could cut out some trails in the woods. There's lots of ups and downs. We could mark them easy, intermediate and difficult. During the summer they could be hiking trails."

"Snowmobiling. We could rent snowmobiles - arrange day trips up the stream to the mountain."

"What about horseback riding?"

"Hunting in the fall? We could have a fall season for hunters and their families."

"You boys won't be here. You'll be away at college."

"We're talking the future, Mum. In the meantime, when we're home we'll have to help keep the place up."

Davy was thinking out loud, "It would be best to start small. Just for the summer until you see how it works. Don't give up your day job just yet. But maybe that lawyer you work for would be agreeable to hiring a student for the summer - the government offers some kind of an incentive. You could take a summer off, do some advertising, and see how it goes. Bed and breakfast - you've really developed into a good cook. Not like the olden days when Annie wouldn't let you into the kitchen."

The boys were still dreaming ahead. "We could build a few little cottages along the stream. Self-contained. Or they could take their meals here at the main lodge."

"Lodge?"

"The house, Mum. We'd call it the lodge. Imagine, people sitting out on the deck like we're doing now, enjoying the sunset. Later in the year as the weather cooled down people would be down in the great room around the fireplace."

"Like I said, you'd probably start small," Davy went on. "All these ideas wouldn't work. Some like skiing and snowmobiling wouldn't mix very well. The nature-lovers don't take to noisy machines. And horseback riding? You might want to contract that out in the future, unless you plan to hire help. It's all just something to think about. But don't sell the property. Don't even think about it. Dream, Miriam, dream."

Chapter Six

Long after Davy and his family had gone back to Toronto, dropping Hannah off in Saint John on their way, long after Joshua and David went back to university in the fall, Miriam looked around and dreamed. Her boys and her property - that's all she had wanted. Now maybe she could keep both; not by holding on to her boys - they both needed freedom to pursue their own lives, but they had made it clear that they would always be coming back. And Chelsea - once she'd thought she was losing her forever, like she had lost Elizabeth so long ago, but Chelsea would soon be sixteen, and Chelsea wanted to come home.

She looked out over her fields down towards the stream, almost hidden behind the trees - with the new growth she would have to go to the upstairs deck to see the flash of blue of the bay - and she could imagine it: Becky and her children coming visiting at the first cottage - not as paying customers of course; Davy back for another two weeks of summer; people from Saint John or Fredericton, coming for a weekend; people from Ontario or the States staying for the week; children running here and there; artists setting up their easels and preparing to catch the sunset through the apple trees; ducks swimming on the pond; little goats frolicking. Sometime, somehow, she would find a way to develop her property.

ISBN 1412016487